The
Final
Score

Carys Jones is a thriller writer based in Shropshire where she lives with her husband, daughter and dog. When she's not writing she can often be found indulging two of her greatest passions: either walking round the local woodland or catching up on all things Disney related.

For more information about Carys please visit www.carys-jones.com or follow her on Twitter @CarysJAuthor

The
Final
Score

CARYS JONES

ORION

First published in Great Britain in 2024 by Orion Fiction
an imprint of The Orion Publishing Group Ltd
Carmelite House, 50 Victoria Embankment
London EC4Y 0DZ

An Hachette UK Company

1 3 5 7 9 10 8 6 4 2

A CIP catalogue record for this book is
available from the British Library.

ISBN (Paperback) 978 1 3987 1204 1
ISBN (eBook) 978 1 3987 1205 8

Typeset by Born Group
Printed and bound in Great Britain by Clays Ltd, Elcograf S.p.A.

www.orionbooks.co.uk

For RG. Always.

Prologue

Dear Mrs Winchester,

I hope this letter finds you well. I have long been an admirer of yours, having studied your career, which took you from the vaulted concert halls of London to the studios of Hollywood, where you performed on numerous iconic film scores throughout the 1970s and '80s. Yours has been an illustrious career and you are admired by aspiring violinists the world over, myself included.

I know that in this, your eighty-second year, you rarely venture far from your home in Shropshire, but I was hoping you'd grant me the honour of being able to interview you. I'm more than happy to visit you in your home to make things easier and more comfortable for you. I'm currently studying for my classical music MA at Liverpool University and as part of my course I'm developing my dissertation with you as the main subject. Like you, I come from a working-class home and endeavour to find a way to a more comfortable life through music.

I hope that you will consider taking me up on my offer as I would so love to speak with you and hear all about what inspired you to become a professional violinist and any obstacles you encountered along the way. You have led a most fascinating life.

I eagerly await your response.

Yours faithfully,
Daniel Layton

I

Now

Connie Winchester waited. Within the jutting shape of the bay window in her lounge, she stood and peered out at her long driveway, dark beneath a pewter sky. The voice on the radio that morning had promised rain. Beneath the blue cable knit of her cardigan, Connie shivered. It was late August but felt more like mid-November. The week had been cold and damp.

Something skittered across the floor behind her. Sucking in a breath Connie turned, weary bones creaking. A flash of ginger and white disappeared through the open door which led to the hallway.

'Urgh, Bach,' Connie fretted through clenched teeth. Her loyal tom cat, who usually whiled away his days stretched out on the plump cushions of the maroon sofa, was unusually active. Turning back to the window, Connie wondered if he could sense her tension. The driveway remained empty. Unable to keep still, she turned to face the fireplace and the carriage clock upon the mantelpiece. It was set five minutes fast, just as Connie liked it. So the clock read five to nine. Which meant it was actually ten to.

'A watched kettle . . .' she muttered to herself, slippers scuffing against the carpet as she withdrew from the lounge and passed over the hallway, shuddering at the draught that always lingered along the stretch of tiles. The adjacent door was already ajar, clearly nudged open by Bach. Sure

3

enough, as Connie entered the kitchen, he began to press himself against her legs, releasing his rocket engine purr. 'Hush now. In a minute, greedy boy.' She skirted around him, made for the countertop and checked for the fourth time that morning the state of her kettle. Full. The teapot – ready. Two teabags were inside, two matching cups and saucers neatly lined up beside it. And next to those a plate of the nicest biscuits Connie had in her cupboards. Fancy iced ones from M&S.

She was not accustomed to visitors. Not since she'd ceased performing and slipped first into obscurity and then old age. Her fingers began to move, pricking at the air. An ancient habit she'd thought she'd shed. Even bent and arthritic, her hands still knew how to move, the speed at which to pluck. Whenever Connie was stressed, she'd mentally revisit Beethoven's *Sonata No. 9*. She'd dedicated her entire eighteenth summer to perfecting it. Back then her fingertips would drip red with blood and her back would be thick with sweat. But she'd been determined not just to learn it but to master it. Her mind played the melody like an old record slipping onto a dusty player. Sometimes she skipped a piece, but more often than not it played. Frantic and wonderful. And so woefully hard. Her fingers began to throb from the memory of it. Over and over, she had played while outside her dad mowed the grass, even as it burned brown, desperate to escape the house, her madness. Because that's what it had been, hadn't it? A descent into—

Bach mewled loudly. Now at his bowl, he nudged it with his soft pink nose then turned dark eyes up towards his mistress.

'No,' Connie told him sternly, fingers freezing where they were held mid-air. 'We have a guest coming. You can

4

wait.' She used to swing her left arm as though still holding a bow, but now only her right wanted to reminisce. With each passing year she became stiffer and stiffer. Connie wondered if when death did come for her, she would have completely turned to stone.

The cat blinked at her, unimpressed. 'I know,' Connie said softly, abandoning the sonata, glancing again to the teacups. 'It's most rare to have a guest. It's usually just you and me, old boy.' At seventeen human years he was close to her in cat years. A distant sound. An engine, but not coming from Bach. This was no purr. Connie startled, nervously smoothed her crooked fingers down the front of her buttoned cardigan and tugged on the upper elastic of her long navy skirt.

She liked to be alone. Days spent reading and wandering around her garden with Bach, when he deigned to leave the house, suited her. It had been a decade since her last interview. And that had been a dull affair; a local paper wanting to revisit her glory days to tie in with the anniversary of one of the films she had performed on the score of. Connie had to admit that it was nice to go back, to remember how it felt to live beneath blue skies and always feel the sun on her face. The final article had been small, lost within the centre pages. Connie hadn't even bothered to cut it out. She had so many scrapbooks full of stories, of her previous adventures.

'So what made you come back to Shropshire?' had been the kind-faced reporter's final question. It was one Connie had faced many times. Few understood why she had ultimately chosen to swap the shine of Los Angeles for the subdued green of her home county. Connie had smiled softly at him. 'I've had my time in the sun. Now I'm ready for a quieter life.' It had felt right to come home.

Connie had tried to stick an ocean between her and her past but that hadn't been enough. Finally she accepted that it never would be.

Bach mewled again. Her visitor was approaching the front door. Connie steeled herself. Considered again how kind the letter had been. So many people had forgotten her, it felt nice to have her ego massaged, to feel like she still mattered. And he was on time. Connie flicked her gaze to the clock mounted on the kitchen wall to confirm as much. He was punctual. That was good. And like she had once been, Daniel Layton was a music student, clearly hungry to learn all he could about his chosen craft. Once Connie's name had mattered in musical circles. Once she had commanded standing ovations whenever she picked up her violin and bow. But she wasn't Connie Winchester then. She was Connie Lipman. So often that time in her life felt like a dream, distant yet just within reach. All she had to do was close her eyes and she was back there. Back in the sun, back with blood-stained fingers.

2

Then

The alarm shrieks at half five. A shrill cry of metal on metal, which burrows deep into Connie's dream and settles in her bones, rattling them. A new day. Same as all the others. Pressing the heels of her hands to her aching eyes before peeling back her thin green curtains, she looks up at a grey, stagnant sky. The row of terraces beneath it already puffing clouds of smoke, adding to the drab sheen that covers the street she lives on. The world she inhabits.

'Come on.' Barely two minutes have passed before the door creaks open, the imposing shape of her mother consuming the threshold. 'You should be up and dressed by now, Connie. You'll be late.'

Not that she ever is. The morning routine is too militant to allow even a shred of tardiness to creep in. The springs of the bed wheeze with relief as Connie gets up; even her slim hundred pounds are more than they can bear. She drags her thick blonde hair out of her face, traps it in a high ponytail and then pulls on her knee-length socks, grey. Pinafore, black. Blazer, navy. All of which were neatly laid out on the chair beneath the window sill the previous evening.

'I don't hear footsteps,' her mother's voice booms up the stairs. She's already in the kitchen slopping lumpy porridge into a bowl and waiting for the hiss of the kettle.

'Coming.' The only mirror is in the bathroom so Connie dashes the length of the landing, pulls on the door and leans against the sink to check herself. Her silver eyes are as dull as the sky outside. She's tired. Wrung out. And it's only Tuesday.

'Connie!'

When she rounds the top of the stairs, she sees her mother lured to the base, face stern. But the angry flush of her cheeks is comical against the crown of rollers framing her wide face, hands wedged against hips covered by the fabric of an apron. 'Your breakfast is ready,' she announces heatedly.

At the small table in the kitchen, surrounded by mustard walls and yellow gingham curtains, faded to almost white, Connie forces down the porridge, made marginally sweet by the scattering of sugar she placed atop it while it cooled.

'I've packed your lunch.' Her mother stomps over to the leather satchel slumped in the far corner by the back door. She peels back the top flap and drops in a paper bag, which lands with a crinkled thud against Connie's notebooks. It will contain a single ham sandwich and an apple. Connie knows this. Because it is Tuesday. 'And no dawdling getting the bus back tonight. I know you've got hockey but your dad is on lates.' Her mother turns her back to her daughter to focus on the sink and the washing-up already mounting beside it. Connie is grateful for this as it permits her to roll her eyes. Her father being on the late shift at the local car factory means two weeks of slamming doors at ten at night when he leaves. And the brief slice of time she has at home in the mornings being spent in suspended silence. That is, if she is running late. Because he'd be home by six thirty, which was when she should be long gone, sitting on the stiff bench of a bus stop waiting to be whisked away to the other side of town. They were two ships passing in the night.

'I'll be at school while he sleeps,' Connie noted as she placed down her spoon and reached for her waiting cup and saucer of tea. It was strong and sweet, just as she liked it.

'Even so,' her mother swivelled back towards the table, wiping damp hands against her apron, 'take care to be quiet. And mind your manners with him, you know how he gets when he's on lates.'

A roll of the eyes. 'I saw that.' Her mother glared, a finger raised and pointed at her daughter. She had eyes like still water; green swirled with blue. Always sharp. Always watching. Connie's flinty, cool stare had been a gift from her father. Along with his lean frame, though she had her mother's height, barely surpassing five feet. At night, after her bath, Connie would press herself against the closed door and stand on her tiptoes, stretching every fibre of her body until she thought they might snap like old elastic bands. She yearned to be tall and willowy like Sarah Clarke at school. She was just sixteen; there was still time to grow. Especially if she kept stretching, willing it.

'If your dad had seen you rolling those damn eyes of yours, he'd have tanned your hide. Be lucky he's not here.' Her mother shifted the direction of both her finger and her stare towards the corner and the slumped satchel. 'At least you're ready with the hockey stick out, violin case too. That's something.'

Connie lifted her head and looked at her belongings. Her stomach rolled at the sight of the curved stick, but the case next to it made her lips curl into a smile. And she remembered why she liked Tuesdays.

'I still think it's too much for you to be expected to carry.' Her mother had returned to the washing-up.

She was right. Connie would have to sling the satchel across her front, prop the hockey stick beneath her arm and wedge the case against her back. But it would be worth it. Because at two that afternoon she'd be excused from double science to sit in the airy music room, which forever smelt like varnish and dust. And there she would remove her violin from the velvet interior. She'd raise it up, press her chin to the plastic rest, reach for the bow and be transported to—

'Mind you don't lose it,' her mother was rattling on, 'because we can't possibly pay for a replacement and a condition of the grammar school is that you all play an instrument. Ridiculous if you ask me. What good can music do a girl like . . .' Connie tuned her out, filled her head with the opening chords of the *Devil's Trill Sonata*, one of her personal favourites. Because that was what the violin did for her. It transported her away from this world into a completely different one, one bright with colour. One without edges. One where she could be free.

3

Now

'Mrs Winchester,' he said her name with a smile. And he was tidy. Connie surveyed him as he stood on her doorstep, flanked by neatly clipped topiary trees in terra-cotta pots, the boy, technically man, who had written the letter. But to Connie he felt like a boy. He was slim with black hair defying gravity above his forehead thanks to a generous application of gel. His opal skin was clear, tight across high cheekbones. And the jeans he wore clung to his slight frame, making him seem as though a stiff breeze might completely tip him over. To his side he hugged a satchel. Square in shape. Old in style. *Vintage*, Connie considered would be the phrase. A flicker of a memory skittered in her mind's eye and then was gone, a mouse darting into a distant hole. Connie shuddered, told herself it was from the cold.

'Come in, come in.' The wind whipped across the step as she ushered him inside. He entered her hallway and then extended his hand.

'I'm Daniel. Daniel Layton. It is truly a pleasure to meet you.'

Connie pressed her palm against his. He felt soft. Her skin was paper next to his. Brittle and prone to rip.

'How do you do?' Her cheeks ached angrily as she offered him a polite grin. Having visitors, in her home. This wasn't Connie. Daniel was glancing around admiringly, noticing

11

the framed pictures that hung on the walls the length of the hallway, neatly positioned between the floral swirls of wallpaper. He stepped away from her, approaching a large print in a gold gilded frame. In the image Connie was young, with eyes that sparkled even when captured in black and white. She was beside a man in a tuxedo and he was gripping an Academy Award.

'Oh my goodness.' Daniel glanced between the old woman and the photograph, reverently touching a finger to the glass. 'I cannot believe I'm actually seeing this. Wasn't this when you worked on—'

A meow. Shrill and demanding. They both glanced down and saw Bach strutting into the hallway, dark eyes peering up at the stranger in his home. He pressed against Daniel's tight jeans, tail poker-straight. 'Aw, is this your cat?' The young man lowered himself to the ground with enviable ease. There, crouched, he gently massaged Bach's head, the cat purring loudly, the sound rumbling out of him in waves.

'Yes, this is Bach.'

'Bach,' Daniel repeated. There was a lilt to his voice. Something regional which Connie couldn't quite place. 'So you've answered one of my questions already.'

'Oh?'

Daniel broke into a fresh smile as he peered up at Connie. 'Favourite composer,' he explained.

'Ah.' Connie nodded, unsure if it was ever fair to say she had a *favourite* composer. In her youth she would cycle through them as she cycled through men. There would be a flavour of the month but nothing lasted. Only her love for the violin endured.

Bach purred ever louder. 'Tea?' Connie offered, raising her voice.

'Yes.' Daniel gave an enthusiastic nod. 'That would be lovely.'

Ten minutes later they were in the lounge, cups and saucers and an assortment of biscuits laid out on the coffee table. Daniel had insisted on carrying it all through for her.

'Here, let me help.' He'd nudged her out of the way, his vibrant energy dulling Connie, dwarfing any rebuttal she might have. And she had to admit it was nice to have help. To not have to carry her tea through across the hallway, counting the steps, watching her slipper-clad feet and fearing if she fell, she'd shatter more easily than the china.

'So?' Daniel had a notebook open in his lap, pen held in his left hand. He was on the sofa, his back to the bay window. And Connie was in her favourite armchair. Sipping from her tea she could see the sky darkening behind her guest. 'Firstly, let me again thank you for agreeing to this interview.'

Connie couldn't meet his gaze. Instead she looked towards the fireplace, to the carriage clock atop it steadily marking each passing second. She remembered buying it at a flea market in Los Angeles. Her throat had been sore from the revelries of the previous night and she'd not slept. In the salmon-pink dawn, she left her hotel and stalked the streets, too elated to sleep. By the time the sky was blue she'd found the market. And her clock. Using the single twenty-dollar bill on her person to buy it.

'It's a beautiful piece,' the woman with a golden tan who looked after the stall told her with a smile that revealed rows of perfect teeth. Everyone in LA was golden. And perfect.

'It is,' she'd agreed shyly. And she so wanted it. Not because of its ornate marble curves, or its delicate roman numerals etched in gold. She wanted it because she wanted to try and capture time. That moment. That morning. When for the first time in what felt like an eternity she was happy, not just pretending to be. She'd managed to exist beyond the music, something she never thought would be possible. Not since—

'I am such an admirer of your work.'

Connie blinked at Daniel, disorientated after being removed from her train of thought.

'I know I said as much in my letter,' he continued brightly, tapping his pen against his notepad.

'Are you studying the violin?' Connie's attention shifted to the far corner, beyond the sofa, at the edge of the bay window where her old case was propped up, never far from her side.

'We're not here to talk about me, Mrs Winchester.' His smile, so bright, so easy, lit up the room despite the dullness of the day. 'This morning is all about *you*.'

Leaning forward, she lowered her cup and saucer onto the table, hoping Daniel didn't notice the tremor in her hands. 'Please,' she slowly leaned back, clasping her fingers together and resting them in her lap, 'call me Connie.'

4

Then

It was always worse when he drank. This was just something Connie came to accept as truth. Hard fact. Like how you'd get wet when it rained. Or feel the bite of the cold when there was snow on the ground.

When her father hit the whiskey, or later in the month when his pay packet was drying out the beer, he was worse. Much worse. Sometimes Connie would look at him and try to imagine the figure her mother had originally married. Had he been softer then? Kinder? Or had his edges always been razor sharp?

'You know how he gets.' That was her mother's mantra, whispered in an anxious breath, eyes leaving her daughter's face to level a steady, fearful gaze at the door. 'It's just the sauce talking, that's all.'

And how the sauce loved to talk.

And shout.

And slam doors. Cupboards. Punch holes in walls.

On the nights when her father idled at the pub after work, when he eventually came home, Connie swore the house trembled with his fury. That even brick and stone was no match for the tempest inside the man who had helped make her. When she was younger, she would cower beneath her covers, press her fingers into her ears and hum as loud as she could, the sound vibrating through her, filling her. Cold and alone, the only music she could make.

'Don't make him start,' her mother would tell her. 'Be a good girl.'

And Connie was good. She toed the line, never straying from it. She went to school. Came home. Worked hard. Studied her way into the best school in the county, did her best to haul herself up from the gutter.

Still he drank.

The front door would slap open and he'd stalk in, the stench of beer, oil and sweat thick on him. On nights when she felt bolder, or perhaps more reckless, Connie would perch upon the tight crest of the landing and lean against the fading wallpaper and listen. Her father would curse as he stumbled around. Grunt. Shout for her mother, who always readily came.

'Why do you get like this?' she'd sometimes ask, on the nights when she also must have felt reckless.

'I put food on the fucking table, I can do as I please.'

Connie couldn't see her father, but she could imagine him attempting a grandiose sweep of his arm as he spoke, but failing, falling against the kitchen table wedged tight against the wall opposite the cooker upon which only two of the four hobs worked. Up on the landing she'd listen and pretend she was hearing a different exchange. One where her father came home attentive, kind, asked her mother about her day. Took her in his arms, kissed her, thanked her for the meal she'd made for him. Perhaps there would be something playing on the wireless, something with sweeping strings and delicate piano. Something they could dance to. And there in the kitchen he'd hold her mother in his arms, just as he had surely done on their wedding day, and sweep her around their small kitchen. For one blissful moment her mother was back in her white gown, back wearing a beaming smile. Back to being happy.

It was while entertaining one such fantasy that he first struck her. Or perhaps that is the first time she could recall being struck. Connie was seven, possibly eight. She had been so swept up in the music she'd been playing in her head, eyes closed, back against the wall, that she'd failed to hear the stomp of boot upon stair. The hot steam of breath through wide nostrils.

'Girl, why are you still up?'

Without waiting for a response, a thick, meaty hand reached for the collar of her nightdress, hauled her up by it, the fabric splitting.

'What time do you call this?' His anger was hot against her face, his free hand holding a Woodbine, slowly unfurling a plume of smoke that curled around them. 'It's too late to be lurking in hallways. That's what whores do.'

'Oh don't, leave her be.' Her mother's voice, plaintive and fragile like a reed, came up from the bottom of the staircase.

'Hush, woman.' He grunted at her without turning his head from his daughter. And that was it. She hushed.

'You should be in bed.' The nightdress was now cutting into her neck; Connie could already feel the red burn she'd be forced to hide the next day. 'Only perverts and creeps lurk around at night. Got it?'

Connie was silent, too stunned to even reply.

'Got it?'

That was when he hit her. Hard and fast against her right cheek, the Woodbine still clenched between his fingertips, still smouldering.

Connie blinked as her eyes smarted, mustering the strength to respond. 'Got it.'

'Good.' Her father dropped the nightdress, let her crash to the floor as he took a long drag on his cigarette. 'Don't let me catch you out here again. Good girls stay in their beds.'

Always with the demands to be good.

Good girls have manners.

Good girls say grace.

Good girls don't talk back.

Good girls study.

Good girls smile.

Be good, Connie. Be a *good* girl.

And she tried so fucking hard. Every day she tried. It was exhausting.

As Connie got older, she got smarter. Some nights she'd still steal out onto the landing, listen to the drunken thumps upon the walls as she perched by the wall, but she always scurried back to bed before her father even reached the hallway. She could sense his movements, the way the cadence in his voice shifted when he was about to ascend to his bedroom and collapse on the lumpy mattress he shared with her mother. During those moments, when everything aligned – when her father worked the right shift to be home before midnight, when her mother hadn't fallen asleep at the table and was still awake to greet him – she studied them. Her parents. Tried to find that flicker of magic that must have once glimmered between them. Because that was what drew people together, wasn't it? Magic? A spark? Connie wanted to see it. Understand. Like any teenage girl, she was keen to learn about the mechanics of love, even if she doubted it dwelled within the walls of her home. She liked to think that it had slowly seeped out over time, like an oil tank with a hairline crack. When in reality, she had a feeling it had never been there.

And as Connie got smarter, quicker, she knew the nights to ensure she was tucked up tight in bed before her father came upstairs, to not even risk being caught at her bedside. Those nights usually came at the start of the month, when the whiskey would have been flowing, hitting that bit harder than the beer ever could. Her father's rasped words at her mother would be louder, more incohesive.

'Where did you put that?'

'How's this hanging there?'

He was just rambling nonsense into the ether. That's when Connie's fascination was surpassed by fear. Over the years she'd become good at avoiding him during his darkest moments, but not good enough. Sometimes he caught her. Twice he grabbed her neck and lifted her clean off the ground, smacked her head back against the hard wall. Both times she lost consciousness. She came round to the pinched face of her mother looming above her like a full moon.

'I told you not to rile him.'

Connie thought of the minotaur she'd read about in school. Half man, half bull, trapped in an endless labyrinth of darkness where it skewered and killed all who were foolish enough to enter. Was that all men? Bullish and cruel?

On the nights when it was whiskey, Connie would lie in her bed, levelling out her breath until it was barely audible at all. Now that she was at the *good* school, working so hard alongside all the girls from richer, more successful families, she hoped she'd done enough to avoid her father's scorn. But he seemed to live to prove her wrong. In bed she would wait, breath held, praying she didn't hear a creak beyond her door. Didn't have to bear the brunt of his anger which always seemed to burn so bright. So hot.

Be a good girl, Connie.

Good girls do as they are told.

Those nights she'd fall asleep tasting the salt of her own tears. She'd try and think of happier things. Better things. Like the kind face of Mr Collins. How the corners of his eyes would crinkle when he spied a bruise upon her neck or cheek. How he'd gently ask if everything was all right before deciding upon the piece for their lesson.

Connie felt so utterly, eternally grateful for Mr Collins. Because of him a crack of light had entered her world when before there had just been darkness. A seemingly endless ocean of it.

5

Then

It had been a day like any other. Classes punctured with the shrewd conflict that could only be perpetrated by teenage girls. Connie tried to drift away from the worst of it, humming to herself, letting her music become a cloud to carry her away.

'And then she told Shirley Danvers about it—'

'But she was lying—'

'God, where *does* she get her hair done.'

Always the same rhythm of bitching. Connie was bored of it. Not that she was ever invited to partake in the mud-slinging. To most of her classmates she was invisible. A scholarship brat.

Only in her music classes did the fog lift. Violin pressed hard against her chin, bow in hand, Connie grew with every note she drew against the strings. She filled her lungs, emptied her mind and *played*.

'Such a natural,' Mr Collins, her teacher, enthused, as he did after every lesson. 'You have a gift, Connie, truly.'

The grades at her primary school had earned Connie her place at the grammar but her skill with the bow had cemented it. She was the best musician there. Everyone knew it. And everyone hated it.

'Thank you.' Connie smiled at Mr Collins as she lowered her instrument back into its velvet bed, stiffening when she heard the sharp peppering of water on glass. It was raining. She felt her shoulders instantly drop. From the school gates it was a half-mile walk to her bus stop. The official school bus didn't go over to her side of town, due to *lack of need* had been the line delivered from the headmistress when Connie's mum had loudly made her case at a parents' assembly a few years back. Currently there were three scholarship students walking the halls. Both younger than Connie. Both from families that had cars and didn't need to worry about the lack of buses.

'Do you need a lift or anything?' While she packed up, Mr Collins had drifted to the large windows that overlooked the playing field. The clipped green grass was devoid of bodies. Hands pushed deep into his grey trouser pockets, he glanced back at Connie, his blue eyes dulled by the ashen light of the room. Many girls fancied him. Connie had heard the whispers in classrooms confirming as much. She supposed he was handsome in a generic way: tall, broad-shouldered with a firm chin that was dimpled in the centre. But like so much at her school, he felt bland. Part of a formula. Everyone overly pronounced their words, wore shades of blue and grey.

'I'll be fine.' Connie snapped her violin case shut, briefly wondering what kind of car Mr Collins had, since clearly he drove. Her parents were slaves to the bus schedule, same as her.

'Driving lessons are expensive, Connie,' her father had gruffly informed her when she'd asked why he didn't have a car. 'Money doesn't grow on trees, you know.'

'Then there's the insurance, petrol,' her mum eagerly chipped in, listing costs on her chubby fingers.

'It's really coming down out there.' Mr Collins rapped his knuckles against the glass.

'Like I said,' Connie hoisted her case onto her back, 'I'll be fine.' The last thing she needed was a car pulling up outside her house, her mother's hawk eyes instantly spying it. The questions would be endless.

Why did he give you a lift home?

Did he ask for money?

Did he only offer because it was raining?

Did you tell him we don't have a car?

You shouldn't accept, charity, Connie.

'Thanks anyway.' She offered him a lazy smile and left the one room within her school that she actually liked.

Mr Collins was right. It really was coming down. Connie was drenched before she'd even passed through the ornate iron gates, swung open and separating the school's emblem of a flying falcon, which gathered neatly together when the gates were closed. It didn't take long for the rain to sink through her blazer, settle against her skin. Connie bowed her head, kept going, socks wet within her shoes. Away from the red bricks, the waiting procession of cars, she headed down a street, past a corner shop whose window burned yellow in the dimness.

Finally the bus stop came into view. A tiny brick shelter set back off the street. Connie hurried her pace. She was almost there when a plume of smoke traced a line through the rain. Connie froze. Someone else was in her usually empty bus stop. And they were smoking.

'Shit,' she whispered the word through lips that were beginning to chatter. She was too cold and too wet. If only she'd had the foresight to take her raincoat but that morning she hadn't wanted the extra weight. The hockey stick and violin case were already more than enough.

'Double shit,' she uttered again. Because if she went home smelling of cigarettes her mother would hit the roof.

The rain pummelled her with renewed intensity, making her decision for her. She darted towards the bus stop, thankful for its shelter. Gasping, she perched on the slim wooden bench beneath a strip of graffiti that read *Fuck Chuck Berry* and beneath that *Danny sucks dick*. Head bowed, she saw droplets falling from the hem of her skirt, joining the dark puddles that swelled at the edges of the bus stop.

'You swim 'ere or something?' The question came from the opposite end of the bench. From the smoker. Connie cautiously raised her head and angled her gaze in their direction.

He must have been eighteen, nineteen. In ripped jeans and a leather jacket, dark hair falling over even darker eyes, a cigarette hanging from his long fingers. 'You're fuckin' soaked.' He cracked a half-smile and then drew on his cigarette, pushing the smoke out into the rain.

'Yeah, um . . .' Connie self-consciously shuffled against the bench, squelching. 'I had to walk over from the school.'

'No shit.' He lightly shook his head, amused. 'No one dresses like a stiff for the hell of it.'

A stiff. Connie felt her cheeks beginning to burn. 'We have to wear the uniform,' she told him sternly. 'It's the rules.'

'Ah, sorry.' He clasped his cigarette between his teeth and raised up both hands in mock surrender. 'I didn't realise you'd end up in jail if you didn't wear the bloody blue blazer.'

'More like a detention,' Connie muttered hotly, pulling on her wet sleeves, wondering just how awful her hair looked now it was completely plastered to her skull.

'You waitin' on the seven?' Cigarette done, he dropped the butt to the ground and crushed it out with the heel of his heavy boot.

'The . . .' Connie frowned, temples throbbing with the promise of a headache thanks to the chill that had now entered her bones. She really needed to get dry. 'Seven.' She nodded, teeth beginning to knock together. 'I'm waiting on the seven.'

'Hmm.' He openly surveyed her and then gazed out on the rain-slicked street. 'I'm just ducking in out the rain.'

'So you live round here?'

'Kind of,' he replied cryptically.

He scratched at his jawline with the tips of his fingers, massaging the faintest trace of stubble. 'So how does a girl who lives over Hadley way end up at the girls' grammar school?'

The directness of the question rendered Connie speechless.

'And there I was thinking you must be smart.' He moved his fingers to brush through his thick hair, drawing it back and away from his face. Chestnut eyes peering over to her, mocking.

'I *am* smart,' Connie responded indignantly, loathing the way it made her sound like her mother whenever she climbed up onto her soap box. 'I earned my scholarship there.'

'You got fire.' The stranger plucked a cigarette that he'd been storing behind his left ear. 'I like that.' He reached into the pocket of his jacket for a box of matches. He was about to strike one when he paused, dark eyes suddenly held on her. 'Sorry, you want one?'

Did he mean a cigarette or a match? Either way the answer was the same.

'No.' Connie knew her voice was a bit too sharp, chest a bit too clenched. But smoking was on the long list of behaviours not tolerated at her school. She knew better than to risk falling foul of the rules, of losing her place there.

All her friends from home smoked at the school she should have gone to. And they wore make-up. And had boyfriends. Their lives weren't sterile like hers.

'Actually . . .'

'Sorry.' The match in his fingers caught, casting a brief glow against his cheeks. 'Remembered I only got the one.'

'Ah.' Connie stared at her lap, feeling foolish.

'Next time.' His mouth widened into a wolfish grin.

Connie blinked, flustered as the number seven pulled in to the kerb. 'I . . .' As she scrambled to her feet he stood up, sauntered over to help her wrestle the violin case onto her back.

'Careful with this,' he smirked as he passed Connie the hockey stick, 'in the wrong hands it could be a weapon.' His own hands were now returning his cigarette to between his lips, dark eyes trailing Connie as she shuffled out into the rain, footing precarious against the slick street and beneath the ample weight of her soaked school goods.

'Th-thank you,' she blurted as the bus door wheezed open.

'I'm Robin.' He eased back beneath the shelter of the bus stop, hair dusted with rain. He exhaled and then pressed his palm to his chest, 'Robin Strand.'

'I'm—'

He waved her onto the bus, raising his voice to be heard over the idling engine. 'You're a grammar girl who gets the seven. I know how to find you.'

On the journey home Connie didn't think about her wet clothes, or the weight of a satchel, or the chill that had settled in her bones. She thought only of the enigmatic boy from the bus shelter. Robin Strand. Whose name she would write a dozen times at the back of her English notebook before falling asleep that night.

LOCAL GIRL PROVED PRODIGY

Teachers at the Blackhill Girls Grammar were delighted to showcase a rising star at their recent open evening. Blackhill resident, Connie Lipman, 14, is a most gifted violinist. She wowed the 200-strong audience with renditions of Bach and Mozart. Her tutor, Mr Collins, remarked 'she has a natural gift, the like of which I have not previously encountered in my career. I look forward to helping nurture her talent during her time here at the school.' To which Connie added, 'I've really fallen in love with the violin.'

Blackhill Girls Grammar is renowned for exemplary exam records and last year was ranked fourth in national league tables. Connie's star is most definitely on the rise and she is one to watch.

6

Now

It started to rain, arriving suddenly. There was no prelude of a delicate drizzle, just the slap of heavy raindrops on glass. Connie gazed at the window beyond her interviewer, watching each drop trace a journey towards the ground before it withered and died. Inside she was dry. Her home warm. But seeing the rain caused her bones to rattle with the memory of a time when her skin was soaked. When her whole world changed.

'Connie?'

'Sorry.' She gave a slight shake of her head and pulled her lips into a half-smile. Her attention returned to Daniel, who was patiently observing her. Connie picked at the tips of her nails, wondering if he'd already written her off as senile. When what she really was, was distracted. The rain did that to her.

'I asked what made you choose the violin.'

'Ah, yes.' It was an extremely fair question. One which made Connie recall a stuffy room with a grand piano wedged in one corner. Mr Collins and his parade of starched shirts. 'I think that, actually, the violin chose me.'

Daniel's eyes widened with interest.

'Well . . .' Connie's back straightened against her chair and she shuffled upon the cushions. Talking about herself, she was unaccustomed to it. A skill that had shrivelled along with so much of her when she ceased to perform professionally. 'I went to a girl's grammar school and it was a requirement for all students to learn an instrument.'

'I see.' Daniel scribbled a note.

'I tried piano. Cello. Flute. Nothing connected with me. Until . . . until I picked up a violin.'

She closed her eyes and for a moment she was there, fresh-faced at eleven, nervously pressing the base of the instrument beneath her chin, her teacher a few feet away, coaxing her.

'Just try,' he was urging, 'you might like this one.'

Connie raised the bow high, drew it against the strings. The sound was an assault on both their ears. But the *feeling*. It vibrated through Connie long after the strings of the violin had stilled. It was like finding a part of herself she'd never known was missing. 'This,' she told her teacher, eyes shining, 'I want to learn this.'

Daniel nodded, absorbing the story. 'That sounds very . . .' He paused to lean forward and sip from his teacup. 'Pure.'

'It was,' Connie agreed as her chest clenched. Coughing against the sensation, she reached for her own drink, needing the warm, sweet fluid to wash down her throat. Daniel was right in his assessment. Her love of the violin had been pure. At the start. And so had she.

'Tell me about your girls' school.' Daniel was holding his pen anew, flicking his gaze between his notepad and Connie.

This was a question Connie had rarely encountered. Most people wanted to know about the instrument, her connection to it, caring little for the educational establishment that was the initial setting for her love affair.

'It was . . .' She considered what to say. So much had changed since her time as a student. But also so much had stayed the same. 'It was my local girls' grammar school.

To get in, you had to pass the eleven plus and then either pay fees or be granted a scholarship. It was a very difficult school to get into.'

'And you were a scholarship student?' The smile Daniel gave her was tight. Sympathetic.

'Yes.' Connie nodded. 'My family could never have afforded the fees.'

'That must have been tough,' Daniel continued to stare at her, 'being around all those children from wealthier families.'

'Oh.' Connie batted away his comment with a sweep of her hand. 'No, it was fine. I hardly registered that things were different. At the school we were all treated the same.'

A gross lie.

Connie knew then as she knew now that if it wasn't for her ability with the violin, she'd have been kicked out of her prestigious school. Cast to the wolves of social ruin to defend for herself. The best she could have hoped for was to secure a place at her nearest school. And that would have been a long shot. But her school kept her on, even when they shouldn't have.

'It must have been hard though,' Daniel pressed, leaning forward, keen. 'To be so different from your peers. Did you make many friends while at school?'

Yes.

Connie still knew their names. The faces they made when they were afraid. But she had not met them *at* school. But she wasn't about to share that inaccuracy.

'I was fortunate to make many friends.'

'And did they stay in your life? After school ended?'

A fire that idled in her belly began to climb up towards her throat, scalding her. Connie coughed, felt the joints of her fingers begin to throb. Her eyes flicked to the wet

30

window. The rain always made her arthritis play up. She considered it some macabre form of punishment.

'My friends have always been in my life.' She raised a bent finger to tap her forehead. 'I keep them all here.'

Daniel smiled in understanding and eased back against the sofa. 'Forgive my bluntness, but you must be grateful to have your memories intact. Some people your age aren't so lucky.'

'It is a gift.' Connie returned her hands to her lap. *And a curse.*

She was again looking to the rain. She wanted to speak of music. Of composers. Of sonatas. Of the times she played so furiously she snapped her own strings, bloodied her own fingers. When the music truly took over. She did not want to speak of school. Of old friends. Because to do so was to think of him. He already invaded her thoughts more than enough.

'Connie?' Her name was delivered suddenly. Sharply. With a jolt she looked across at Daniel. 'Sorry,' he added more softly. 'You were zoning out again. And I was just saying that I really want to focus on your early years, that initial introduction to music.'

The rain lashed against the window and Connie forced herself to smile. 'Of course.' But she didn't want to go back there. Because going back meant returning to him and she wasn't sure she had the strength to revisit those days.

7

Then

A week later he found her again. The sky was eggshell blue, the red of turning leaves burning against it.

It had been a long week, Connie's every waking hour scheduled and accounted for. When she wasn't eating or sleeping, she was travelling. And in the snippets of any spare moments, she could claim she was having to study. She was sixteen and utterly depleted. She'd look around at the other girls at school and wonder if their gaze was as glassy, their days as long. Which of course they weren't. They fell asleep on plush mattresses beneath soft sheets, not on a stiff single bed listening to slamming doors vibrate through the thin walls of a terrace. When shouting rose up through the floorboards, Connie struggled to tell if it was her parents or her neighbours thrashing out a twilight argument. The jumble of sound became a toxic lullaby. Most nights exhaustion would claim her before she'd managed to figure out who it was shouting somewhere down below.

So when Robin appeared at the bus stop, leaning against the bricks, arms folded over his chest, Connie was so surprised and so fatigued that for a moment she wondered if she were dreaming. That her seven days spent yearning for him had somehow made her manifest an hallucination.

'Grammar girl.' He nodded as she came closer.

'Bus stop boy.'

His half-smile widened. 'I prefer Robin.'

'And I prefer Connie.'

His brown eyes shone. 'Touché.'

Connie edged around him with her assortment of bags, instruments and sports gear, letting her load fall against the bus stop bench.

'You always carry that much shit?'

'On Tuesdays, yes.' Connie straightened and massaged her throbbing shoulders. Only a bumpy bus ride and a twenty-minute walk to go and she'd be done for the day.

'What about weekends?' He stared at her and Connie noticed how smooth his jawline was. Freshly shaved.

'W-weekends?' She struggled to focus.

'Yeah, you have to carry all this shit with you on weekends?'

'What? No. At the weekends I . . . I have to study. Practice.'

'You make it sound like this is all some dress rehearsal.'

Connie squinted at him, trying to read his dark eyes. 'I mean, it is,' she stated primly. 'Your time at school is a rehearsal for adult life.'

He snorted and dramatically leaned out of the bus stop, gesturing up to the clear sky. 'Take a look around, *Connie*. The show has already started, why waste your time in rehearsals?'

At the top of the road her bus came into view.

'Saturday.' He clicked his fingers at her. 'I'll meet you here.'

'I'm meant to be studying. At home.'

He dragged his fingers through his hair and then withdrew a cigarette from his jeans pocket. 'You're a smart girl,' he told her, this time fumbling for a light. 'I'm sure you'll figure out a reason to be here.'

Connie stared at his jacket. The tears in his jeans. The mud on his boots. And then when she looked at his full lips and warm eyes, she felt a current move through her body like the time the light switch in her room was playing up and she pressed it and clear got pushed across two feet back, onto her bed.

'Time you start living, *grammar girl*,' he teased. Connie opened her mouth, mind churning desperately for some smart retort, but her bus had arrived and Robin was sauntering away, a plume of smoke snaking around him like he was a train withdrawing from the station.

She watched him, eyes growing sore from lack of blinking.

'Come on, love,' the bus driver called impatiently, grey moustache twitching, 'I've not got all day.'

The lie had been surprisingly simple to fabricate and execute.

A whole day of violin practice with Mr Collins. She told her mother. *He wants to nurture my talent.* The lie was not questioned, merely embraced.

On Saturday morning, instead of getting up and peering over her timetable of study for the day, Connie woke up at seven and pulled on her best pair of jeans and favourite pink cardigan. Her mum gave an approving glance over tea and toast, which meant that Connie was toeing the line of looking smart yet not immodest. Her hair was drawn back in a high ponytail that she planned to remove the second she rounded the corner and was beyond view from her mother's watchful eyes.

When Connie arrived the bus stop was empty and she felt her cheeks begin to burn with shame. They hadn't even agreed a time to meet. How foolish she had been to think his offer genuine. To have spent the latter end of the week wishing away every minute, every hour, her stomach feeling blissfully sick like she was riding on the waltzers.

Thirty minutes passed and just as Connie was quite certain she was going to forsake her plans and return home, catch up on all the studying she had already missed, he appeared. Only he wasn't alone. Robin approached the small brick shelter, hands stuffed into the pockets of his leather jacket, flanked by a boy with a blonde buzz cut and bad acne and a very pretty girl. Connie stiffened, reached for her elbows, satchel knocking against her side, the apple she'd packed for lunch rolling around inside it.

'You showed up.' Robin pinned her with his gaze, lips lifting to smile.

'You planning on serenading us or something?' the girl asked scornfully, breaking the spell Robin was casting. Connie inhaled nervously and looked at her. The girl was pointing to the violin case wedged in the far corner of the bus stop. She had jet-black hair that stopped suddenly at her chin. Blue eyes framed by thick eyeliner. She wore black pedal pushers that hugged every curve and a mono-chrome polka-dot top that emphasised the paleness of her skin juxtaposed against her hair. She was the prettiest girl Connie had ever seen. Exquisite, like an exotic bird.

'Ignore Wren,' Robin objected, poking the girl with an elbow. 'She's always hostile to newcomers.'

Connie smiled nervously, glancing between them all, trying to figure out how they slotted together.

'And this is Arthur,' Robin continued and the other guy nodded. 'Everyone, meet Connie.' Hands still in denim pockets, he bowed in her direction.

Wren pursed lips that were painted bright red, arched an eyebrow shaped like an oversized comma. 'I don't know about her.'

'Well I do.' Robin broke free of his entourage and came to stand by Connie. It was like shifting the angle of the sun, she was instantly warm. 'Connie here is a grammar girl, so she's smart.' His hand clasped her shoulder, drew her close to him. She could smell cigarettes and soap. 'And she's from the bad part of town. So she's a realist.'

'I still don't know,' Wren objected.

'Well I do.' Arthur began to turn back the way they had come. 'Because I trust Robin. So let's get out of here already.'

'Come on.' Robin released her shoulder but lingered by her side. 'Let's go.'

'Go where?'

'To our place,' Robin explained. 'I think you're going to love it there.' Grinning eagerly, Connie walked in step with him, thoughts lighting up her mind like fireworks.

He had his own place.

He must be successful.

Sophisticated.

He was everything Connie aspired to be. She followed Robin and his friends away from the bus stop, down the street and deeper into town, not realising that she'd left her first love behind, tucked up in the corner of the shelter, abandoned and alone.

8

Then

The moment Connie picked up a violin, she loved it. It was difficult to explain the feeling, the synergy. Something just felt *right*. And she felt the same way about Mr Collins. Kind Mr Collins, who always had a smile for her whenever she entered the room.

She liked the way Mr Collins understood her, and the way he seemed to truly see her. Not like the other teachers did, through a lens of disinterest. No, with Mr Collins it was different.

'You play beautifully.' It was the first compliment he gave her over the violin, given on a dusky October afternoon when leaves tumbled past the classroom window and there was a bite in the air. Connie kept that compliment tight, wrapped it safe within her memory and would gently unravel it, listen to it anew, when the nights were the darkest at home. While her father thundered around downstairs, she replayed Mr Collins's words. Over and over. They never lost their magic. Their power.

'I think this is something you should be taking seriously,' he'd informed her solemnly one Friday, when half the school were out stretching on a field, preparing for a cross-country run. 'Why don't I speak with Mrs Watson about offering you additional tuition – private music lessons?'

Mr Collins must have seen the flash of panic behind her eyes as he hastily added, 'Of course, at no cost to your family, Connie. It is in the school's best interest to nurture a talent like yours.'

Connie had been nervous when she went to see hard-faced Mrs Watson, who was never without a cluster of pearls clasped to the sagging skin of her neck. The formidable head of year had the power to take it all away, to deny Connie extra lessons, to deny her the bolthole she had found within music. Within Mr Collins.

'He says you've quite a talent for the violin.' Mrs Watson squinted across the expanse of her desk as Connie squirmed in a stiff chair opposite, hair still damp from the shower of rain she'd had to dash through across the common area to reach the office. 'An exquisite instrument, truly. You'd of course be an asset to the school if you could obtain up to Grade 8. Which Mr Collins has assured me you can.'

Connie blushed, face poker-hot. She wasn't accustomed to someone having so much faith in her.

'Do you believe you can make the grade?'

Connie went to speak but Mrs Watson pressed on. 'It's no easy feat. It will take dedication. Considerable commitment on your part. You will of course need the extra classes that Mr Collins has suggested.'

'Yes,' Connie gushed eagerly, 'I'll do the work, of course.'

Because I'm good, she thought. *I'm so very, very good. I always follow the rules.*

'Well, that's settled then,' Mrs Watson concluded, doing something she rarely did: smiling. 'I always trust the judgement of Mr Collins. He's been such a,' a hand clasped to her chest and for a second a dreamy look passed over Mrs Watson's hard face, 'well, a breath of fresh air. We are truly lucky to have him. And don't you forget it.' Her expression solidified into its usual mask of slight contempt as she stared at Connie again. 'You're most fortunate to have a teacher such as Mr Collins offer you tutelage. Don't go wasting such an opportunity, you hear?'

'I won't.' Now Connie's mood was souring. Mrs Watson didn't need to say it but Connie would read her expression like a poorly written book.

Someone like you.

It was an effort to square her shoulders and leave the office with her head held high.

A scholarship student.

So many people said the label with a sneer in their voice. But not Mr Collins. He didn't care where she was from or that she had to take the bus home. He just cared that she could play. The further Connie walked away from Mrs Watson's office, the better she felt. Already her head was filling with music, with the hours she would spend along with Mr Collins practising. Perfecting. Her face had broken out into a wide smile as she re-entered the common, not even caring that the rain had picked up.

'Everything all right?'

It was about a month later, during one of their tuition lessons, that Mr Collins noticed the blue tint of a bruise close to Connie's collar. Feeling self-conscious, she'd re-angled the violin beneath her chin and stared so intently at the music sheet open before her that her eyeballs began to ache.

'Connie?' A hand upon her shoulder – warm, gentle. 'You know you can always talk to me.' The hint of a squeeze. Connie shuddered, snapped her eyes shut. But that was a mistake, she was back in the darkness of her bedroom, hearing her father's wheeze just beyond the thin door, waiting for the twist of her doorknob.

'I'm—' She couldn't do it. She couldn't say *I'm fine.* Not to Mr Collins with his kind eyes and attentive stare.

Connie wilted, violin slipping from her grasp, which her teacher deftly caught. Then he folded himself around her while she wept, seeming to understand that she just needed to cry, to release it all.

'I'm sorry things are bad at home.' His voice was so soft as he rubbed her back. 'But you know you're safe here, don't you? With me.'

Connie sniffed, breathed in the dust and oil of the music room, the cologne of Mr Collins. She did know that. The music room, her violin. This was her safe space. Within these four walls she could let the melody guide her, the notes block out the shouts and screams from home, which were always snapping at her heels no matter how much distance she placed between herself and her front door.

'You can always talk to me,' Mr Collins assured her. Connie leaned into him, thinking how lucky his sons were to have such a wonderful father. How different it must feel to not fear the man at the head of the table, to possibly even actually like him.

'I'm sorry.' Connie began wiping her eyes with the back of her hand. 'Really, I don't mean to start blubbing and ruining practice.'

'You're not ruining anything.' Mr Collins kept his hands on her shoulders and smiled at her. 'I just want to know that you're OK.'

'I'm . . .' Connie felt a pulse beneath her bruise, reminding her how sore her skin was. 'I'm glad I can come here. To play. To . . . to get away.'

'Of course.' Mr Collins nodded knowingly. 'This is more than a music room for us, isn't it? It's a sanctuary.'

'Exactly.' Connie flashed him a brief smile.

'There we go.' He beamed at her. 'That's better. You're so pretty when you smile.'

Her entire face burned. Though it was more than her face, it sunk down into her bones, into the innermost, most intimate parts of herself. She burned so hot, so sudden, she feared she was about to burst into flames.

'Is there anyone you can . . . talk to? About things at home? Any friends?' He watched her intently, studying her pale face. Connie hung her head, suddenly cold.

'No,' she rasped. 'The girls here . . .' She sighed as she thought about her lonely lunch hours, how she'd always have to sit at the very back of the library to avoid hearing the barbed whispers aimed at her. 'I'm not like them, I'm, you know, on a scholarship so . . .' She bit her lip, hating how needy she sounded. How immature. The taunts followed her throughout the day.

Have you seen she gets the bus?

Her uniform is second hand, I can tell.

She doesn't even have a record player, she told me. Can you believe it?

'What about back home?' Mr Collins wondered. 'Do you have friends from when you grew up? From your neighbourhood?'

'I did,' Connie's stomach curdled with all the unpleasant memories surfacing, 'but when I got accepted here, they kind of, well . . .'

'They abandoned you?' Mr Collins was so close she could smell the tea he'd drunk at break-time on his breath.

'Yes,' Connie admitted, shamefaced, a single tear sliding down her cheek. 'They stopped wanting to have anything to do with me.'

'That all sounds terribly lonely.'

'Yeah.' Connie blinked, trying to stop any further tears. 'It is.'

'Here . . .' Mr Collins handed her a handkerchief from his pocket. Crisp, white cotton. As Connie dabbed

41

at her face with it, she smelt the freshness of outside, imagined it drying on a line in a large garden, fluttering in the breeze. 'I hope you know that you can always talk to me.'

Connie nodded. 'The . . .' She gestured to the violin Mr Collins had returned to the velvet lining of its case. 'The music helps.'

'I'm glad.'

'When I'm playing, I feel like I'm . . . like I'm not myself anymore. Like nothing else matters. Just the next note and the next.'

'Spoken like someone with a gift.' Mr Collins remained close to her.

'It's all I want to do,' Connie admitted. 'I think about it all the time. Playing.'

This made him smile. 'That's good to know.'

And it was true. Connie heard music wherever she went, as though someone had installed a record player in her brain that never switched off. She provided a soundtrack to her parents' arguments to smooth them out; she added the swell of strings over the patter of rain when she was sitting on the bus on the way home. Music had a way of making everything more beautiful, more wonderful. And when Connie played, she became a part of that beauty and wonder. She became better.

'You know, you can use the music room anytime,' Mr Collins told her.

'Oh?'

'Not just for our scheduled sessions. Whenever you feel upset, alone. Come here.' He eased away from her, towards the violin which he gingerly raised from its box, presenting it to her like an offering from a wise man. 'Come see me, come feel the music.'

Connie took a deep, steadying breath, reached for the violin, the wood always smooth beneath her hands. How easily her fingers closed around its neck. When it slotted beneath her chin, it was like sliding a piece of a puzzle into place. The pulsing behind the bruise on her neck began to ease. Connie felt a stillness wash over her.

'You were made for this.'

With a start she realised Mr Collins was still watching her, observing the serenity pass through her.

'The music, it's like it's a part of you,' he went on. 'It's truly something to see. One day you're going to be the most exceptional player.'

'Thank you.'

'Music can take you places. Literal places, Connie. If you let it.'

'I hope so.' She eyed her sheet music, keen to resume playing, her moment of weakness passed.

'If you let *me*,' he held her in a sincere gaze that made her heartbeat quicken, 'I think I can help you become the truly amazing violinist you were clearly meant to be.'

Connie felt excitement passing through her like an electric current. It was exhilarating.

'Together we can do this, if we have trust. If we have commitment.'

'I'll do it,' Connie told him, breathless with anticipation for all that might lay before her. 'Whatever it is, whatever I have to do, I'll do it. I just want to play.'

And get away.

There was nothing she wouldn't do to place even more distance between herself and her front door. To not hear her father's angry stumbles in the night. To not hear her mother's defeated cries come the dawn.

Mr Collins was smiling at her. 'Good girl, Connie.'

Mentally wrapping another compliment to devour later, Connie beamed and raised her bow, preparing to play.

Still her teacher watched her, grinning, admiring her performance. 'You're such a good girl.'

9

Now

The tea was cold. Yet still Connie eagerly drank it, needing the sweetness. She was grateful for the rain continuing to tap against the window as it helped to silence the ghosts from her past who were now rattling their chains. This hadn't been her intention. She'd wanted to spend her morning discussing music, her time in the sun.

'I moved to London when I was nineteen, shortly after completing college. My first job was—' She attempted to control the interview but Daniel was too swift, too informed. He interrupted her with youthful ease, not caring that his words tumbled over her own.

'At the Royal Opera House. I know. Your very first gig was second chair at a performance of *The Nutcracker*.'

'You've done your research.'

'It's all online,' Daniel said modestly, a gentle blush staining the porcelain of his cheeks. 'On your Wikipedia page.'

'My . . . what?' Connie frowned, sipped more tea. She assumed he meant the internet. That thing which Connie had never quite grasped.

'Never mind.'

'It was a big thing, back then,' Connie continued, keen to only venture down the more solidly paved pathways of memory lane. 'Moving away. But my parents were happy for me to follow my dream.'

Something lodged in her throat. Her cup shook against its saucer as she lowered it to the table and then gently pressed a hand to her mouth to cough hard, the sensation reminding her how flimsy all her muscles now were. How everything which held her together was now threatening to fall apart.

'Are you OK?'

'Fine,' she announced hoarsely. The taste of tea now all but completely gone. Replaced by bile. And Connie knew why. She'd always made such a terrible liar, prone to nervous twitches and panic attacks. Her parents had not been unhappy for her to move to London; they had seemed relieved. She could still recall their faces as she told them, a salmon summer sunset blossoming over the garden outside as they gathered around the kitchen table, the smell of the Sunday roast still lingering thickly in the air.

'London?' Her father's bushy eyebrows had shot up, her mother's hand quickly finding his, fingers intertwining atop the gingham tablecloth. Across from them Connie sank into her chair.

'You've found a job there?' her mother wondered gently. Hopefully.

'Yes. With an orchestra.'

'Well . . .' Her parents shared a look that Connie couldn't quite read. It was akin to the expression her mother wore when they had to put their cat, Mildred, to sleep several years earlier. 'It's for the best,' she had declared stoically, fussing the black cat one final time.

'It will be good for you,' her father announced. 'London. A new place. New adventures.'

Connie should have been grateful for their support. That they weren't trying to barricade this door to a new life for her. The width of the table felt like it was expanding, leaving her woefully alone on the other side of it. They wanted her gone. She could see it in their eyes. Perhaps they had never truly forgiven her despite their proclamations. Perhaps—

'But those early days with music,' Daniel bustled on, pen scratching against paper. 'They must have been so . . . so *extraordinary*. That falling in love for the first time.'

'With . . .' Connie lowered her hands to her lap and internally lamented her mind for being slow. She should have been listening to the young man, not thinking back on times she'd fought so hard to forget. 'Falling in love with *music*?'

'Yes,' his smile was so earnest, 'of course.'

Connie mirrored his expression. Because that had been her first love. Music. Her time with the violin, the moments when she was lost to the notes, swept upon the wave of a melody that she never wanted to leave.

But first loves rarely endure.

'I want to know about that early connection. About who taught you, at the school, how they shaped you as a student and a musician.'

Mr Collins.

Connie clenched her hands together so tightly her fingers began to grow numb. 'Really, I can assure you that my time at school was exceptionally dull.'

'Somehow I doubt that.' His gaze pinned her. The clock on the mantelpiece ticked, the rain whipped the windows. 'I bet it was fascinating,' Daniel continued. 'Because, like me, you come from a working-class family. Yet somehow you found your way into what is an elitist career.'

'My story is very boring,' Connie heard herself insisting. 'I just worked hard. Focused on my studies, my lessons with the violin, and when an opportunity in London presented itself, I seized it. Therein my career truly began.'

'So you'd classify yourself as a good student?'

Connie felt the thump of her own heartbeat in her ears. Eight decades and still going. Something pressed against her leg. With a start she jerked her knee up as Bach sidled past her, tail high, meowing loudly before launching himself onto the spare half of the sofa and turning several times, claws kneading the thick fabric.

'He's a friendly one.' Daniel watched the cat out of the corner of his eye.

'Territorial more like.' Bach was purring, paws continuing to prick at the sofa. 'He's just letting you know this is his space. Don't trust him when he shows you kindness.'

'Ha!' Daniel released an easy laugh. 'Sounds like a smart cat.'

'He watches out for me.' Connie felt the tension in her hands begin to ease as Bach curled his ginger body into a tight ball and closed his eyes.

'So it's just you and him here, in this big house?' More notes being scratched.

'Yes. It's just myself and Bach here. But we keep each other company.' The clock above the fireplace loudly chimed to announce the half-hour.

'Tea.' Connie thought of the cold contents of her cup and began to raise herself up using the armrest of her chair. 'I think it is time for more tea.'

10

Then

'How could you *lose* it?' Her father's voice was thunder.

'Connie, what the hell were you thinking?' her mother demanded shrilly from where she was hiding in the hallway. It was Sunday evening and the sky was dark. Connie had hoped that her secret might remain uncovered for a few more days. Back on the bus, giddy from her day spent with Robin and his friends, it took three stops for Connie to realise something was missing. That she was unsettlingly unburdened. She'd raced back to the bus stop by school only to find it empty. Her violin was gone. The panic that shredded through her soured what had perhaps been, up until that point, one of the greatest days of her life.

She had listened to records while lying on the floor upon a faded rug, Robin by her side. He chained his way through cigarettes and chatted, filling the air with smoke and grand ideas. And Connie drew both into her lungs, into her soul.

'The world,' he'd turned to tell her, pupils wide, 'isn't how most people see it. It's not about working yourself to the bone. It's about being happy.'

Robin and his friends lived in an end terrace not unlike Connie's home, except his lacked carpet. Or a lock on the front door. Or glass in all of the windows. And where the wallpaper peeled away, there was graffiti and crumbling plaster. 'It's a roof over our heads,' he told her proudly as he'd ushered her inside, 'and it's ours. We get to make the rules, do as we please.'

The term *squatters* flitted through Connie's mind but she ignored it. 'The place is great,' she'd told him earnestly. Mattresses on floors, a kitchen that smelt of old grease and tobacco. It wasn't homely, yet it was liberating. Shoes could be worn in all rooms. You could sit wherever you wanted. Through Connie's eyes it was a teenage utopia.

'Do you know what it *cost*?' her father raged, cheeks ruddy from the ale he'd been consuming in the Duck and Sow since noon. 'Thirty pounds, Connie. Thirty. Pounds.'

As she faced him, she kept her gaze steady, hard. But her body was betraying her, a tremor snaking up her leg.

Connie had originally hoped that she wouldn't need to tell her parents about the missing violin. That Monday would arrive and she could explain to Mr Collins, see if there was one at the school she could borrow. Knowing it was gone filled her with a strange sorrow, which left her hollow. But thoughts of Robin eagerly filled the space. The way his hair fell into his eyes. The lopsided smile he wore when he was talking to her. How animated his hands were when he talked about music. And books.

She had been in the bath when there was a knock at the door. Tucked up within an ocean of bubbles she felt safe. Serene. Studying her toes as they dipped below the surface and back up again, considering if she should paint them, like Wren did, Connie suddenly heard the mumble of voices below and froze.

'We need to talk.' It didn't take long for her mother to appear in the doorway, letting all the warm air escape onto the landing, leaving the bathroom cool and damp. 'Get some clothes on and come downstairs.'

Connie had idled over drying herself, putting off facing the firing squad for as long as she could.

'I just had a gentleman at the door,' her mother began primly, but the hands wedged against her wide hips belied the truth of her demeanour. 'And strangely, he had your violin case with him. Said he'd found it in the bus stop. Thank God it had your name and address written inside.'

'I . . .' Connie dragged her fingers through still wet hair. 'I forgot it coming home yesterday, it was such a blur and—'

'Yesterday,' her mother interrupted. Voice hard. 'Yet you said nothing.'

'I know but—'

'What a deceitful little thing you're becoming.'

Connie bulked. Stunned. All she did was work. Go to school, attend lessons. Do as everyone told her to. And suddenly she was *deceitful*.

'Look, Mum—'

'And know that I'm telling your father when he gets back from the pub.' The words seemed to suck all air out of the room. Connie struggled to breathe, struggled to find her voice.

'Please . . .' she whispered quietly. Desperately. 'Please don't.'

A look of regret washed over her mother's tired features. 'Maybe if you'd told me right away when it happened,' she reasoned, mouth puckered. 'But you didn't, you lied.'

'I didn't lie!' Connie quickly corrected her.

'A lie of omission is still a lie. I'm telling your father.'

'Why!' Connie demanded, feeling hot tears on her cheeks. 'The violin has been returned, why tell him?'

Her mother squared her shoulders, made herself as tall as she possibly could. 'Because in this house, my girl, we don't keep secrets.'

Connie had checked the clock on the far wall. It was just past four. The pub had closed at two but her father would have laboured over his walk home, listing from side to side. Smoking with friends as he staggered through town. He usually stumbled through the door just after five, giving him time to eat his dinner before heading back for the seven o'clock reopening and one final session of the weekend.

As the sun dipped low in the sky, Connie struggled to eat any of her roast chicken and gravy. Just as the pudding was served her mother unpinned her grenade.

'Albert, our Connie went and lost her violin yesterday.'

Ignoring the jam and custard in front of him, he ordered his daughter into the lounge, so that they could 'properly discuss' what had happened. But he never discussed anything. He only ever shouted.

'How could you be so *foolish*? So *reckless*?' her father raged at her. 'We work *so hard* and this is how you repay us!'

Connie felt her patience snap. It was like someone clicking their fingers beside her ear and awakening something long dormant. 'How hard *you* work?' she demanded, breathing heavily through her nose. 'You know nothing about hard work. I go in to school every day. I study. Every day. I practise violin. Every day. Even at weekends. All you do at weekends is drink.'

The slap was sudden. Sharp. And even though her father's hand was flat when it connected with her right cheek it connected like a punch. Connie staggered back, hands reaching to where there was now a fire within her face.

'You watch your mouth, girl,' he snarled, words slurring together. 'Or I'll be giving you a black eye next.'

Fingers still pressed to her cheek, she turned and ran. Away from her father. Shoving past her mother in the hallway, out the front door into the darkness, ignoring the cries which followed her into the cold night.

LOCAL TEACHER HONOURED

Local music teacher, Mr Collins from Blackhill Girls Grammar, received the Mayor's Commendation this past Saturday at an awards ceremony held within the town hall. Mr Collins was hailed for his passion and dedication to his students, most notably Year 9 student, Connie Lipman, who underneath his tutelage has advanced to Grade 8 on the violin in record time.

Ms Lipman played a rousing rendition of Vivaldi's *Four Seasons* at the event. Mr Collins said that seeing her play marked one of his proudest moments in teaching. 'Giving the gift of music to students, seeing them light up when they play, brings me both joy and comfort.'

There is an open day at the school on 20 June, where Mr Collins will be present to speak with prospective students.

II

Then

Connie would never recall how exactly she made it to Robin's doorstep. Like a homing pigeon, some internal guidance had taken her down dark streets, to the bus stop, helped her fumble in the satchel she'd had the foresight to grab before fleeing from home, show her bus pass to the driver who'd let her on, concealing any misgivings he may have had about a young woman travelling alone after dusk.

Her cheek still throbbed. There was ringing in her ears.

But the violin was returned. Blinking back tears, she clung to this thought as the bus bounced along quiet streets. But still her father was furious. Still she wasn't enough. He was always telling her to study harder. Play more. Even though her predicted O level grades were all looking good. More than good, great. It was never enough.

When her stop came, Connie hurried off the almost empty bus. There was a bald man engrossed in his copy of the *Sunday Express* and an elderly woman at the back who appeared to be asleep. Neither acknowledged Connie's departure. Only the driver gave her a tight, 'take care'. And then with a hiss of hydraulics the bus was gone. Connie alone beneath a lamppost.

Things were different at night. This had always intrigued Connie. Her welcoming driveway suddenly thick with shadows, unfamiliar. The slim back garden a tangle of green grass and hydrangeas in the day. In the dark there were corners she couldn't see, that the glow from the open back door couldn't reach.

The streets Connie had followed Robin and his friends down felt different now. Longer. Lonelier. So many of them were as dark as the dense sky overhead, no welcoming rectangles of yellow. Connie kept her steps light and quick, the cool of the night seeping in even quicker thanks to her damp hair. Then she heard it. The scratchy, soulful voice she'd heard on the radio. Elvis Presley. 'That's All Right'. Her mother would hum along to it when she was washing up. Only now it was carried on the stiff night air, drawing her in. Connie followed the music to the final house in a row of darkened terraces, where the flimsy front door was wedged ajar with a dog-eared copy of *War and Peace*. And there was light within. Faint and flickering, like a candle.

It was like stepping through the looking glass. Once inside the house, the pain in her face eased, the bite from the cool evening cowered in the street, unable to follow her in. Music and warmth enveloped her and Connie floated as though in a dream through rooms filled with faces she didn't know until she arrived in the front room. The only relic of its time used as such was a fireplace now filled with glowing candles almost burned down to their wicks. Lying on the floor, stretched out long, his head tilted in the direction of the record player in the far corner, eyes closed, was Robin. He looked so peaceful. So content. The record jumped, Elvis's smooth vocals suddenly awkward as he repeated the same line. Robin's eyes snapped open at the disruption. And he stared straight up at Connie, who was gazing down at him, mouth growing dry as the realisation that she was there uninvited began to creep up her spine.

'Robin, I—'

She sensed Wren and another girl. Blonde, even prettier, at her back. Circling.

'Connie . . .' The smile he gave her was so wide, so whole, that she couldn't help but beam back at him. 'Hey, you made it.' He nimbly got to his feet and then embraced her, arms wrapping tight, drawing her close. Holding her a beat longer than a family member would. He smelt of smoke. And beer. 'I'm so glad you made it. We were just about to head over.'

'Head . . . over?' Connie's smile began to falter. Robin was holding her shoulders, still smiling at her, hair falling into his face, cheeks rosy.

'The fair?' Now he glanced behind her, at Wren and the blonde. 'We have to go to the fair. Remember?'

Connie studied his face for some hidden smirk, a sign of cynicism. But no, his words seemed sincere. He clearly believed that he had invited her along to the fair, that her being in his home was not some strange coincidence. So Connie began nodding, happy to go along with the pretence. 'Yes, the fair, right.'

She'd heard about the fair. From the newspaper. Seen the adverts on lampposts around town. She knew her old friends would be going. Stuffing their faces with candy floss and toffee apples. Shrieking as they spun around on the waltzers. It was there for three weekends out of the month, just on the edge of town in a field usually filled only with dying wildflowers at this time of year. Connie hadn't even asked her parents about going. Knew it wouldn't be allowed. Weekends were for studying. Playing violin. And no one from the grammar school was going. For different reasons to Connie. None of them would be caught dead on that side of town. Where the beer was cheap and gardens didn't come with fences.

They walked to the fair. About a dozen of them. Though Connie couldn't be quite certain of the number, it was difficult to do a head count in the dark. Robin was at her side, arm slung casually over her shoulder. The other thrust deep into his pocket.

Arthur was loud, singing Elvis as he strolled hand in hand with Wren. Which made the barbed looks she kept throwing back at Connie all the more confusing.

'You excited?' Robin asked, voice high with mirth, as they walked. 'Your folks happy to let you stay out late?'

'No . . . I . . .' Connie chewed her lip, reluctant to get into it. Not here, surrounded by people she didn't know. And not now, where the night felt alive with promise. She didn't want to risk puncturing that and letting the magic slip away. Next to Robin she wasn't thinking about her parents, about the frantic phone calls they'd surely be making, about how they'd face each other across the kitchen table, faces like stone, and wonder where their golden girl had gone. 'I mean, yeah, sure.'

Connie felt the pulse of the fair before she saw it. Gleeful cries. The tinny melody of a carousel. The crackle of sparklers. As the group turned a corner it came into view, distant and sparkling, a fairy tale come to life.

Arthur whooped with approval and sped off, dragging a reluctant Wren along with him. Robin's pace remained the same, languid and steady. He leaned in close to Connie, whispered in her ear, 'Ready to have some fun?'

The fair was packed with bodies. The air a tangle of sugar and cigarette smoke. Robin hooked his arm around Connie's waist and guided her. First to the candy floss stall.

'Here.' He handed her a pink fluffy cloud.

Then they went on the waltzers. Robin was forever waving to people. Saying hello. Nodding in greeting.

Everyone knew him. And Connie could have been mistaken but she was certain he didn't pay for anything. That at every stall, every ride, people just let him on. Just handed him food.

'Do you have friends who work here?' she asked loudly over the din.

His brown eyes settled on her, crinkling in the corners. 'Some.'

Growing up, the waltzers were always Connie's favourite. She loved to spin herself into oblivion. She was wedged up against Robin, her thigh pressed to his, as they clutched the central bar and turned, turned, turned. The lights from the fair blurring behind them. Connie's mouth was still sweet from the candy gloss. And she stared at Robin, at the streak of lights behind him, at the glow he seemed to always hold in his gaze, and she feared she was suddenly so happy, so buoyant, that if she weren't holding onto the grimy surface of the bar she'd simply float away, become just another star in the sky.

'This . . . this is my favourite,' Robin declared when, hand in hand, they found themselves at the base of the big wheel. He'd slipped his hand into hers when they stepped off the waltzers as though it were the most natural thing to do. Connie didn't care if people were looking, if old school friends were there and whispering about her. She just cared that Robin never let go.

'Come on.' He pulled her forward and together they climbed into a carriage that swung precariously the second they stepped inside. For a moment Connie withdrew, felt the unpleasant cold stab of fear in her gut. 'Hey.' Robin spread his arms to stabilise the carriage, expression boyish and hopeful as he stared at her. 'Come on. I've got you.'

Up they went.

The fair beneath them grew smaller. A model village instead of a living thing. Alone and aloft Connie was so aware of her breath. Of the manic beating of her own heart.

'Hey.' Robin's warm fingers grazed her cheek. 'What happened here?'

'It . . .' Her chest clenched, eyes burned with the need to cry. 'It's nothing.'

'It looks sore.' His gentle touch continued to stroke the place her father had hit.

'I . . . I lost my violin,' she blurted suddenly, desperately. 'And my dad, he was so . . . so angry at me and . . .' She burrowed her face into Robin's shoulder, drank in his scent, his warmth, just as she started to cry.

'Hey, hey, we'll find it,' he assured her as he gently stroked her hair. 'If some light-fingered idiot lifted it, I'll find it. I promise.'

'No, no . . .' Sniffing, Connie eased back, cheeks blotchy. 'Someone found it, returned it.'

'They did?' Robin's eyes seemed sharper. More focused. 'Then why was your dad so mad at you?'

'He . . . he . . .' Connie hiccuped, struggling to speak. 'I disappointed him. L-losing it like that.' She squeezed her eyes shut, leaned into Robin. He held her, stroked her back as they swung above the fair. Above the town. Above the entire world. And as her breathing levelled out, Connie realised it had been no accident, leaving her violin. That a part of her had never wanted to see it again.

12

Then

It was difficult to know when it first happened. In Connie's mind it was sudden, like a streak of lightning suddenly bursting like a firework in the sky. The reality, she suspected, was surely different, full of gentle rumblings that foretold what lay ahead. But late one January evening, shortly after she'd passed her Grade 2 violin exam, things began to change for Connie.

The first time always felt the most significant. When Connie played it all back in her mind, it felt woefully clichéd to note that the evening had unfolded like any other. Yet it truly had.

Connie had returned home from school in darkness, as was normal during the long winter months. Sunlight only existed when she was already locked within school. Her journey on the bus, her long walk to and from the gates, they happened when the sun had long dipped beneath the horizon. It made her commute all the more unnerving. The times that Mr Collins offered to drive her to the bus stop she readily accepted. Yearning for the light of his car, the comfort. Mr Collins forever so kind, so keen. So overfilled with joy with each exam she passed.

After this last exam he'd kissed her cheek and made it burn. 'You're such a star.'

On the night everything changed, Connie had sat at the back of the bus, head filled with the gentle pluck of violin strings, fingers flexing retrospectively as she went over her practice from the day. Outside it was dark, quiet. The world hard and frozen. Bowing her head against a bitter wind, Connie left the bus and walked home, steps light and brisk. When she got home, warmth and the sweet smell of rice pudding rushed to greet her, causing her stomach to release a slow, steady growl.

'Shut that door, you're letting all the heat out!' her mother had called sharply from the kitchen where she bustled about in her apron, face flushed. Out of sight, Connie rolled her eyes and closed the door.

'Wash your hands before dinner.'

She'd barely crossed the threshold to her home and already orders were being flung at her like arrows.

'And don't go leaving any bags in the hall for your father to trip over. He's on afternoons this week now.'

Connie froze.

Afternoons meant a five o'clock finish. Which meant ample time to sit in the glow of the fire in the Fox and Heathers. Ample time to drink. And then a slap of cold when he staggered home hours later, the alcohol set in deep.

Fuck.

Connie knew he was meant to be on the night shift, ten until six, creeping in just as she left for school, leaving the house quiet and still while she slept. Now he'd be thundering in just shy of midnight. Connie felt her stomach hit the floor, no longer hungry.

'I said come and wash yer hands.'

'I'm not hungry,' Connie called loudly.

'You'll eat when I say you eat.' Her mother appeared in the doorway to the kitchen, filling it, blocking out all warmth and light. 'Don't start with me, young lady. I've had enough of a day to contend with, rushing round sorting things for your father.'

Connie could just picture the black telephone in their hallway ringing shrilly, her mother bustling towards her, annoyed at having to sacrifice the cigarette she'd surely been enjoying in the cramped front room while she listened to songs on the wireless. A shift change was never a good thing. It brought disruption, tension.

'I thought he was on nights.' Connie stared down the hallway at her mother.

'So did I.' Her mother threw her hands up in despair. 'God knows what's going on at that bloody place. But mark my words, he'll be pissed about the change, lord knows it.'

'Gives him more time in the pub,' Connie remarked sourly.

'Don't you start, Connie Lipman,' her mother fired hotly at her. 'Watch your lip and be a good girl. You hear?'

'I hear.' Connie stalked towards the kitchen, the light, the food. Despite her misgivings, her body was reacting to it all. She ate two bowlfuls of rice pudding before heading up to her bedroom to finish her homework and read. She told herself that everything would be fine. And other than the information about the change to her father's schedule, it was.

At eight Connie slipped into her long-sleeved nightdress, combed her blonde hair, drew it back in a plait, padded down the landing to brush her teeth. When she returned to her bed, she noticed the bulge under her blankets where her mother had placed a brick hot from the oven, wrapped in newspaper, to try and bite back some of the cold. Already ice streaked across the outside of her bedroom window.

When midnight came, there was no melody in Connie's mind. She was deep asleep, the pudding from earlier thick in her stomach. She failed to hear her father come home, hear him curse and scold the air as he slammed the front door, and stomp towards the kitchen to eat the food laid out for him on the table.

It was dark when Connie awoke. And cold. So, so cold. It took her several long, panicked seconds to realise she wasn't in bed. With a gasp she noticed she was standing up, feeling the ice of tiled floor beneath her feet. Eyes wide, she looked about but it was all so impossibly dark. She thought to reach out a hand but realised she was holding something. Something smooth. Cool.

What is happening?

Light. Sudden and blinding. And along with it a buzzing so loud Connie felt like it was clawing into her skull, pressing against the soft tissue of her brain.

'Argh!' she screamed, reached for her temple as something clattered to the floor.

'Saints alive, foolish girl!'

Her mother's voice. Connie turned, sensing a shape moving in her direction but her vision was blurry, too quickly drawn out of the darkness.

'What have you done?'

Her mother's hands were guiding her down, onto a chair, then pressing a glass of water between her palms.

'Here, drink?'

'What . . . the . . .' Gradually Connie noticed the tiles on the floor. The shape of the cupboards. Smelt the lingering sweetness of rice pudding. She was in the kitchen. She was home.

Why the hell was she in the kitchen?

Her gaze instantly tipped skyward, fearful.

'He's passed out,' her mother assured her stiffly. 'Herd of cows passing through couldn't wake him. You're lucky.'

'I'm . . .' Connie took a sip of water from the glass. It tasted like iron. With a grimace she lowered it from her mouth.

Her mother loomed over her, one hand pressed firmly to her temple, lips pulled thin and tight. 'Soon as I 'eard a creak on the stairs I thought, oh no, here we go again.'

'Again?' Connie echoed, the word leaving her as a croak.

'I quickly checked your bed and sure enough, empty.'

'Empty?'

'What are you? A bloody parrot?' Her mother shook her head in dismay. 'What am I to do with you? If your father finds out, he'll blame me for sure. And Christ knows what's wrong with you.'

'With *me*?' Connie began to shiver, the cold of the room drawing up too tight against her bare legs, pressing through the cotton of her nightdress.

'Do you remember nothing?'

Connie shook her head, thoughts foggy.

Her mother released a deep sigh. 'Just drink your water.'

'But I—'

'You've been walking in your sleep again,' her mother explained with disdain.

'Again?'

'Usually I'm quick enough to catch you on the landing, turn you around and place you back in bed.'

'I don't—'

'They say don't wake a sleepwalker. Worst thing you can do is wake them.'

'But, Mum, I—'

'And now this time I find you down 'ere. With that!'

Connie glances to the floor where her mother is pointing, to where a heavy-duty kitchen knife was lying upon the tiles.

64

'I—'

'Stupid, stupid girl. Could have cut off your own toes dropping it like you did. Lord knows why you grabbed it. Maybe you were going to peel me some sodding potatoes.'

'I don't . . .' Connie hiccuped against a developing sob. She had been in bed. Asleep. A good, deep sleep. And then suddenly there was darkness. So much of it. 'Mum, I don't . . .' She threw her mother a helpless look.

'Hush, hush now.' Her mother knelt beside her and stroked at Connie's cheeks with her rough thumbs. 'You're OK, that's what matters.'

'This has happened before?' Connie asked fretfully.

'Few times, yes,' her mum confirmed. 'It all started around the time school did. When you took up the violin. I figured it was, perhaps, you know, stress. That you'd grow out of it. But . . .' She gazed into Connie's eyes, looking pained.

'I didn't know.' Connie felt so small. So afraid. So cheated by her sleeping self. 'I didn't know I was doing it.'

'I know. I know.'

'I didn't—'

'We just need your father not to catch you. That's all.'

Her mother cast a backwards glance towards the knife upon the floor. For a moment neither of them spoke. Connie was unsure why her sleeping self had grabbed it from the drawer, but she was certain it hadn't been to peel potatoes.

'You're awake, you're fine, that's what matters.' Her mother kissed her cheek hard and then doubled back to grab the knife, returning it to its drawer, which she closed with a loud flourish, causing cutlery to rattle.

'Why am I doing this?' Connie asked, still shivering, even though she knew her mother wouldn't hold the answer.

'Look at you, you're freezing. You'll catch a chill down 'ere. Back to bed with you. I'll place another brick in the oven and bring it up.'

Connie rose to her feet, body tense and out of sorts. A part of her felt like she was still in a dream. She padded over to the door, the taste of iron still in her throat. 'Mum?' She glanced back to where her mother was busying herself lighting a match for the stove.

'Hmm?'

'Thank you.' Connie lingered by the darkness of the hallway; they couldn't afford to turn on every light in the middle of the night. Few down their street could. 'For . . . for looking after me. Not just tonight but—'

'Don't mention it.' The match spluttered to life in her mother's hand. 'I'm just doing my job, just being your mother.'

'I know but . . . ' Connie peered towards the shadows that swelled against the stairs, unsure what she needed to say. What she should say.

'To bed with you,' her mother nudged again. 'We didn't work for you to be in that school just to be taken sick and stuck in bed with a fever. Go on, off with you.'

Connie nodded and reached for the banister, began climbing up to the landing. Already she could hear the guttural roar of her father's snoring reaching down from his bedroom. As she slipped deeper into the darkness, she didn't notice her mother reopen the cutlery drawer and pull out the knife Connie had been holding, the sharp one usually used for carving meat. Her mother held it towards the light, turned it over, studying it, a deep worry line furrowed into her brow.

When Connie climbed back into bed, sleep claimed her quicker than she'd expected. The next time she woke, it was to the sound of her mother's knuckles rapping upon her door.

'Time for school, Lady Lipman, let's go.'

The events of the previous night drifted far from her mind as she ate her porridge and prepared for the day. But in still moments, she thought of it. Of the knife she had held. Of the darkness. And, most troubling of all, how it had not been the first time it had happened. Which surely meant it also wouldn't be the last.

13

Now

'It was in London.' Connie stirs the spoon in her cup, the tea warm and fresh. 'I can still remember how it felt, that first moment, to play as part of such a grand orchestra. To think that I was being *paid* to play. That it was my job.'

She so wanted to go back there, to that day, that memory. When the sky was an icy winter blue and her home had become a stuffy flat above a chip shop. But her dreams had shifted from sand into something real. Something from which she could build a future. She needed to only close her eyes to be back in the thick darkness of the theatre, to smell the dust rising off the lamps, the musk of the velvet chairs.

'But I really want to focus on your early days as a violinist.' Daniel smiled wanly at her, his fresh cup and saucer of tea on the table before him, untouched. 'On your *study* of the craft.'

Connie winced.

'Back when you were a grammar school student, taking those first tentative steps with the instrument.'

Bach raised his head, narrowed his yellow-ringed eyes, turning to peer at the stranger on the sofa.

'Can you tell me more about those days?'

Connie sipped at her tea. She'd made it too weak. Bach lowered his head to his paws, gaze now fixed on his mistress. Neatly placing her cup upon the saucer, she lowered the china duo down to the coffee table. Her wrists were beginning to ache, the damp outside trying to seep into her bones, infuriate her arthritis. 'I fear I've told you all I can about my time as a student.'

The rain against the window grew louder. Branches of a tree in the driveway fluttered madly, like someone desperately waving for attention. All of its leaves already gone. Winter was imminent. Connie could sense its approach each morning as she pushed open the back door and allowed Bach to trot out, tail held high. He had a cat flap but refused to use it.

'Stubborn old mule,' she'd tut under her breath as he strode towards the lawn, wondering how she'd ended up with a pet who so mirrored her. Would Bach always have been a crotchety old cat, or had living with a crotchety old woman turned him into one?

'Was there a teacher at the school who particularly influenced you?' Daniel gazed her, ever patient. Pen ever poised atop his notepad.

Mr Collins.

Connie gave a curt shake of her head. 'No one that springs to mind.'

'When I attempted to research your early career . . . ' Now Daniel was moving, removing his notepad from his lap and leaning towards his satchel resting against the foot of the sofa. Connie looked at it, the faded leather, the buckle clasp. So very like the one she had slung across her slim shoulders every morning for school. She'd always found it strange how cyclic fashion could be. Leather jackets, polka dots, winklepicker boots, they all drifted in and out of style. She was thinking about her own bag, about how the leather softened over the years, the ends of the straps frayed. How once she spilt a bottle of Coca-Cola over all her books and it stained the base of her bag.

'. . . the earliest mentions of your career begin in London . . . ' Daniel was leafing through a stack of papers he'd taken from his bag. From her position in the armchair, Connie could see dates, newspaper articles. '. . . when you performed at the Royal Opera House.'

'Right.'

'There are some earlier . . . ' He riffled through his pile of printed information. 'Articles in your local paper about your achievements. And before that—'

A roar. Within the chimney, rushing out through the empty hearth. The wind was picking up. Connie dutifully shuddered. Really, she should light a fire. But the thought of carrying first the wood, then getting on her knees to place it within the grate, was just too much. She was thankful for the heating system she'd had installed a little over ten years ago. It kept the house cosy, warm. Even on days when the wind howled down the chimney.

'Like I've said, those early days were very dull. Lots of lessons. Lots of studying.'

'There was a scandal . . . ' Daniel's eyes widened in triumph as he found the article he'd been searching for. 'It occurred while you were at the grammar school and involved . . .' He leaned forward, slim body extending with ease, proffering the paper and the article printed upon it to Connie. His fingers were long, as were his nails. Clenching her jaw, Connie turned to the fireplace, fixing her attention on the clock above it.

'I don't need to see the article to know what you're referring to.'

She heard the flutter of paper as Daniel withdrew and returned it to his stack. 'It must have been incredibly . . . traumatic.' His voice was soft. Careful.

'Please.' Connie twisted to look over at him, searching his pale features, noting the chickenpox scars which mottled his forehead, 'I want only to talk about events which are linked to my career.'

'Is that not linked?' Daniel flicked his gaze to the papers now piled beside him, the top one bearing a copy of an article Connie didn't dare look at directly. She knew what it would say. How reading it would make her feel. 'Because I don't see how it couldn't be. When that happened it must have been a huge blow for you and—'

'It was in London,' Connie loudly repeated her earlier comment, a steel edge creeping into her voice which she had feared had long since diminished. It felt good to know she could still do it, could still fill her lungs with fire when she needed to. 'My first paid concert. For the *Nutcracker* ballet. I was still a teenager and I was playing Tchaikovsky within a world-renowned orchestra. To a packed house. So my career was just fine, I can assure you. What happened was not a . . .' She had to pause, not for dramatic effect, but to catch her breath, '*huge blow* for me. My craft did not suffer. So, please, let us focus only on the music. For that is why you are here, it is not?'

14

Then

It was past midnight when she returned home. Giddy from sugar, from the thrill of the fair, body still pulsing from being in such close proximity to Robin, Connie floated along the streets. Only when she pushed open the little gate at the edge of her garden did she notice the glow within the windows and seize up, fingers tight against the metal latch she was suddenly unable to close. Her parents were still up. There would be questions. Slung at her like an endless assault of arrows. Connie's chin dropped to her chest, legs crumpling like paper. She wasn't sure she had the strength to walk the few feet down the thin strip of a path to her front door.

Her mother found her there some ten minutes later, buckled beside the gate. 'Do you have any idea how worried we've been?' she demanded angrily as she hoisted her daughter up, gripping her firmly by the armpits. 'Your dad and I have been beside ourselves.'

Inside, the house was warm. Connie peered into the living room, at the embers glowing in the hearth, illuminating the slumped figure of her father in his beloved armchair, a trail of spittle running down his chin. 'Yeah, he looks *real worried*.'

Her mother spun her around so fast that Connie felt dizzier than she had on the waltzers. Thick hands gripped her shoulders, fingers reddened by years spent washing clothes and dishes. 'Now you listen here.' Her mother's voice was low but sharp. 'We're to have no more of this running off, you got it? You go to a *good school*, Connie. If you keep your head down, get good grades, you'll have a decent future. Don't you want that?'

'I . . .' Connie peered beyond her mother, to the stairs, desperate to climb them and fall into the soft embrace of her bed. Dry fingers clutched at her chin, directed her gaze back towards the current conversation.

'You have a gift with the violin. A gift. It's something that could take you places. Do you understand?'

Connie nodded.

'We need you to keep playing. Keep studying.'

Connie was silent as a sole tear fell down her left cheek.

'Play the violin. Get the grades. That's all you need to do. Don't slip up now.'

Connie's chin began to tremble as it was released from her mother's grip. 'But—'

'Not another word out of you. Bed. Now. When your father wakes, leave him to me.'

The next day was hard. Connie was tired, sluggish. But she woke up on time, muscles aching. She dragged herself onto the bus, travelled beneath a pewter sky to school where she drifted from classroom to classroom. Attending lessons. Making the right noises when prompted. And while her body was there, her mind drifted through town, over to where the fair was packing up to leave. She was thinking of blurring lights and carousels. She was thinking of Robin Strand.

Tuesday brought with it her violin lesson. A time when she usually came so alive, felt so free. But, as the day before, she was distant, distracted. Something which Mr Collins quickly picked up on.

'Are you with me today?' he wondered brightly, dimples appearing in chiselled cheeks. 'Because it feels like you're far away.'

Connie smiled weakly. 'I'm just tired.' The instrument tucked beneath her chin felt heavier than usual.

'It's a tough year with all the studying. The exams. The pressure.' Mr Collins tipped his head to the right as he watched her, arms folded against his lean chest. As usual he wore a waistcoat over his shirt. Always dapper. Her mother had loved that about him.

'So well dressed,' she had gushed following a parents' evening. 'Such a gentleman.'

Even Connie's father had agreed. 'He's an upstanding sort.' Then his tired eyes had settled on his daughter. 'You should be grateful he's taken you under his wing.'

'From the top,' Mr Collins ordered, waving a finger in the air. 'I need to really *feel* what you're playing.'

As Connie began her sonata again, he closed his eyes, drifted to somewhere else. With each pull of her bow, Connie's thoughts edged further and further away from school. Closer and closer to Robin. She was wistfully gazing out the window when she noticed the first spatter of rain against the glass and caught her note awkwardly, the sound jarring and sharp. A cat in pain.

Mr Collins's eyes flew open. 'What happened there?' Before Connie could answer, he looked to the window, hearing the slap of the rain that was quickly growing in fervour. 'Would you look at that weather? That's October for you.'

Connie knew that her lesson was almost over so she was hurriedly returning her violin to its case, already wondering if she might see Robin at the bus stop. Or, if she was quick enough, there might be time to hurry over to his house.

'Let me drive you home.' Mr Collins's hand was on her back. 'I don't like to think of you out there alone, getting wet.'

'Really, I'm fine.' She shied away from his touch. His offer.

Besides, she thought, *I'm not alone*.

But Robin wasn't at the bus stop. He didn't materialise for the rest of the week. Each day felt more torturous than the one before. And at home her mother monitored her every movement. Even going to the bathroom, she'd hear the thump of footsteps coming up the stairs, checking her. Waiting to see if she'd cracked a window and tried to escape.

Thankfully her father's shifts meant that she could easily avoid him. Which was for the best. So she only had her mother's overvigilance to contend with.

'Where did you go on Sunday night?' she'd question over breakfast and dinner.

'To a friend's.' Connie kept her reply simple. Basic.

'Which friend?'

'You don't know them.'

'I know everyone.'

This was true. And her mother probably did know Robin and his friends. Or at least would know *of* them. Connie sensed that their existence would be notorious in town. A cluster of young people living together, shirking their commitment to society, their education. Being free. But her mother never talked of them, which wasn't surprising. She refused to discuss anything in the house that she felt might destroy Connie's innocence, might lure her away from her studies. Her music. Connie wasn't allowed to watch television or listen to the radio unsupervised. All the books she borrowed from the library were on the school's reading list.

By Friday Connie felt exhausted by her longing. She was sick of it being cold, of the days feeling damp. Of her studies. Even of her violin. Everything in her life felt so dull compared to the brightness of Robin. She dragged herself to the bus stop, satchel heavy upon her shoulders, aware that a weekend of being trapped in her bedroom awaited her. And there he was.

Connie saw the curl of smoke snaking out of the bus stop first and her heart nearly leapt clean out of her chest. She was beaming when she came to face him, leaning against the back wall, one hand deep in his pocket, the other tipping ash from his cigarette onto the street. 'Miss me?' he asked with a casual smirk. Connie's face burned from the awareness that she was giving too much away. 'How's school?'

'Ridiculous,' she blurted earnestly. That week she'd learnt about the way the Tudors raged against one another, how fractions worked, how to recite the periodic table backwards and to say the Lord's Prayer in Latin. And now, facing Robin, it all felt utterly pointless and completely ridiculous. She knew he'd have spent his week *living*, not hiding within musty books.

'You should come hang with us this weekend,' he offered, raising his cigarette to his lips. Connie frowned and he must have read the fear which bleached her face. 'Or, you know, stay as long as you like.' He exhaled a grey trail, which drifted up towards the sky. 'I know how it is,' his chestnut eyes crinkled with understanding, 'feeling misunderstood, like you don't belong. Everyone at my place felt like that. Lost. We're all strays. But together, we're a pack.'

'You want me to just come and . . . *live* with you?' Connie wasn't sure she was understanding. She had a home. And school. So much school to contend with. And her parents and—

He was suddenly beside her, fingers warmed as they grazed her cheek. 'You just strike me as someone who wants to be free, that's all.' The violin tucked up beneath her arm. The satchel draped over her. The textbooks within it. It was all so unbearably heavy. And her violin . . . her music . . . Connie closed her eyes. Focused on his touch upon her skin. She wanted so desperately to be free.

15

Then

She left when it was dark. When the moon was round and ripe. It was easy to slip out while her mother slept and her father was out working. Connie heard the motor engine rumble of her mother's snores echoing along the slim landing as she crept from her room, school satchel clenched to her side, violin case tucked under her arm.

She'd thought about leaving it behind. Letting it gather dust in a corner of her room. But it was as though the strings of her violin had entwined her, were able to drag her back. It was the music. The dizzying high she felt when she played, the way she left her thoughts, her world.

Connie had made it as far as the top of the staircase when she doubled back to grab her instrument. She'd hoped she could be without it. Without the music. Without the memories. Because now, more often than not when she played, she flinched. A muscle memory she hadn't intended to adopt. But now her violin was at her side and she was at the base of the stairs, then in the hallway looking at the front door, the glint of a loose chain and a single dead bolt all that stood in her way. In the darkness Connie waited, the smell of roast beef still lingering in the air. She waited for the floorboards overhead to creak, for her mother to come thundering down the stairs, cheeks flushed in rage. But all she heard was the steady tick of the carriage clock in the front room. Marking every second. Connie waited an entire minute and then slipped out into the night.

Robin was awake when she reached his house, shaken by the dark, barren streets. She would soon learn that he didn't keep regular hours. That like a lion he drifted between sleep and wakefulness whenever it suited him. Whenever he sensed prey.

'You're actually here.' He embraced her like they were old friends. Connie beamed at him while her thoughts hung on the *actually*. Had he not thought she'd do it? Was his offer not genuine? 'Come, come.' One hand was pressed to her back as he ushered her inside. The air was hazy and bleary-eyed guests lined the walls, some still propped up, others slumped to the ground, expressions glazed. 'I'll find somewhere for you to put your stuff.' He led her up the bare staircase, towards a distant door and into a room lit only by the moon, the walls streaked with damp. The room was small, barely able to accommodate the sole mattress spread on the floor. 'I freed up some long-term residents as I figured you'd want your own space.' His hand moved lower on her back. Connie traced the walls with her nervous gaze, noticed the latticework of graffiti racing across it like a stream of consciousness. As her eyes adjusted, words jumped out at her. *Life. Lies. Dreams.* From a distance it seemed rambling, incoherent. Nervously she placed her satchel and violin case on the mattress, instantly thinking of her bed back home and its floral sheets and soft pillows. 'It's a big step.' Robin drew close against her as he heard the whimper escape her lips. 'But it will be worth it.' His breath was hot on her cheek. 'I promise.'

When dawn came, the sky sulked. Clouds had crept in and blotted out the sun, making Connie's room feel even colder and more unwelcoming. Without even the sheen of moonlight to coat it, it was looking more like a prison. Spine pressed to the wall, knees to her chest, she was wedged atop the mattress and had been that way for hours, waiting for sleep that never came. It felt like the house beyond was alive. Voices wafted in beneath the door. Sometimes euphoric in laughter, other times screaming. And music pulsed from beneath like a heartbeat. Connie looked out the curtainless window, at the slate rooftops and the bleak sky. She tried to anchor herself in reality, in the moment. What time was it? Seven? Half past? She should have been on the bus by now, on her way to school, close to her stop. What had her mother done when she'd entered Connie's room while the stars still shone, peeling back the soft sheets to find not her daughter but a hastily scrawled note.

I'm sorry but you wouldn't listen. Don't try and find me.

Connie knew her mother would be more than mad, she'd be furious. She'd grip the note between her raw, plump fingers and wait for her husband to return home from his shift. Was she now smoothing it out against the kitchen table, blinking back tears and wondering what to do. Wondering whether to look for her daughter. Wondering where to look?

There was a rap against the door. 'Hey.' Robin peered in at her, hair messier than usual, eyes red, as though he'd been sleeping. 'You manage to get any sleep?' He drew himself up beside her on the mattress, his lean arms bare in a white t-shirt. Connie just shook her head, unable to speak. She knew that if she opened her mouth, it would all come tumbling out – her doubts, her worries. Her fear that this was all so awfully, horribly wrong. What was she even

80

doing, running away like this? She went to a *good* school. She was set to have a *good* future. Why jeopardise that?

'We worked so hard to get you in there,' her mother had said that awful day. 'And you're so talented, Connie. We can't let that go to waste.'

'It's OK.' Robin leaned his head against the wall and peered up at the ceiling, at the fissures in the flaking paint. 'I struggled when I first came here.'

Connie tilted her gaze to study him. In profile she could see a kink in his nose which hinted at a poorly healed fracture. And his jawline was shadowed with stubble.

'It's hard to let go of the world, of what came before,' he continued, his voice taking on a dreamlike quality. 'But if you're here,' his tone suddenly firmed as he slipped a hand into the pocket of his jeans and then pressed something into Connie's palm, 'it means you'd been waiting to run away. That you're like the rest of us.'

Looking down at her hand Connie saw a small knot of paper obscuring her fate line.

'You put it on your tongue,' Robin explained. 'And it makes everything better. It makes everything *real*.'

Connie peered at him, unconvinced.

'It's legit, my mum took it all the time. Her doctor gave it to her, said it was some new drug that worked wonders, that helped cleanse the mind.'

Connie looked down at her palm. Her mind definitely did need cleansing. Robin leaned in close, hair falling into his eyes. 'Trust me.'

Outside the slick of grey was lightening. How long until her name was called at morning register, until her school noted her absence? Connie placed the paper on her tongue. It was so light, tasting of nothing. Like eating a cloud. As it melted it left a chalky residue.

'Like I said, my mum took it all the time.' Robin pressed a kiss against her cheek and Connie lit up, smiling wide. And then he got up, making for the doorway, pausing as an afterthought occurred to him. 'At least, she took it until she died.'

Connie blinked. Was it just her imagination or were the colours in the room shifting? And then Robin was gone and she was alone.

LOCAL STAR A CRACKER

If you're planning on taking in a performance of *The Nutcracker* by the Royal Ballet this festive season, you may spy a familiar face. Not on the stage but within the orchestra. We are proud to report that Connie Lipman, graduate of Blackhill Girls Grammar, will be performing with the orchestra. At the young age of nineteen, this is an honour usually bestowed upon more seasoned performers. Ms Lipman told us, 'I'm so grateful for this opportunity to play with some of the country's best musicians while we accompany truly wonderful dancers. I couldn't ask for a better Christmas present.' What a way to make the season shine. We couldn't be happier for young Ms Lipman. If you can't get yourself to London this December, the Lydia Dowling Company are putting on their own performance of *The Nutcracker* at Blackhill Theatre. Tickets are still available and the show runs until Christmas Eve. Do consider going along to support the local arts. Who knows, the next local star might be within their midst.

16

Then

There was something about playing the violin. How easily it came to her. How abundantly. Connie had tried other instruments. The piano. The clarinet. The guitar. None resonated with her the way the violin did. There was something about the way she had to pluck and saw at the strings, lean into the instrument, let it feel like it was a part of her. And how she adored to listen to it. It could be haunting, plaintive, soulful. Connie was quite certain the violin made the most wondrous sounds she had ever heard.

'You're very good at it, but I don't get it,' her mother would often muse. 'I'd much rather a nice piano. Or a trumpet. Along with a good crooner. That's what music is.'

Connie knew that Mr Collins understood her fascination with it. Her obsession. Sometimes, while playing, she'd steal a glance at him as he stood across the room, or perched on a stool by her side, and she'd glow when she caught the wistful look on his handsome face, the curve of a smile on his full lips. Knowing that she'd put it there, that her music had done that, it ignited something within her. Spurred her on to do better, to do more.

'There's something about the way you play,' Mr Collins told her just after she'd completed her Grade 4 exam and passed with flying colours. 'You don't just play the violin,' he explained, looking into her eyes, 'it's like you're doing battle with it. It is both terrifying and beautiful.'

Terrifying and beautiful.

Another compliment she stored away and withdrew on dark nights. When she played, she put everything into her music. All her anger. All her fear. Her frustration. With every pluck and pull of each string, every sweep of her bow, she dug deeper, harder. The music overtook all other thoughts, as if she were sailing upon an ocean of it and could no longer see land. When Connie finished playing, her body felt slick with sweat, breathing shallow. It was the greatest feeling she had ever had, one she was keen to capture again and again.

'The girl is certainly good,' Mrs Watson commented one afternoon when she peered around the door. She was staring at Connie but her comments were directed towards Mr Collins, who rose from his stool to look back at her. 'Though her talent is raw. Far too raw for many formal environments.'

'It's the rawness that makes her great,' Mr Collins countered, 'the rawness that will make her exceptional.'

'The diamond needs more polishing yet,' Mrs Watson remarked, arching an eyebrow and pursing her lips.

Every day when her lessons finished, Connie went over to the music room. She withdrew her violin from its velvet case and played. Over and over. Until her fingers were numb, until they bled. Mr Collins remained unfailingly at her side. Always with a kind comment, a smile, a hand upon her tired shoulders, telling her how wonderful she was. How *good*.

Through it all, the sleepwalking persisted. Some nights Connie went out into the garden, feet damp upon the grass, a glassy moon overhead. Other nights she managed to venture out the front door, into the street, through the front gate, wandering like a lost soul past dark houses. Her mother was never far behind.

'Christ, again . . .' She'd grab her daughter, hustle her back to the house, head bowed and glowing with shame. 'Are we going to have to tie you to that bed of yours?'

If her father ever became aware of her nightly antics, he never said anything. Connie supposed he was either working when it happened, or in a sleep akin to a coma following a session at the pub. She wondered if her parents discussed it in her absence, although she highly doubted it. Her sleepwalking was surely just another burden for her mother to shoulder alone.

'I mean, it can't continue,' her mother said one morning as she sipped her tea, the shadows beneath her eyes darker than normal. 'Last night you made it past the Morgans at number thirty-eight. What if I hadn't woken up? What if you just kept going? Chills me to my bloody bones to think what might happen to you.'

'I'm sorry.' It was all Connie could say. And she *was* sorry. Deeply. But how could she be accountable for what she did in her sleep? And more pressingly, how could she make it stop?

'Emily Beadle at number sixteen reckons it is stress-induced.' Her mother gave Connie a suspicious look from across the table.

'You've been talking to Mrs Beadle about me?' Connie asked as she chewed her toast, which tasted like sawdust in her mouth. It had been left too long on the grill, grown too hard and too brittle beneath the heat, though she didn't dare say as much. She'd need to try and grab something at school if she could. A biscuit. Anything.

Her mother exhaled loudly. 'Trust me, I didn't *want* to. Last thing we need is people round here gossiping. But sooner or later, someone is going to see you walking down the road like a bloody spectre. And I don't want *that*. So

I saw her, yesterday, when I went to get eggs and milk. She used to work as a nurse.'

'I didn't know that.'

Mrs Beadle reminded Connie of an owl with her large glasses and the startled expression she always seemed to wear. She was a slip of a woman, always dwarfed by whatever plain dress she was wearing.

'Hmm, yes.' Her mother sipped her tea thoughtfully. 'Back during the war. She's seen some things. Was on one of those ships. Nearly drowned, you know? Barely escaped with her life. You wouldn't think it, would you? Such a timid thing she is.'

Connie said nothing and just continued to chew the arid toast within her mouth.

'Anyway, so I saw her when I was waiting with my basket, and it was pretty quiet, so I just asked, you know. I said, "Mary, what do you know about sleepwalking." And, let me tell you, it was the most I've ever known her talk. In all the years of her living down the road.'

'Oh?'

'She was telling me she saw it a lot. Sleepwalking. Back when she was a nurse.'

'Did she?'

'Yes.'

'Oh?' Connie watched her mother expectantly.

'Said it was a sign of trauma.'

'Oh.'

'Which makes sense for the men on those boats, doesn't it? I mean, the things they must have seen. It doesn't bear thinking about.' Her mother lowered her cup to its saucer and stared at her daughter. 'But with you, it doesn't make sense. What do you know about trauma?'

Connie was silent.

'You live in a good house, go to a good school. I told Mrs Beadle, it had to be something else. And she said no, usually trauma. Then she asked if your father was having trouble.' This made a deep scowl settle upon her mother's face. 'And I told her, no, of course not. He's managing fine.'

Connie forced down her chewed-up toast, felt it slide down the back of her throat, thick and tasteless.

'Because he is managing. He has his *ways* of managing. And considering some of the stories I hear, we are lucky.' Her voice hardened, still staring across at Connie. 'Very lucky. Your dad came back to us able to work. Able to provide. I thank God for that every day. As should you.'

Connie felt anger rising within her like the tide coming in. Soon everything would be drowned by it.

Be grateful.

Be a good girl, Connie.

Be good.

Be good. Be good. Be good.

'You know *nothing* about trauma my girl,' her mother declared sharply. 'If that school of yours is getting too stressful, you need to toughen up. Understand? If your father can come home, hold down a job, a marriage, a family, despite what he's seen, what he's had to do, you can go to class. You can read your books and you can work hard, understand?'

Just be good.

'I want an end to this sleepwalking business. I need you to figure it out. I won't have you bringing shame to our door.'

'You think Dad's OK?' Connie hissed out the words, needing to grip the wood of the table between her hands. 'You think he's all right? I *hear* him. Every night. I hear him shout and yell, throw things. I hear it all, Mum. And then do you know what he does? He comes upstairs and—'

'Do not,' her mother slapped the table so hard that her teacup rattled within its saucer, 'do not speak ill of your father, do you hear?'

'You think it's OK that he hits you? Hits *me*?'

'Connie, I'm warning you.'

'I'm just—'

'No!' Her mother pushed back her chair, got to her feet, crossed the space between them in a single step and hauled Connie to her feet. They were almost the same height, eye to eye. 'You be respectful of your father in this house, you hear? You think going to that fancy school gives you the right to judge him? It does not. You need to sort things out, Connie. You need to be good.'

Connie felt her heart rate climbing. How she longed to scream. To reach for her violin and play it so hard the strings split.

'This world is not built for women who aren't good.' A sadness crept into her mother's voice, dragging down the lines that bordered her mouth. 'You need to remember that.'

Her mother suddenly embraced her hard, pushing their bodies together. 'Just do your work, school will be over soon and you'll have the grades. The chance. The chance to do better.'

'Mum—'

'Stay away from boys, from trouble. Then you'll start sleeping again and all will be well.'

'It's not boys,' Connie said quietly, voice muffled against the softness of her mother's cardigan.

'I don't want you climbing out that bed again.' Her mother withdrew from her, cupped Connie's chin in her hands. 'I don't want the neighbours seeing, or worse, your father catching you.'

They both glanced briefly at the floor, where the knife had once been that Connie held in her sleep.

'Be good, my girl, be good.' Then her mother held her again, even tighter, as the clock ticked by another minute.

'I'm trying,' Connie admitted. She was trying so hard, with every fibre of her being, that she feared the effort of it all was going to tear her apart. 'Really, Mum, I'm trying.'

'I know, sweetheart,' a wet kiss upon her cheek, 'I know.'

17

Then

Music. Distant and lilting. Connie stares at the walls. They seem to almost . . . ripple with it. As though each chord is striking the foundations of the house. The melody is familiar like a half-forgotten lullaby.

I should be at school.

The music grows louder. Sharper. The sky outside has a sheen to it, as though the leaded collection of clouds has hardened into sterling silver.

I should be in school right now. I should be studying. I should be in my mathematics class. Learning how things add together. Multiply. Change. Because things do change. I'm changing. Ever since I picked up the violin I have been changing. Multiplying. Subtracting.

Connie is on her feet, fingertips pressed to the wallpaper, tracing a tear in the design.

Like a fracture through time. A break in something beautiful.

She can't stop thinking. Her thoughts begin as a breeze, flitting through her mind, but quickly gather speed and momentum, becoming a tornado that sweeps her up.

The music keeps playing.

It is far enough away that Connie can't quite grasp what it is. But she hears strings. Fevered and fast. Difficult to play. And now her hands are aloft, trying to mimic the notes she hears, the frenzy of them. But she can't keep up.

I have to play. That is my gift. My talent. And in the music . . . in the music I'm free. Like a bird set loose from a cage to sweep and soar.

A starling passes the window, snatching her attention.

I need to play. I need to play and I need to be free.

Her hands are still threading the air, playing along to the music she hears. She closes her eyes, tries to *feel* the music, just as the house around her does.

Robin slips in and out of the room but she doesn't register his presence. Now there is only the music. A sonata. She's sure of that. Maybe even her favourite one. The one she plays in her mind to calm herself, to quieten the voices, her fears.

Because if I play well enough, I will be free. If I play well enough, it will all have been worth it. If I—

She doesn't remember opening the window but now she's peering down at the scrubland of garden beneath her. A neglected lawn, overgrown and cluttered with litter. She's stretching so far out that her lungs fill with cold, crisp air, and when she glances down, her body quivers with a surge of vertigo.

I need to be free, to fly like a bird. I need to leave my cage, spread my wings, if only to escape the music. To escape the—

A hand clasps her shoulder, drawing her back. Wren is at her side, beautiful and delicate like a porcelain doll.

'Easy there, new girl,' she says, guiding Connie back to the stained mattress upon the floor and then pressing a glass of cold water into her hands. 'How much did he give you?'

'I can hear the music and it is calling me and . . .' Connie looks beyond Wren's annoyed, pretty face and studies the walls. Still they pulse. Still they carry the beat from the music. The movement is becoming more manic, causing the wallpaper to rip and bulge. 'Don't let the music take me,' eyes bulging, she peers up at Wren, 'it's trying to take me. Because it is supposed to save me, but when I'm there with my violin and playing then—'

'Drink.' Wren presses the glass to Connie's lips. It is cold. Icy water slides down her throat. Wren's fingers close around her wrist, also cold. 'Your pulse is racing.' A strained sigh escapes from her purple painted lips. 'He should know better than to leave you alone after your first dose. Not everyone has a good experience. Not that he listens when I try and tell him as much.' She releases Connie's wrist. 'I'll stay here until it passes, 'kay?'

Connie's hands are now pressed to her ears. 'I just want it to stop. The music, please.' All around her it was becoming louder, more urgent. The strings that delivered each note on the verge of snapping.

'Sweetie, there is no music. At least not for the rest of us.'

Connie blinked, confused. Wren's face came in and out of focus beside her.

'It's what he gave you,' the girl beside her is explaining. 'It's meant to mellow you out. But it doesn't always work that way.'

Finally the walls became still again.

'Here.' Wren wiped a tissue across Connie's cheeks.

'Have I been crying?' Slowly the sheen in the sky faded. Her thoughts slowed.

'Quite a bit.' Beside her Wren got up, sensing the storm had passed. 'Seems music really stresses you out.'

'No.' Connie dragged the back of her hand across the base of her nose. 'Music is my . . . the thing that makes me happy.' She felt out of sorts and adrift from the day, like she'd just woken from a deep nap. What time was it? 'I love music.'

'Sure.' Wren was disappearing through the door. 'Come down and grab something to eat when you feel up to it, OK?'

'How long have I been here?' Connie wondered groggily.

Wren pursed her lips in disapproval. 'Wow. He must have given you a hefty dose.' Then she added, scowling, 'He must really be hoping you stick around.'

'Look, I—'

'Downstairs, eat,' Wren ordered tersely. And for an absurd moment, Connie felt like she was still back at home, being beckoned down for dinner by her mother. In the kitchen she'd find battered fish and chips, or a hearty stew. Connie's stomach clenched with hunger and regret. Already she was homesick. 'You'll feel better once you eat,' Wren offered her a half-smile.

'How long have you been here?' Connie ventured. Everyone in the house must have come from somewhere, left behind something.

'What is time but a man-made construct?' Wren replied vaguely.

'I don't—'

'I've been here long enough to know you need to eat. Come on. And when I see Robin, I'm going to give him such an earful about being reckless. He's going to get somebody killed one of these days if he doesn't watch out.'

18

Then

So many days passed in the same way; blurred and strung out. Velvet nights gave way to shimmering days. Within the unkempt walls of the house, Connie drifted. She mimicked what the others did, how they'd snatch food from whatever was laid out on the slab of a kitchen table. It was solid and concrete, like it belonged in a mortuary. Connie was sure she'd heard Robin boast that he'd stolen it from a building site. But then perhaps that had been a dream. The more time that passed, the more her dreams seemed to blur with her waking moments. So often Robin would appear at her side, press something into her palm and then smile his Cheshire cat grin.

But the morning he didn't find her, the voile dropped and her vision cleared. The room was once again grimy, bare. And she was alone. Head pounding, Connie tried to tame the thoughts which ricocheted at her.

What day is it?

Are my mum and dad looking for me?

Are the police looking for me?

What must school think?

Drawing in a deep, steadying breath, she recalled the note she had left upon her pillow. Written in her neat, cursive hand. The style her school had instilled within her. If her parents had read that then surely they wouldn't come looking for her. But then what did they think she was doing? Hiding? Running away?

Connie unfolded and stepped over to the window, realising her feet were bare but she still wore the shirt dress she'd left home in. Now though it was creased beyond recognition. She gazed at her grainy reflection in the glass. What *was* she doing? Closing her eyes, she tried to find calm but in the darkness there was only madness. Because that's what this was – madness. She should go home. Return to school. Return to—

Her fingers twitched. A reflex. A desire. She needed to play. Almost stumbling over her own feet, Connie reached for her violin case and unclasped it, briefly surprised to find her instrument still inside. Someone could so easily have stolen it while she meandered between dreams. It felt good to hold it, feel its firmness. Breathe in the scent of old wood and varnish. Connie rested it beneath her chin, lifted the bow. And she played. The *Devil's Trill Sonata*. A haunting piece. One she had not quite yet mastered.

She escaped into the music. The rhythm. The pace of her bow, the pressure of her fingers against the strings. She came alive.

'Wow.'

Connie gasped, chest heaving, sweat beaded on her brow. Lowering the violin, she blinked at the figure in the doorway, the music slowly releasing her from its spell.

'That was incredible.' Robin stepped towards her, a white t-shirt hugging his chest tight, jeans loose at his waist, his feet bare like her own. 'You can really play.'

She knew she was blushing. 'N-no. Not really. That piece, I'm not doing it justice.'

'Didn't sound that way to me.'

Connie smiled at him. 'Thank you.'

'It sounded . . . intense.' He came closer, hands in pockets, head tilted. His jawline sharp, freshly shaven. Chestnut eyes glossy and alert.

'It's an intense piece,' Connie agreed, violin now pressed to her hip. 'It's based on a dream a French astronomer had.'

'He dreamt he went to the moon?' Robin reached out and swept a strand of golden hair out of Connie's eyes.

'No,' she whispered, feeling breathless again. 'He dreamt he made a pact with the devil for his soul.'

Robin's eyes crinkled in the corners. 'Sounds like a good dream.'

He smelt of cheap cigarettes and strong coffee. He was so close she could see the black which swirled within the brown ocean of his eyes. The hand that had touched her hair now drifted down her bare arm, moving lightly, easily, causing her flesh to prickle with delight. 'I like having you here.' He locked eyes with her.

There had been so many thoughts. So many worries. But now they were all swept away. Connie stared at him, not daring to move, not daring to breathe. When his lips met hers, she dropped the violin. It clattered ungracefully to the ground but she did not care. Robin now had one hand on the back of her neck and one on her hip, drawing her in to him, letting her drown in him. She kissed him back, forgetting everything, tasting the cigarette, the coffee. Beyond them the sky grew dark and it began to rain.

19

Now

'I am of course here to learn about the music.' Daniel's smile was smooth. 'But a person is the sum of many parts. That is what I am trying to explore within my dissertation. *Who* exactly is Connie Winchester?'

Connie shivered even though the room was warm, the fire crackling ravenously in the hearth. She crossed her arms at the wrists resting on her lap, back as straight as she could make it. The need to present herself well, to be seen as a lady, had been ingrained so deeply within her time at school that it felt like it was welded to her DNA.

'Sit up straight,' her mother would snap.

'Legs crossed at ankles, arms at wrists,' her teachers would demand of all the girls. It gave Connie an air of gracefulness her old friends who lived on her street resented.

'Thinks she's above us,' they'd scoff loudly as she walked by, back straight, chin high. Forcing herself to be one of the grammar girls. They didn't see how lonely she was. How she longed to be with them. How could they? When her waking hours were spent being taught to appear aloof, distant.

'Honestly, I was just a working-class girl who was fortu-nate enough to be able to play the violin well.'

'Exceedingly well,' Daniel gushed. 'Your version of the *Devil's Trill Sonata* you recorded when you played with the London Symphony Orchestra gives me chills. Truly.'

Connie nodded. She knew the piece. Knew it better than she did the layout of her own home. She liked that it was fraught. Haunting. But whenever she played it, a tear would trickle down her cheeks and the audience would always erupt in rapturous applause, assuming that she had been so swept away by the power of the music, the emotion in the melody. They were wrong.

In her mind she could hear the opening notes. And uninvited he crept into her mind, a shadow on her senses. He lingered in the background, never truly leaving her thoughts.

'An impressive feat to climb to the heights you did, considering your humble beginnings.' Daniel gave her a salesman smile, briefly abandoning his notes. 'Did you always know that you wanted to play the violin professionally?'

'Well . . .' Connie breathed deep, felt the rattle in her lungs that reminded her she'd smoked too much for too long. But when she was young it was seen as glamorous, what everyone did. Like most eighteen-year-old girls, Connie had swooned at the image of James Dean casually holding a cigarette in the posters for *Rebel Without A Cause*. Though he was gone before the film even came to the cinema, a car crash out in LA. A star that burned too bright.

'So did you?'

Connie shook her head, stared at the young man across from her. Her mind had wandered, she saw that in the small crest of annoyance that appeared between his eyebrows. She didn't mean to. She wanted to focus. But it was too easy these days to be carried on the wave of a thought. To let it pull her downstream, towards something deeper, darker. James Dean had been the ultimate idol with his

98

red leather jacket and jeans. So dangerous. So desirable. Connie knew some girls whose parents wouldn't let them go and see his movies, but hers never tried to hold her back. Had learnt not to grip her too tightly.

'Initially I wasn't aware that playing professionally was a thing,' Connie admitted. 'Being part of an orchestra, it felt a million miles away from my little town in the Midlands. And at school, girls were groomed for more sturdy forms of employment. Like teaching or being accountants or working with medicine.'

'Did your teacher guide you towards the path you ultimately took? Because you didn't go on to university as I'm sure many of your peers did. Was that their influence?'

Now Connie frowned and her chest throbbed. 'It . . . um . . . he . . .'

Kind Mr Collins. Handsome Mr Collins.

'He always encouraged me with my music.'

'I see.' Daniel was once again taking notes. Connie let her gaze stray past him, to the window and the sweep of driveway beyond. Still it rained. Bouncing in the puddles that had gathered, the sky dark and potent.

She was thinking of Mr Collins. How he was always immaculately dressed in a three-piece suit. How he had two children, boys, both under five. Everyone at the school adored him.

'Would you say that the violin was your first love?'

'My . . .' Connie readjusted herself in her armchair, bones wincing at the movement. Playing the violin had been a passion. An obsession. 'Tell me, Daniel, how would you describe love?'

His cheeks blushed pink and Connie wondered if it was perhaps a feeling that had thus far eluded him. He was, after all, young.

'I would describe love as something all-consuming. Something that endures.'

'Ah.' Connie nodded sagely. 'So something all-consuming that is fleeting, is perhaps not love, but infatuation?'

'I suppose.' He shifted awkwardly, dropping her gaze, pen still gripped between two lean fingers.

'But the violin and I, we endured. We weathered many storms, but still I held my desire to play. So in that respect, yes, it was my first love.'

'Your greatest love?' Daniel ventured.

Connie laughed. She had to admire his bravado, even though his interest in learning about her as a person beyond being a musician perplexed her. She wasn't a celebrity. She had been in proximity to them during her time in Los Angeles. But she herself wasn't famous. Not really. Hers was not a household name.

Daniel's eyes crinkled mischievously. Connie felt like she was starting to like him.

'Not my greatest love, no.'

'So who had that honour?' he quickly asked.

Connie smiled primly. 'That, my dear boy, is something an old lady gets to take to her grave, I'm afraid.'

'Shame.' Daniel dropped his pen to scratch at his chin. 'I felt like I was about to get something really juicy there.'

'Points for effort,' Connie commended genially.

'Oh, I'll keep trying.' He grasped the pen with renewed vigour. 'Trust me on that.'

Connie released a fluttery laugh, hoping that her interviewer didn't sense her unease. Or her fear.

20

Then

Wren liked to talk when there was no one else around. When the boys were sleeping and the house was unusually still. She'd find Connie in the kitchen, at the table, chin resting in her hands. And it was often dark. Though everyone kept to erratic sleeping patterns, Connie found that she and Wren were the most restless during the night.

'We're like cats,' Wren said with a sly smile. 'Never truly settled. Always sleeping with one eye open.'

Connie didn't want to agree, especially when she always had the unshakeable feeling that Wren didn't really like her. Which made these clandestine conversations all the more strange. Connie suspected that Wren was choosing these quiet moments to probe her, to find something wrong, an undeniable flaw that would be enough for Robin to banish her from the house. From his life.

'I can't sleep.'

Connie had been at the house a month, possibly more. Possibly less. Time seemed to stop working properly there, at least in her mind. She was in the kitchen, staring at her hands, when Wren walked in, dark hair falling into her eyes. Candles flickered upon the table and Connie felt an ache in her bones that hinted that she might be getting sick.

'How long you been here?' Wren dropped down opposite her.

Connie said nothing, continued to look down at her hands. How long *had* she been down there? She had an uneasy suspicion that she was sleepwalking again. That she'd begun the night beside Robin and somehow found her way down here. Though it all felt murky and unhinged, like trying to look at a photograph through a filter and being unable to see it all.

'You get nightmares too?' Wren cocked her head at her, like a bird studying something small that amused them.

Connie shook her head.

'Course you do.' She could hear the smirk that had drawn across Wren's lips. 'We all get nightmares here. Some worse than others. For me, they are pretty bad. What about you?'

Connie shrugged.

'You can't stare at your damn hands all night. What happens in them? Your nightmares?'

'Nothing.'

'Bullshit.'

Connie looked up sharply, knowing she was being goaded but too tired to stave it off. The candlelight that flickered upon Wren's face made her seem ethereal and beautiful. Connie felt so naïve and awkward beside her. Maybe that was why Wren seemed to despise her so; because she wasn't worthy of her place beside Robin. At least in Wren's dark eyes.

'I see my grandmother.' Wren leaned across the table, a sense of mischief twisting her features. Making them uglier, dangerous. 'I see her sputtering her last breath.'

'I don't—'

'What do you see? And don't say nothing. Nothing is a lie. Nothing is boring. Nothing is an insult to me.'

Connie squared her jaw, was silent.

'Everyone here,' Wren gestured to the ceiling, to the sleeping bodies just a few feet away from them, 'sees something. It's why we are here, princess. Because we did something bad. And I'm not talking about lifting some shit from a shop.'

'Robin hasn't done anything.' The words were sharp from Connie.

'Hasn't he?' Wren said with a knowing look. 'Does he keep it from you, princess? All the dark things that haunt his nightmares?'

Connie heard it then. The slur in Wren's voice. She was drunk. On something less pungent than beer or whiskey. Something you almost couldn't detect. Like gin or vodka. How she'd come about it, Connie could only guess.

'Right before my grandmother died her eyes bulged.' Wren expanded her own gaze theatrically, puffing out her cheeks. 'And then, boom.' She clicked her fingers loudly, causing Connie to jump. 'She was gone.' She saw Wren smile in triumph when she clocked her reaction. 'And dead bodies go cold quick. Anyone ever tell you that?'

'I'm going back to bed.' Connie stood up and Wren mirrored her, the two of them positioned either side of the table.

'Why don't you sleep?' Wren demanded. 'I find you here most nights.'

'Why don't *you* sleep?'

'What goes on in that pretty little head of yours? Who did you hurt? What are you running from?'

'N-nothing. No one!' Connie louder, with more emotion than she'd intended.

'You lie,' Wren purred, remaining frustratingly calm and collected. She stalked around the table with feline grace, edging closer to Connie. 'I see in you the same fucked-up crap that brought us all here. There's blood on those hands.' She reached for Connie's wrist and Connie snatched her hands out of reach, pressing them against her chest, beneath her armpits, and stepping back from Wren. From her dark intensity.

'Does he know? Have you told him?' Wren asked, glaring at her.

'I'm not—'

'The little innocent act doesn't work with me.' Wren lunged forward, grabbed Connie's chin in her hand, long nails digging into her cheeks like talons. 'You're as broken as the rest of us. He sees it. Of course he does. You come down here to hide from your demons same as me. So don't act like you're better, or above it all.'

Connie slapped at Wren's hand, knocking her away, face flushed.

'That's more like it.' Wren grinned wickedly at her. 'I knew it was in there, that fire that landed you in trouble.'

'Look, I don't know what you're talking about,' Connie stated haughtily. 'I come down here because I can't sleep because of. . . because of the stuff Robin gives us. That's all.'

'No.' Wren shook her head and gave her a wry look. 'You come down here because you can't stop whatever is playing on your mind in a loop. You can't look away, can't make it stop. Just like the rest of us.'

'You're wrong.'

'Bad things have a way of haunting us, Connie. Especially when we try and push them down.'

'So what's your bad stuff?' Connie demanded, sounding shrill and girlish, which she hated. 'What have you done that's so bloody awful?'

'You ever killed someone?' Wren whispered, gazing at her, toying with her. 'Ever watched the life drain from them?'

'You're ridiculous.'

'And you're a fool,' Wren called after Connie as she turned and stalked out of the kitchen. 'I won't let you make a fool of him.' Wren's voice followed her out of the kitchen, only fading when she reached the stairs.

I'm a good girl, Connie reminded herself as she climbed to the landing, heart pounding. *I'm a good girl*. Wren was just wrong, that's all. She'd say anything to get Connie to leave the house. Anything at all.

21

Then

'We're running out of money.' Robin delivered the statement factually yet lightly as he perched on the edge of the mattress Connie was still lying upon, pale threads of sunlight stretching across the bare floorboards.

She felt groggy, his presence having awoken her from a dream. Or rather a nightmare. Connie drew herself up against the wall, rubbing her eyes, remembering how it felt to have copper strings wrapped around her wrist, pulling ever tighter.

'Are you all right?' Robin moved to sit beside her. 'You seem a little spooked.'

'Just a . . .' Connie traced the inside of her wrist with her thumb, catching on the ridges of her veins. 'I just had a bad dream, that's all.' She didn't want to admit that she'd been having more of them. That in the darkness, great strings stretched up from the floor and wrapped themselves around her like hungry vines, how she'd squirm and try to scream for help but she couldn't make a sound. When her mouth gaped open and she thrust air up from her lungs all that escaped was dust, like she had become some empty vault.

'The stuff can do that.' He reached for the hand that was stroking her wrist, entangled it within his own. His skin was so warm. 'It manages to reach into your dreams sometimes. We should ease off. At least for a bit.'

Connie felt herself nodding although she still hadn't quite grasped what *the stuff* was. Only that they were all on it, leaving them all in a limbo between sleep and wakefulness. 'How long have I been here?' She turned to him, trying to grasp onto something solid, something real. Time was steady, constant. Reliable.

'Doesn't matter.' He flicked the question away, strengthened his grip on her hand. 'Like I said, we're running out of money. So I need you to help Wren get some more.'

'Running out of . . . money?' Connie looked at the cracked walls, the mould fanning out from the far corner and bleeding across the ceiling.

'Money. Cash. Dough. Bread. Whatever you want to call it.'

'But . . .' Her mind was so sluggish, still bound within her nightmare.

'This place doesn't run on air.' He released her to cup her chin with his hands, gazing into her eyes. 'We need food, clothes.'

'But you squat here?'

Robin winced. 'Yes. But sadly we still need money to survive.'

'Do any of you work?'

The left corner of his mouth jerked upwards in amusement. 'Do any of us have *jobs*? Come on, Connie. The working world is a construct to keep us all within our place. To keep us all on our knees. No, we don't *work*. We live. There's a difference.'

Connie wasn't sure there was. She felt an ache growing behind her eyes as she tried to understand. 'So how do you get money?'

His hands were still cradling her face. He chewed on his lip as he studied her. 'We take what we need.'

'You *steal*?'

Robin kissed her, hard and firm, silencing any further questions. As he drew back, he kept his hands to her cheeks. 'We take only what we need to survive,' he repeated gently. Softly. Like he was explaining something simple to a child. 'No harm, no foul. Like I said, the working world is a construct. We don't use money to buy fancy things. We don't own a car, or a house. We get our clothes from charity. But food doesn't come for free.'

'So . . . how do you get money?'

He kissed her again. Deeper this time.

'Wren will show you.' He withdrew as Connie's heart beat hard in her chest. 'Just follow her lead, OK?'

Connie was about to reply when he kissed her again and she forgot what she was going to say.

22

Then

Wren made it sound so easy. So effortless. 'We go in, we talk to the guy, we laugh at his terrible jokes, whatever it takes to keep him engaged.' She was almost swallowed by the shadows of the street where she leaned against a red brick wall, cigarette clasped between elegant fingers, nails painted red.

'I don't understand.' Beside her Connie felt foolish, even though she'd been stuffed into a similar outfit of pedal pushers and leather jacket, a scarf the same red as Wren's nails tied around her neck. While Wren looked sexy and sophisticated, Connie feared she looked as awkward as she felt. These clothes, which were tight to her hips, stretched across her breasts, these weren't clothes she had worn before.

'You'll be fine,' Wren insisted back at the house as she traced a kohl pencil around Connie's eyes. 'Just follow my lead.'

Now, they were away from the comfort of the house, in a part of town Connie had never seen before, amongst red terraces. A dog began to bark somewhere nearby, angry and insistent.

'All you have to do is smile and look pretty.' Wren dropped the butt of her cigarette to the ground where the faded ember glowed upon the pavement. She studied it for a second and then ground the tip of her boot against it.

'So it should be pretty easy for you.' The smile she gave Connie was hollow. It made her shiver within the foreign clothes, even though the night was balmy for October.

Shoving her hands into her jacket pockets, Wren began to strut along the street, heels clicking, marking every step. Connie scurried behind, afraid to lose her in the dark. They rounded a corner and stopped. Wren pulled Connie to her side and pointed across the street to a pub with sash windows and a door open wide. The Hangman's Noose. This close, Connie could see that the paint on Wren's fingers was chipped, and her mascara had dusted her cheeks, which now looked like marble, streaked with her blue veins.

'Landlord's name is Big Cooper. We go in, lean over the bar, pout our lips, smile at him. You know.'

'I don't know.'

Wren laughed dryly before rolling her eyes. 'Right.'

Dogs kept barking. Connie searched the golden windows of the pub for signs of movement but all seemed still within.

'It's quiet on Tuesdays,' Wren noted, sensing her apprehension. 'Hence why we are out here looking like a couple of desperate whores.'

Connie frowned. Tuesday. It was Tuesday. So that would mean . . . had she been gone over a week? The days folded together so oddly in the house; it was almost impossible to keep track. One moment there would be blue skies, then the next, impenetrable darkness. Nothing seemed to move as it should, as though time didn't operate quite the same within those neglected walls.

'Come on . . .' Wren stretched to look both ways down the street. 'Robin needs to hurry up. I'm not waiting out here all night for him.'

'Robin is coming?'

'Jesus.' Wren's dark eyebrows pulled together. 'He really didn't fill you in, did he? Typical. Yes, he's coming *here*. But no, he's not coming in the pub with us. That part we do alone.'

'What part?'

Wren exhaled loudly. Angrily. 'While he takes his time, he's stuck me on babysitting duty.'

'I just . . .' Connie tugged at the tight sleeves of her jacket, feeling her skin sweating beneath it. 'He told me you'd tell me what to do.'

'Why exactly are you here?' Wren turned to her, eyes gleaming despite the darkness. She didn't need the make-up to make her beautiful. But the added effect was both stunning and terrifying. To Connie she seemed like a girl from a record sleeve come to life. Otherworldly and glorious.

'Robin asked me to come. To . . . to help you.'

'No.' Wren spoke slowly, stretching out the word through her crimson lips. 'Why are you at the house, with all of us. Little princess like you must surely be missed.'

'I . . . I was invited,' Connie declared, an edge of indignation creeping into her voice. Robin had wanted her there. Had *asked* her to come. Wren seemed amused by this.

'Sweetie, we were all invited. But why did you come? What are you running away from?'

Connie blinked, feeling hot in her uncomfortable outfit.

'Robin is like the pied piper for lost souls,' Wren continued. 'Everyone in that house has a story, something they're running from.'

'So what about you?' Connie asked. 'What are you running away from?'

'Oh no, princess.' Wren glared at her. 'Just because Robin likes you doesn't mean the rest of us do.'

Connie felt winded by the remark.

'I'm not about to share my story with you. Why the hell would I?'

'But you asked me mine!'

Wren stepped closer, towering over her in her heeled boots, the smell of cigarettes and beer tumbling off her in waves. 'I asked because I'm pretty sure your reason for being here will bring us unwanted heat. But of course Robin doesn't see that. All he sees is,' she waved a hand up and down, 'is this. And he's blinded to it as usual.'

'As usual?'

Easing away from her, Wren clicked her tongue in amusement. 'He really does like them pretty and dumb,' she muttered to herself.

'Wait, I—'

A sound, like a trapped bird, travelled from further up the street. 'That's it.' Wren tightly grasped Connie's elbow and tugged her towards the open door of the pub. 'Follow my lead. Keep smiling, and keep your tits up. Got it?'

There wasn't a chance to reply as Connie was thrust into the Hangman's Noose, Wren still clutching her elbow, pulling her up to the wooden bar. The air was thick with smoke and stale ale and Connie was struggling to breathe.

'Evening, ladies.' A man with several chins and a receding hairline greeted them with a toothy smile. 'What can I do you for?'

'Showtime,' Wren whispered under her breath.

GOLDEN GIRL

Blackhill-born Connie Lipman, now Winchester, has been wowing classical music fans over in the sunshine of Los

112

Angeles, California. And she's recently turned her attention to playing on film scores to great success. Connie was part of the ensemble orchestra for *Due Tides*. Her violin solo features in a pivotal moment in the film when star Desmond DuValier contemplates his future upon the white cliffs of Dover.

This weekend *Due Tides* won the prestigious Academy Award for Best Original Score. Thanks, we are certain, in no small part to the efforts of our own Mrs Winchester.

Connie has informed us that she will be returning to her home county later this month and will be bringing her shiny new Oscar along with her. Among numerous press appearances, she will be visiting her former school, Blackhill Girls Grammar. Connie has said of her recent success that the school 'played a formative role in moulding her into the musician she is today'.

If you want to see *Due Tides* and hear Connie's phenomenal performance for yourself, the Clifton Cinema on North Road will be showing it every night at 8pm until the end of March in honour of Connie's triumphant win.

23

Then

Connie Lipman had been brought up to be *good*. To do as she was told. To work hard. To not make waves. And as she stood beside Wren in the dingy lights of the Hangman's Noose, she felt something shift even though the sticky floor beneath her didn't move. The iron tankards on the shelves didn't tremble, the horseshoes tacked to nails on the beam across the bar didn't loosen and fall. And yet everything changed.

'We're lost,' Wren purred to the barman, elbows propped on the slab of wood peppered with faded beer mats, chin resting in her hands.

'That so?' His eyes grew wide with interest as he looked between Wren and Connie, taking in their make-up, their exposed curves. 'Isn't it a bit late for you to be out, just the two of you?'

'We're older than we look,' Wren smirked. Her boot, out of sight from the barman, stretched out to kick Connie.

'Yes . . .' Connie agreed tensely, feeling her heart trying to climb up into her throat, 'much older.'

An old man tucked away in a far corner began to cough, guttural and raw. And something beneath that. Something coming from behind the barman, a swift waterfall of sound, like keys or coins falling. Wren was quick to seize his attention before it wavered.

'And we're good girls.' She grinned at him, though her smile was one a good girl would never wear. 'So we don't want to walk around all night getting lost.'

'Best ask for directions,' Connie added stiffly, not quite sure what her part in this pantomime was, just that she had to play along.

'Where are you trying to get to?' The barman propped a thick arm close to Wren, tossed the small towel he was holding upon his shoulder.

'Clapham Street.' Wren didn't miss a beat. As the barman stroked his cheek, the man in the corner hacked up some more of his weathered lungs and Connie heard again the soft chime of movement somewhere beyond. They'd passed Clapham Street on their walk to the pub; Connie could recall staggering past it as she struggled in her heels.

'Ah, you're not far.' The barman smiled kindly at them. 'Just out, take the first left, onto Glower Street, right, then left again and you're there. Visiting friends, are you?'

'Something like that.' Wren was easing away from the bar, lips still held in a beckoning smile. 'Thank you *so* much for your help.'

'Can I get you anything while you're here? A Cherry B? Or a Babycham?'

'We're fine.' Wren's fingers closed around Connie's wrist, drawing her back from the bar. It was time to go.

The cold air hit them like a fist. It had been warm within the pub, the gentle flames of a fire in the hearth keeping everywhere cosy and the old man in the corner's lungs clogged. While they'd been inside, the autumn night had sharpened from mild to chilled. Connie shuddered as Wren hurriedly guided her back the way they had come. All the way back to Clapham Street, keeping a fierce pace.

Connie tottered awkwardly behind her, chest and heels starting to burn. 'Wait,' she gasped.

'We need to get out of here,' Wren replied tersely, still walking, heels clacking loudly, drowning out the dogs that continued to bark.

'Please . . . I'm just . . .'

'We can't hang around as he'll notice soon.'

'Notice what?'

'The money.'

'Money?' Connie didn't want to catch up to what was happening. Not truly. Because that wasn't who she was.

'That it's gone.' Wren turned on her heel and released the words like a whip, letting them crack against Connie's cold cheeks.

Connie tugged her hand free of Wren's grip, wrist throbbing where her chipped nails had held on too tight. 'Wait.' The street they were on was deserted. And dark. The further they walked from the pub, the fewer lights were on inside the houses. 'You stole his money?'

'Technically, Robin and Arthur stole his money.' Wren pressed her hands against her hips. 'We merely provided the distraction. Now come on, if we hang around here, we risk getting caught.'

'I don't—'

'There's a safe in the back. Arthur knew about it from when he used to wash dishes there a few years back. Big Cooper is too trusting and too dumb to keep it locked. So while we kept him looking one way, they popped in round the back and helped themselves to it.'

'That's stealing!' Connie began to feel hot. Too hot. 'You can't just *steal*, you—'

'Fuck off with your righteousness,' Wren snapped. 'Robin told you we needed money. Did you think he

116

was going to go and shake down some tree in the back garden? Wake. Up. *This* is how we survive. How we get to live our life hidden away. Nothing comes for free.'

'And . . . and how does *he* survive?' The hand that pointed back the way they had come, towards the pub, was trembling. 'That's *his* money, Wren. What he worked for. What he's earned.'

Wren stepped close, nostrils flared. 'And he got that money selling booze to lowlife losers who spend night after night wedged on ratty bar stools trying to forget about their miserable lives when they should be at home, taking care of their family, not frittering money away.'

Connie blinked, felt a tear slice down her cheek. Tasted salt. That was her own father's routine, to sit night after night in the darkness of the pub, nursing a pint.

'You don't want to get your hands dirty, fine. Run off back home.' Wren pushed her shoulders, causing Connie to stagger back. 'But I'm pretty sure you're in no hurry to go back.'

There was a lump gathering in Connie's throat which made it hard to swallow. Wren was right. All that waited for her back home were her father's fists and her mother's disappointment. She'd told her parents everything and they made her feel like there was no place for her.

'You want to keep hiding out with us?' Wren asked.

Connie could only nod.

'You want to keep taking the stuff? Keep being around Robin?'

'Yes,' her response was hoarse.

'We do this again, don't fight me.' Wren tucked a strand of raven hair behind her ear and then sidled up beside Connie, linking arms with her as they continued to walk down the street. 'I don't have it in me to always be fighting,' she added softly, gazing into the distance. 'I've done enough of that.'

'So is that why you're here,' Connie ventured, 'because you had to keep fighting someone?'

'No more questions.' Wren didn't release her arm, nor did she resume her frantic pace. Together they walked quietly through the streets, back towards the house, towards Robin and the others. And as they walked, Connie wondered if the old barman would weep when he realised he'd been robbed, if she cared about money as desperately as her own father did, always guarding it with the ferocity of a dragon with its gold.

24

Then

There was money in the house. Food on the stretch of table in the kitchen. Drugs in Connie's system. Robin slipped it to her almost as soon as she came back from the Hangman's Noose, Wren quickly easing from her side as they entered the house.

'You did great . . .' Robin's lips pressed against her. And then he pressed something into the palm of her hand.

'I'm not—' It was loud in the house. A record was playing, a manic jazz piece packed full of trilling trumpets. People lined the walls. Laughing. Shouting. Connie shrank in their presence. Some faces were familiar, many were not. 'I don't like stealing.' She stretched onto her tiptoes to whisper in Robin's ear. He grabbed her then, by the wrist, and guided her through the melee, up the slim, steep staircase to what had become her room. Though as they entered, the small scrap of floor lit only by the moon, Connie's heart clenched as she realised it looked more like a prison cell.

'We're not stealing . . .' Robin closed the thin door behind them, muffling the worst of the noise that echoed through the foundations. '. . . We're *reallocating*.'

'I don't understand.' Connie shivered, the room almost as cold as the night beyond. Robin draped an arm across her shoulders and led her to sit beside him on the mattress that was her bed.

'Money, wealth, it should be distributed equally. Like, no one should be rich. No one should be poor. We should all be *comfortable*.'

'But—'

'Are your family rich?'

Connie shook her head.

'The school where you go, are most of the girls there from rich families?'

'Yes.'

'Do they get dropped off in nice cars while you have to catch the bus every day?'

'Yes.' The sting of jealousy stabbed her in the stomach. When the Bentleys and the Jaguars pulled up at her school gates, she'd stare at them, marvel at the gleaming metal, imagine what it must feel like to be driven about in one.

'Do you think the parents who own those cars work harder than your parents do?'

'No.' The word was small as it left her. She needed to breathe more strength into it. Her father worked hard. He drank hard too, but her mother always said that was to silence the voices that had followed him home from the war. Connie noted the fearful look in her mother's eyes when she said this, so never pressed her on it more. 'No. My dad he . . . he works like a dog at the metal works. Does night shifts. Weekends.'

'Exactly.' Robin's fingers stroked her shoulder, his body pressed against hers creating much-needed warmth. 'We should all share things equally. Because nobody is better than anyone else. No one should *own* a house. We all just live as and where we need to. When we need to.'

Connie peered round at the blank walls. 'Like you're all doing here?'

'Yes!' he said loudly, elated. He reached for her chin and turned her face towards his. Dark hair tumbled into his eyes, a soft smile on his lips. Lips which she couldn't help but stare at. 'Here, we live as we should. As everyone should. And the stuff we take,' he kissed her gently, 'it just helps us exist. Helps us try to build a bridge between this world and the next.'

'The next?' But Connie's question was muffled. He was kissing her again. Harder, deeper, hands beginning to roam across the clothes that had previously felt so uncomfortable but now she barely noticed they were there. Her skin was molten beneath his touch. She wanted to latch onto what he had said, to focus on what he was trying to tell her. But as his tongue met with hers, it became impossible to think about anything at all.

When the dawn came, he was still in her room. They'd slept curled together and as silver dawn light crept across the floor, Robin had shifted. Once he was gone, the cold of the morning nipped at Connie and she soon awoke, stretching and rubbing her eyes to see him leaning by the window, peering out at the grey morning.

'You OK?' She felt stiff as she staggered to her feet, noting she was still wearing the clothes that Wren had lent her. Clothes she would need to return.

'I'm fine.' He raked a hand through his hair, drawing it back off his face. 'I just struggle to sleep without the stuff.'

Connie looked down to her hands, which were empty. At some point she'd forgotten about what he'd slipped to her when she came home. 'What is it?' She studied him, the clean lines of his jaw, the softness of his lips, the dimple to the left of his right eye which hinted at a previous battle with chickenpox. 'What do we take?'

'It's . . .' He shrugged, pushed his hands into his jeans pockets. 'It's like taking a drink. It loosens you up, opens your mind.'

'Drugs?'

121

Another shrug. 'I suppose that's one label for it.'

'You have another?'

'I've heard it called LSD.' He raised his head to lock eyes with her. His were red-rimmed. He looked tired. 'But really it's just medicine. That's how I came to know about it. Because my mum had to take it.'

'Did she take it . . . a lot?'

'Yeah.' His head dipped to gaze at his bare feet. 'After my dad didn't come home from the war, she started acting . . .' He expanded his lungs, kicked at nothing. 'She was acting strange. The doctors said it was some . . . delusion. She'd just start screaming in the middle of the night and stopped washing and stuff. They tried everything and eventually they gave her . . . that stuff. And,' Robin tapped at the smeared glass of the window then pressed his forehead to it, 'when she was on it she kept saying he came back. That he was with us again.'

Connie padded the short distance between him and stood at his side, gazing out at rooftops and a clotted sky.

'Everyone thought she was crazy. That she was having,' he made quotation marks with his hands, '"a psychotic episode". But I believed her. I think when she was on the stuff, she found a way to see him again.'

'Is that why you take it? Because you want to see your dad again?' Connie gently placed her hand on his forehead. His skin was like ice.

Robin nearly choked on a dry laugh. 'Hell no. My dad was an arsehole. It's better he didn't come back, trust me. But the stuff . . . I think my mum was onto something with it. That it can be like this bridge to the other side.'

Connie looked at him, remembering how it made her feel when she took it. Like time was fluid, like her thoughts were an endless chain she needed to piece together.

'About a year ago I sought out my mum's doctor, got him to give me some, because I wanted . . . you know. To see her.'

'To see your mum?'

Robin turned his back to the window. Looked at the floor. 'Yeah, she . . . she jumped from the window of our flat.' He twisted to glance at Connie, his brown eyes glistening. 'We lived on the fifth floor.'

The tidal wave of his pain washed against her, carrying her along with him. But Connie reached for him, held him, keeping them both in place. 'Oh my God,' she muttered breathily. 'That's . . . that's just awful.'

'She told me she thought she could fly.' Robin held Connie to him, she could feel his heart pounding in his chest. 'I knew she was on the stuff again. Even though she wasn't supposed to be. I tried to stop her but . . .' A sound got strangled in his throat.

'It's OK,' Connie whispered. 'It's OK.'

'I'm sorry,' he sniffed and released her to drag the back of his hand across his raw eyes. 'I shouldn't have said anything. I don't talk about it. I just . . .' He held her in a steady gaze as a tear slid down his face. 'I feel like I can trust you.'

'You can.' Connie leaned up to kiss him, tasting salt. She'd heard love songs before. Been kissed before. But she'd never thought it could be like this. Robin was telling her everything, all his secrets. All the things he kept stored closest to his heart. Perhaps that meant she could trust him with hers too. And maybe this time she'd be heard.

25

Then

There were nightmares. Many of them. Connie had hoped that perhaps being away from home, being somewhere new, they might abate a little. Robin even promised that the drugs he so keenly slipped to everyone would help: 'They take you somewhere else, somewhere better.'

But still the nightmares came. The worst ones were when Connie awoke in a cold pit of her own sweat, heart thrashing in her chest, hands instantly reaching for her neck, feeling the throb of a phantom touch still closed around it. Robin rarely stirred. Beside her, he slept deeply, lost to his own thoughts and dreams. Sometimes, in the pale early morning light, Connie would sit, legs pulled to her chest, and watch him. Wonder about the world he had come from. The things he had seen.

'We're all monsters here,' Wren had slurred to her during one of her drunken jaunts down to the kitchen, where Connie also went whenever sleep evaded her. Or worse, when she sleepwalked away from her bed. 'It's why we get on so well.' Wren had grinned wide at her. Manic. Connie had shuffled away, dismissing the comment. Yet it kept coming back to her, unbidden. She watched Robin sleeping. There was nothing monstrous in the curve of his lips, the soft lace of his eyelashes falling on pale skin. He was boyish and beautiful, his edges not yet fully roughened out by manhood.

Monsters.

Connie felt that Wren was the only monster amongst them. The viper in the nest. With her dark talk of dead bodies, her constant desire to try and push Connie to the edge.

Connie's nightmares troubled her. If she was having them, she assumed she must also be sleepwalking. If she closed her eyes she was back there, hands on her neck, a voice from her past hot and rough in her ear: 'You need to learn to shut up.'

But I'm a good girl.

Connie awoke with a shudder, the same thought echoing in her mind over and over.

When was good, good enough?

The house around her felt like it was getting colder. She didn't want to think how it might cope once winter truly set in, when there was hard ice on the ground. She recalled with a pained familiarity the newspaper-wrapped brick her mother would provide for her on bitter nights.

Her mother.

Thinking about her made Connie put her head in her hands and moan. Was her mother sick now? Frantic at the thought of what might have become of her only daughter? Did she keep a vigil at the window every night, anxiously waiting? Or was the public shame of it too great; did she keep the curtains tightly closed and barely venture out? What were people saying about her? That she was no good. Had gone astray.

And how was her father coping?

Connie's breath caught in her throat, she coughed, dislodging it, eyes smarting. No, she wouldn't picture him fireside in his favourite pub, a glass clasped in his grimy hand, eyes bloodshot. She wouldn't picture him at all.

Once, Robin found her by the window, staring out at the darkened street, forehead pressed to the glass.

'Connie?' He tentatively tapped her shoulder and she gave a jolt, eyes blinking rapidly. 'Is everything all right?' His voice still thick with sleep.

'W-what?' Connie turned, glanced at the mattress they used as their bed. How many steps had she taken to reach the window? Five? Six?

'What are you doing with that?' Robin gestured to her hands and Connie glanced down, stunned to see her fingers tightly closed around a rusty screwdriver.

'I . . .' Connie let it fall from her grip and land with a dull thud upon the bare floorboards.

'Are you OK?' Robin carefully turned her body to face his. How glorious he looked in the moonlight. Brown eyes glistening with concern, a tumble of hair falling over his forehead, lips so ripe Connie could kiss them all day.

'Yeah, I'm . . .' She drew in a feathery breath, still held by the captor of sleep. Had she been dreaming as she drifted from the bed? Where had she found the screwdriver? Downstairs? In the bedroom?

'Were you planning on doing some fixing up around the place?' Robin joked, but there was a nervousness to his tone that also made Connie uneasy.

Were you planning on peeling potatoes?

She looked down at the hand that had held the tool, turning it over, distrusting each of her five fingers. 'I don't . . .' She gave a long sigh. 'I'm sorry, I'm just tired.'

'Nightmares?' he asked with such kindness, such sincerity, but in Connie's mind she heard Wren, saw the crook of her knowing smirk.

We're all monsters here.

'No, no, I'm fine. Really. I just . . .' She glanced back

at the mattress, wishing her subconscious self would cease betraying her. 'I'm just tired.'

'Sure.' Robin kept looking at her, unconvinced.

'Really.' To prove her point, Connie walked over to the mattress, lay down in her usual spot, which held no warmth. Had long had she been absent from Robin's side? How long had she been staring out of the window before he found her? What was she even looking for? 'Can we go back to sleep now, please?'

'OK.' Robin raised his arms up over his head, stretching. 'But I'm a bit awake now.' He gave her that grin, the one he used whenever he wanted something. The one she could never refuse.

'Is that so?' Connie smiled back at him, grateful for the distraction. She didn't want to consider what the presence of the screwdriver meant. Or what she was doing at the window. She had felt so sure that if she left home, the sleepwalking would stop. That she would be well.

Be good.

'I don't like it when you're not next to me,' Robin murmured as he lay down beside her, drawing her into his arms.

'Me neither.'

'This is where you belong.' He kissed her lips gently. 'You belong with me.'

'I know.' And in that moment, she did. It felt right. She leaned into him, kissing him hard, doing her best to forget about the screwdriver abandoned on the floor.

26

Then

It was late. The dark sky was pricked with stars and it was cold. Connie was in the kitchen, wrapped in a woollen knit cardigan several sizes too large. It hung down to her knees but she was glad of the extra length, the warmth it provided. Her hair was scraped back in a severe ponytail, slick against her head. It felt greasy. She needed to shower but she tried to avoid the sparse bathroom as much as possible. There was black mould that snaked the length of the bathtub and the water was rarely warm. Not like at home where her mother would scrub the enamel until it shone, where the bath would be filled with water boiled downstairs.

Connie lowered the spoonful of porridge she'd been about to eat from out of a cracked blue striped bowl. She thought of home. Of her parents. Of what they might be doing at that moment. Had they resigned themselves to her absence? Thinking she would return when ready? Or were they sick with worry? And guilt? Connie jabbed at the lumpy contents of the bowl. What about school? Had the girls there worn her name out on the playground and along the hallways? Were people speculating about where she'd gone or did no one care?

The kitchen door slammed and Connie realised she was no longer alone.

'You're jumpy,' Wren stated as she lowered herself across the table from her, slender in a green turtleneck sweater and jeans. Her dark hair looked damp, as though she'd just showered, skin flushed and dewy. Connie sagged behind her bowl, painfully aware of how she must look in contrast. 'Taking too much of the stuff makes you jumpy,' Wren added as she reached for a red apple perched in a small pile of fruit in the centre of the table. Connie had no idea whose job it was to acquire food for the house but someone must do it, as every couple of days the cupboards were replenished. Probably using the money she'd helped Robin steal. Connie nudged her bowl away, appetite completely gone.

'I've not had any today.' Connie massaged her cheeks, which felt too hollow, skin too thin, like paper that could rip at any moment.

'Hmm.' Wren's scrutiny was swift and severe. Even without eyeliner framing her gaze, it was still dark, still sharp. 'Whatever. You're his new pet, so he'll keep plying you with treats until he gets what he wants.'

Connie looked down at her hands, which she'd clenched atop the table, nails bitten down lower than they'd ever been before. She'd taken drugs that day, she knew it would be clear to someone like Wren, who knew the tell-tale signs. Each time Robin found her in the house, he pressed something into her hand. Either that or kissed her. And it was all blurring together. Her time with him. Her thoughts. The days. It was like living on the waltzers. Her world had become both beautiful and confusing.

'What does he want?' Connie hated that she asked, but the question slipped from her unbidden. The drugs were doing that, making her resolve sloppier, dopier. She should have bitten her tongue, left the room, instead she played into Wren's hands. She knew girls like Wren, they were multiple at her school. Girls who were as cruel as they were beautiful. Though none of them had the air of sophistication that Wren did. She had seen things. Done things. Enough things to seem jaded by it all, even though she could barely be eighteen.

'Come on,' Wren smirked. 'You can play the nice girl act for him all day long. He loves it but I see through it.'

'I don't know what you're talking about.'

'Are you a virgin?'

Connie turned to stone. She didn't move. Didn't respond.

'Because that's what he wants,' Wren continued. 'That's what he likes.'

Connie had to remind herself to breathe as Wren loomed large across from her, a cobra preparing to strike a mouse. Hands spread upon the table, Wren leaned forward. 'He'll take what he wants from you, and then drop you.'

'Is that what he did to you?' Connie found her voice.

Wren gave a laugh more like a cackle, easing back down, reaching for her apple and taking a large bite out of it. She chewed loudly, smacking her lips together. Then, wiping her mouth with the back of her hand, she smiled at Connie, eyes bright with mirth. 'You really like him, don't you?'

'I—'

'Is that why you don't run home to Mummy and Daddy?'

Connie steeled herself with a deep breath. Sure, she could just run back home. She'd be punished for her absence, but she would also be swiftly sent back to school, expected to carry on as though everything was normal. As though nothing had ever happened.

'See?' Wren wagged a finger at her, chewing on a fresh piece of apple. 'That look . . . where you look scared. That's why we might one day be friends. Maybe.'

'Why aren't we friends now?'

Wren scoffed. Ate more apple.

'Seriously,' Connie pressed. 'You've not liked me since I got here. Is it because you like Robin? Is that it?'

'Everyone likes Robin,' Wren replied breezily. 'Just look around. He's the reason anyone is here. You've met him, you've fallen under his spell just the same as everyone else.'

'Do you love him?' That was the thing with the drugs, they'd muted Connie's inner voice. Thoughts she'd normally keep close, not release, flew all too easily from her lips. She watched Wren straighten, eyes widen just a fraction.

'Do you think you have something special with him?' she asked mockingly. 'Do you think you're the first girl he's doted on here? Do you think you'll be the last?'

Connie felt something with Robin. Something beyond the drugs. Beyond the liberation of being away from home, away from what had happened. When she was around Robin, things made sense. And when he kissed her . . . she lost track of everything. That had to be love. Didn't it?

'He tell you about his mum?' Wren cocked her head, left side of her mouth lifted in a playful smirk.

'I should go . . .' Connie didn't want to be toyed with further.

'He tell you that she jumped from a window?' Wren called after her as Connie scurried towards the kitchen door. She was just in the hallway when Wren's final question landed against her back, arriving there like a dagger.

'He tell you that the police think he did it? That he pushed her?'

Connie slammed the door shut and ran down the hallway, feeling sick.

27

Now

'Was there ever a time when you didn't play the violin?' Daniel's question pulled her back into the room. Connie cleared her throat, played for time. The air in the lounge was beginning to smell like damp earth, carried in on a cold breeze through the fireplace. The sky was still lead. Window peppered with raindrops.

'In an interview you did with . . .' Now it was Daniel's turn to venture down memory lane, to pull open the drawers within his mind until he found what he was searching for. 'The *LA Times*.' He clicked his fingers, the information quickly retrieved. Connie envied the sharpness of it, the speed. Sometimes an hour could pass while she fought to recall why she had slipped into the kitchen. Usually Bach would mew and press against her legs, eagerly reminding her. 'It was just after you played on the Oscar-winning score for *Due Tides*. You said that you played every day. Religiously. For at least an hour. You said it was essential to keep your muscle memory sharp.'

Connie nodded. She remembered both the interview and the quote. Back then she believed what she was saying, the importance of it. And she would play daily, bathed in a rectangle of pure golden sunlight. She'd played until her arm ached, until her fingers throbbed. She'd play like she was a schoolgirl again, desperate to improve. Desperate to be free. Connie closed her eyes, feeling weary. 'I did say that, yes.'

'So.' Daniel tilted his head as he watched her, his gaze noting every sigh, every wilt in her posture. 'Was there a time when you didn't play daily?'

With a fluttery breath Connie opened her eyes. The young man slid in and out of focus. Damn her failing eyesight. Just another part of her that was being eroded by the inevitable river of time. 'I used to believe it was imperative to play daily. To constantly be working on your craft.'

'Used to?'

Connie looked to the window, wondered how long it would continue to rain for. Surely her front garden was already soaked enough? What she wouldn't give for a slice of sunlight, a sliver of blue sky to remind her of those years spent in America, when her world was warm. When she'd placed as much distance as she could between herself and home.

'It has been many years since I picked up a violin.' She smiled thinly at her interviewer. 'Perhaps close to a decade. The mind is willing but,' she extended her fingers, highlighting how they no longer stretched out fully, how some joints were swollen, always bent, 'the body not so much. But I remember every sonata. Every note. How much pressure to apply. When to release the bow.' Gently she tapped a thin finger against her temple. 'I forget so many things these days. The day of the week, when to pay the milkman. But the music, the music never leaves.'

'I suppose it is a part of you?'

'It is.' And Connie liked that part. The part that played. Always had. It was the part that had ultimately saved her. She pressed a hand to her mouth, coughed loudly, needing to disguise the sob she desperately wanted to release. While music had saved her, it had also provided the noose that nearly hanged her. It always perplexed her, how something could be both the worst and best thing in someone's life.

'It's great that you can recall all the music.' Daniel smiled, but it quickly fell away. 'But you've still not answered my initial question. Did you always play daily?'

No.

'Yes. I was extremely dedicated to my music.'

'Even as a young woman, when there were so many . . . temptations to lure you away from study?'

A mask of indifference settled on Connie's features. *A young woman.* Connie felt her there so often, lingering behind old bones and sagging skin. The packaging had changed but she had not.

'I know that I have struggled.' Daniel pressed a hand to his chest. 'Girls. Boys. They can be a distraction. Especially when you're young, footloose and fancy-free.'

'Ah.' Connie smiled genially. 'It is definitely harder to focus on one's studies when there are, as you call them, *distractions.*'

Bach jumped down off the sofa, landing almost silently upon the carpet. Tail high, he strutted out of the room without a backward glance.

'But at the risk of being a bore, I was always completely dedicated to my musical studies.'

'That's not boring at all,' Daniel commented, though an edge had crept into his voice. 'I applaud your dedication. Clearly it helped you get to great heights.'

Connie turned to glance in the direction her cat had gone. She was lying. Why was she lying? The young man was well meaning, wasn't he? Merely trying to unpick who she was. And he'd said himself that he became distracted from time to time. Didn't everyone? Wouldn't it help his own endeavours with music to see her as human? Fallible?

A tense sigh escaped from her lips. 'Maybe I wasn't always *completely* dedicated.'

Daniel's eyes widened, spine straightened. 'Oh?'

'I . . .' Connie shook her head dismissively. 'I was young and foolish once. As most of us are. I neglected my music. It didn't last long but . . .' Her voice trailed off, unable to finish her own sentence.

It didn't last long but *it changed everything.*

She had always tried to be closed off to reporters. Her entire career, she hid behind the music. Even her late husband, Albert, didn't know the full truth about what had happened. She couldn't risk him knowing, letting it sour all that they had. Connie had vowed to take her secrets to the grave, just as her parents had done for her. The final thing they actually managed to get right.

'I'm wittering on.' Connie snatched a glance at her clock. 'And time is getting away from us. I feel like we should start discussing my time over in America; that was when the really exciting things began to happen.'

'No.' Daniel's smile didn't reach his eyes. 'I'd like to keep our discussion right where it is.'

Rain pelted the window and Connie shuddered.

HOUSE OF HORRORS

Frank Collins, Blackhill resident and beloved music teacher at Blackhill Girls Grammar, and his wife, Barbara Collins, were found murdered in his home on Breckheath Street in the early hours of this morning. Authorities were alerted by a neighbour shortly after 4am when figures were seen vaulting over an exterior wall. Previously, screams had been heard.

When police arrived on site, they discovered Mr and Mrs Collins still in their bed. Their sons, Colin, five, and Marshall, three, were found weeping at their parents' sides, disorientated and blood-soaked, still trying to wake their mother and father. Signs of forced entry were revealed downstairs via a broken window.

Police Constable Alan Stevens said it was the most horrific case he has come across in his thirty-year career. 'This appears to be a home invasion of the most grotesque kind. To stab someone while they sleep is just heinous and it is unimaginable to think it happened here in Blackhill. We urge residents to come forward with any and all information they have. We will find the attackers. In the meantime, we ask that everyone be vigilant and keep doors and windows locked at all times.'

If you have any information relating to the crime, please call 01902 641996.

28

Then

'Why don't you play anymore?'

He found her crouched in the cement wasteland that passed as the garden. Connie had pressed herself against the back wall, pressing her knees to her chin, feeling as strangled as the weeds that fought for life between the cracks in the slabs. She couldn't, wouldn't look at him.

'I said why don't you play anymore?' His footsteps scuffed against the ground as he approached her, joining her by the wall in a swift collapse of long limbs. The sky was flint. He leaned back and gazed up at it, legs stretched out long while Connie remained compressed. 'It's pretty cold out here.' Goosebumps crept up the lean flanks of his arms. The t-shirt he wore was crumpled and he smelt faintly of mildew. Connie felt herself frown as she tried to calm her thoughts. 'Is everything all right?' He seemed unnerved by her silence. 'I mean . . . I like it when you play but . . .' Robin picked at the leaves of a dandelion, its flowers long since taken by the wind. 'It's been a while.'

Has it?

Connie felt the fog of her fear briefly disperse. How long *had* it been since she had played? In her mind she still heard music. When she drifted through the house, when she stood beneath the shower that dripped tepid water onto her. But when had she last actually *felt* it? Actually *played*?

'I don't . . .' Her fingers twitched in anticipation. She itched to play. But now something blocked her. The drugs, the way they loosened her mind. Memories had returned unbidden to her dreams. Of dark rooms. And hands. Things she had fought so hard to bury. 'Why are you here?' Sudden and swift, she was once again clutching the axe she needed to grind.

'I came looking for you.' He reached for her face and Connie darted just out of reach, her eyes wide, almost frantic. 'Hey.' Robin quickly withdrew his hand. 'What's got into you?'

'Why are you *here*?' Connie said more determinedly, scrambling up to her feet. She felt the first drops of rain land on the crown of her blonde parting. The chill in the air told her that was more was on the way. 'In this house.' She gestured to it. To the bare windows, the cracked walls laced with graffiti. 'What are you doing here, Robin? Are you hiding from the police?'

He also stood, eyes dark as he dipped his chin to stare at her. 'I guess you've been talking to Wren.'

'What's going on here? What is all this?' She gestured again to the dilapidated terrace, hand dancing like a manic kite. 'Did you—' She ran out of air and let her arm fall to her side.

'If you intend on finishing that sentence, you should leave right now and never come back,' Robin said coldly, but a flash of pain swept across his face.

A moment passed and the rain fell around them.

'I just want to know what's going on,' Connie admitted quietly as it began to soak into her clothes.

Robin peered up at the sky, let the rain streak his cheeks. 'Well . . .' He pushed wet hair back with a hand that trembled ever so slightly. 'This is where I came to hide. Same as you.'

'No, you started this.'

'I was the first.' He nodded briefly. 'But others quickly came.'

'Are the police after you?'

He pinned her with his gaze, eyes as deep and potent as the strongest coffee. 'Maybe. It's been a while.'

'They think you killed your mother?'

Robin's jaw clenched. A stiff nod of confirmation.

Did you?

The question was on her tongue but Connie couldn't quite breathe life into it. Not when she could still recall the pressure of his mouth on hers, how intoxicating it was, how liberating.

'She jumped,' Robin offered so quietly the hiss of the rain almost drowned him out. His dark hair was plastered to his head. 'She thought she could fly and I wasn't quick enough to stop her. I knew no one would believe me, so I ran.'

Connie began to shiver in her wet clothes.

'So now you know.' Robin stepped closer to her. 'So your turn. Why are you hiding here?'

She felt grateful for the rain. It hid the tears that were now falling. Chin quivering, she reached for him. 'Because no one would believe me, either.'

In the house, in her bedroom, the soaked clothes had to come off. They dropped to the ground with a heavy thud as they shed them. Laid bare, Connie pressed her hands to her chest, seeking to cover herself. Robin showed no such modesty, striding over to her and taking her wrists in his hands, guiding them to her sides. Connie could barely breathe. Her teeth knocked together from the cold and nerves.

'Do you want this?' He whispered the question into her collarbone, his breath warm. Her body responded before her mind could, reaching for him, drawing him closer. She trembled beneath his touch, clung to his back as he rested above her. If he sensed it wasn't her first time, he didn't let on.

The air felt thick and musky, after. The rain had moved on but left a pale grey sky behind. Tucked in the crook of Robin's arm, Connie leaned her head upon his bare chest, listened to the rise and fall of each breath, marvelling at the closeness of it all. As they were entwined, he idly stroked her arm, the light outside dwindling. Connie glanced around the room, noticing her violin box propped in a corner, gathering dust.

'Why were you asking why I don't play anymore?' Her heartbeat sped up. *Did he know?*

'Well.' He kissed her forehead, leaving a simmering heat upon her skin as though her were branding her. 'I hadn't heard you for a while.'

'I've just not felt in the mood.' Her fingers fluttered, a melody played in her mind. Music was like her heartbeat, ever present. But now when she played, the memories no longer remained in the shadows; they surged for the light, for recognition. Connie closed her eyes and gave a sigh of defeat.

'Did something happen?' He moved to cup her face in his hands, his voice soft with concern.

'Not here.'

Robin stroked her cheek with his thumb. 'Where?'

A tear dripped down Connie's cheek. 'Please, not now,' she whispered, 'I don't want to ruin this moment.'

He kissed her. Held her close. 'Would it help if you sold it?'

Connie stiffened. She had not considered parting with her violin in such a way. It was her most treasured possession.

Glancing over at the case, she felt her stomach lurch. But it was tainted. The violin. The music. All of it.

'How do we get it so that you can play again?' Robin asked. Connie sniffed, unsure of the answer.

'I don't know.' She rubbed at her eyes which felt raw.

That night she slept curled against Robin, his strong arms protectively wrapped around her. She stared into the darkness, unwilling to give in to sleep in case the nightmares found her. With only moonlight to guide her, she stared at the elegant curves of her violin case. She knew the weight of it so intimately from the years she'd shouldered it to school and back. Knew every crack and kink across its dark surface. Perhaps selling it was the answer. The trade-off she'd need to make to stay in this life and completely sever her connections from her previous one.

29

Then

'Can you do bad things?'

It was a question Wren liked to ask of Connie, more as a taunt. 'I bet you can,' she'd add with a purr. 'I bet you can do *really* bad things.' Connie managed to maintain a dignified silence though she wanted to point out that she was a good girl. She didn't *do* bad things. Bad things were done to her. She always put her time and energy into doing better, being better.

Running away.

Often, her chest ached when she thought for too long about home. About all she had left behind. About Mr Collins frowning and pacing each time she failed to turn up for a music lesson. Had he gone to her parents, turning up on their doorstep wearing his most gracious smile? 'I'm just worried about Connie, it isn't like her to fail to turn up for school. She's usually such a good girl.' Or would he keep away from there, knowing too many of the secrets Connie kept stored up too tight. Would he know to fear her father?

Of course, Connie had done bad things. She surmised that everyone surely had at some point in their lives. Running away, for example, would definitely be considered a bad thing. But Connie knew it depended how you looked at things. Objectively, yes, it was bad. But subjectively, no. It was quite the opposite.

'Could you hurt someone?' How Wren loved to probe. Always with that feline stare of hers, alert yet aloof. 'Could you kill someone?'

'Wren, enough!' Arthur finally shut her down, shaking his head with disapproval. 'When will you learn to just let people be?'

'When they stop keeping secrets,' Wren told him while continuing to stare at Connie.

'Like you don't have secrets enough of your own. Stop being wicked.'

This made her smirk. Wren loved to be wicked.

Connie liked to think that *no*, she could not hurt someone. Not intentionally. So of course no, she couldn't *kill* someone. And yet . . .

The question triggered something in Connie. A memory she fought so hard to forget. It had happened almost a year ago. Her father drinking more frequently each evening, excusing his behaviour as simply 'being festive'. Each night he came in, he slammed the door harder, spouting crueller and crueller taunts at his long-suffering wife. Connie listened from the landing, from her bedroom, feeling rage coil within her. Finally it was all too much. When he came trudging up the staircase, reeking like a brewery, Connie was waiting for him at the top, a thunderous expression twisting her young face.

'To bed with you.'

'You can't speak to her like that. Or me.'

He looked at her like he was seeing her for the very first time. And he didn't like what he saw. His lips curled with contempt. 'What did you just say to me?'

'I said—'

The question had clearly been rhetorical as before Connie could answer, he slapped her. Hard. But the burn in her face was nothing compared to the fire that grew within her, molten and dangerous. With a scream of fury, she lashed out, fingers and nails extended, scraping a hand across her father's face, digging as deep as she could, feeling flesh tear.

'You little bitch.'

Despite his drunken state, his reactions were impressively quick. He grabbed her wrist with such force he almost snapped it. And then he headbutted her. Connie recalled his face coming fast and sudden towards hers, like a freight train, but then there was nothing. Only darkness.

When she came to, she was in her bed, her mother above her, morning light glowing behind her head like a halo. She was dipping low over her daughter, a damp flannel in hand, mopping Connie's brow.

'What did you do? Foolish, foolish girl,' she muttered when she saw Connie's eyes flutter open. 'You looking to get yourself killed?'

Connie went to reply but managed only a groan. Everything hurt but especially her face. She felt as though someone had smacked her with a cricket bat. Tentatively she raised her hand to her nose, finding something wet and sticky at the base of it.

'Ow.' It was woefully tender. Then, journeying upwards, she felt something sticky between her eyebrows, then a mound in the centre of her forehead.

'You're lucky he didn't kill you. *Foolish girl*. What have I said about avoiding him when he drinks? You know how he gets. What were you thinking?' Her mother patted the flannel against Connie's nose, wincing as though she shared the pain that bloomed from it. 'I don't think it's broken. But we need to wait for the swelling to go down to be sure.'

'He . . . he attacked me,' Connie rasped.

'Hmm,' her mother clicked her tongue, 'by the looks of him you got a few licks in of your own first.'

'Wait, I—'

'Looks like a cat had him. Like I said, you're lucky, Connie. Very bloody lucky.'

'What . . . what time is it?' Connie registered again the morning light, felt her internal body clock jolt with alarm. She tried to sit up but her mother's hand was firm on her shoulder, forcing her back down.

'There'll be no school today, not looking like this. At least it's Friday, you should have cleared up enough by Monday, God willing.'

'Mum . . .' Connie sagged against her pillows, defeated. Sore.

'Stay away from him,' her mother urged through clenched teeth. 'Especially when he drinks.'

'Why did you marry him?' Connie wondered earnestly as she gazed up at her mother.

'You ask that like you think women have choices.' Her mother gave a rueful shake of her head and then continued to dab at Connie's battered face.

'You do though, Mum.'

'Sometimes I forget how young you really are.' Her mother looked so old in the pale morning light, so worn out.

On cold mornings Connie's nose still ached from the beating she'd taken that night. Though it wasn't crooked, she felt something was wrong within it. And she remembered how it felt, that moment when she'd lunged at her father. How filled with anger, with rage, with hate she had been. How in that moment she could have happily killed him.

30

Then

She barely remembered seeing him. But it was the feelings that still curdled within her as she clung to Robin, weeping, barely able to speak.

'Your girl just suddenly turned,' Wren remarked somewhere in the distance, her tone dull without its usual sharpness. 'I've no idea what happened.'

Of course she had no idea. Connie barely understood it herself. Her fingers dug into the thin fabric of Robin's t-shirt, trying to anchor against flesh and bone.

Just an hour earlier she and Wren had been on a park bench studying a small corner shop across the street. Around them the light was dwindling, twilight quickly being devoured by night. From her position on the bench, Connie could make out the boxes of fresh fruit in the window, the cheery welcome sign.

'The guys need to hurry up.' Wren stamped her feet with impatience and to stave off the cold. Her heavy boots rustled in the grass that surrounded the bench. 'Like seriously, we've been here twenty minutes already.'

Had they?

Connie didn't like how thick her thoughts were, how slowly they stirred in her mind. Lately it seemed that she was only sharp when she was high. In these, her regular hours, it felt like everything moved at a crawl, even the beating of her own heart. Robin was insistent that they couldn't go outside high. 'You need to focus,' he'd told Connie when she pressed him. But she did focus on the drugs. It was like switching from an oil lamp to an electric one. Everything was sudden, instant. Bright.

'What is taking them so bloody long?' Irritated, Wren got up, stalked towards the cover of an oak tree and withdrew a cigarette from the pocket of her worn leather coat. Connie watched the flicker of a flame briefly illuminate her companion's face. Wren, pale as bone with eyes lined with thick kohl. She looked unearthly. But more demon than angel. As Connie watched her, she thought of what she had tried to do, to place in her mind. That Robin was a killer. Wren exhaled a long trail of smoke through pursed, blood-red lips. Connie let her gaze wander up the trunk of the tree, along its gnarled, almost barren branches. Nearly all of its golden leaves had been stripped. Connie knew that the air would soon smell of bonfires. Days were beginning to turn to months since she'd left home.

Run away.

She flinched as she corrected herself. Had she run away? Was she now in hiding like Robin? Like the others?

Connie looked again to the raven gloss of Wren's hair. What had she done to warrant a place in the house? Were the police searching for her too? Connie's mouth parted to send a question across the space between them but Wren moved suddenly, footsteps small and fast as she returned to the bench like a startled bird. 'Someone's coming,' she gestured to the glow of the shop, cigarette clutched in fingers, a conductor for Connie's attention. Wren leaned forward, eyes narrowed. 'Is it Robin?'

It wasn't. The square shoulders. The light but firm gait. The thick hair. The three-piece suit. Connie blinked. And then kept blinking, eyes growing sore. She was wrong. She had to be wrong. Was she somehow still high? Was this all an hallucination? Because why would he be *here*?

Connie's hands gripped the slat of bench beneath her, fingers digging into old wood. She felt her teeth grinding together. She realised she didn't know where *here* actually was. She'd just followed Wren from the house, down streets and alleys until they arrived at the park. Until she was told to sit tight on the bench and wait for Robin's signal. Was she near home? The school?

'Shit, are you OK?' Wren was pressing a hand against her back but Connie didn't feel it, could only keep looking ahead at the shop he'd now disappeared into. What was he buying? Something for home? Something for his family?

'Connie, are you all right?' Wren was speaking louder now, tone urgent. The sight of him approaching the window of the shop to admire some tomatoes was like a starter pistol. Connie leapt from the bench, turned and ran. Deeper into the park. Deeper into darkness.

She kept running until she returned to the house, unable to account for how she'd got back there. Like a homing pigeon she'd somehow sensed her way. Wren pursued her, shouting for answers that never came. Only in Robin's arms did Connie stop.

'What's wrong with her?' The question was fired at Wren, who sullenly removed her coat in the hallway, scowling.

'Like I said, I don't know. Why are you even here?' she demanded hotly, turning the enquiry around. 'We've been out there in that shitty park freezing our arses off waiting for you.'

'We got delayed,' Arthur offered from somewhere nearby.

'More like you got high.' Any voice. Connie shuddered against Robin, feeling spent and hollow.

'Stay out of it, Charlotte,' Robin cut sharply, arms wrapped tightly against Connie.

'*Were* you getting high?' Wren's cloud of perfume blew close. Cheap yet heavy. She always wore enough to linger in a room long after she'd left. 'Is that what's going on with her? Is she fucking high, Rob?'

'No, she's not high. Shhh, shh . . .' He was stroking Connie's golden hair, trying to soothe her. 'It's OK, you're safe now.'

'She just took off.' Wren was stomping towards the kitchen and Robin coaxed Connie to follow, the room warm thanks to the stew that was on the hob. Though the smell of cooking meat made Connie want to retch.

'OK, why? What happened?' Robin looked between the two women, face pale.

'Shopkeeper get wise?' Arthur asked as he opened a cupboard and rummaged around for a bowl.

'No.' Wren crossed her arms against her chest. 'We didn't leave the bench.'

Connie's fingertips throbbed with the splinters she'd got from clutching the bench. She'd held on too tight, as though the grass were trying to drown her.

'So what happened exactly?' Robin rubbed circles against Connie's back, intermittently leaning down to kiss her forehead.

'We were there on the stupid bench. Waiting.' Wren leaned against the kitchen counter, raising her chin. 'I got up for a smoke.'

Arthur found a chipped blue bowl and began ladling stew into it. From her position against Robin's chest, Connie watched him. His movements weren't fluid like her mother's at mealtimes, but he was proficient. There was gravy seeping over the sides that he didn't bother to mop up, and splotches left upon the hob. But his bowl was full. The kitchen was soiled but the world hadn't ended.

'Someone entered the shop.' Wren was now tapping her forehead, replaying events of the evening. 'Some . . . some guy.'

Connie froze. She didn't breathe. Didn't move. In her chest her lungs began to ache with the desire to exhale. But how could she breathe when everything was about to fall apart? Somehow they were here, at the cliff edge. And Wren was about to push her over.

'A guy?' Robin's voice lifted. Still Connie wouldn't breathe. 'What guy?'

'Ask her.' Wren pointed a painted fingernail at Robin's chest. 'She's the one who lost it when she saw him.'

Robin's hands settled on Connie's shoulders and eased her back from the reassuring pulse of his heart, just a fraction. Lungs burning, she gasped, felt the soreness of her eyes from all the tears she had shed. 'Is that what's wrong?' Robin squeezed her shoulders as he probed. 'The guy going into the shop. Did you . . . do you know him?' His jaw clenched. Whether in jealously or disappointment, Connie couldn't tell. She could only nod. Yes, she knew him. Fresh tears scorched along old pathways. It was the man who stalked her sleep.

'OK, well . . .' Robin swept his palm against her cheek, taking away some of her tears. 'Who is he, Connie?'

No one.

She knew that's what she was supposed to say. Had been trained to say. *No one. It was nothing.* With a whimper she remembered her parents' faces, drained of colour and pinched with fear. She'd spoken this truth before to those who were meant to love her. Gazing into Robin's eyes, she studied the rich brown that gave way to a black centre.

'Connie, who is he?'

Her voice was hoarse as she spoke. 'Mr . . . Mr Collins. It was Mr Collins.'

31

Now

'How did you feel when you stopped playing music?'

There was a greedy interest in Daniel's eyes that Connie didn't appreciate. Was he trying to pull her down? Was his entire dissertation, this whole interview, just some twisted interpretation of his jealousy? Connie had seen it before. Many times on many faces. They'd look to undermine her at any given chance. Be flippant of all she had achieved. Insist that it was *just music*.

Connie gave him the flat smile she always gave them. It was never *just music*. It was an extension of who she was, of her soul. But there had been a time when she'd been so conflicted she gave it up. Old hurts burned within her, suddenly fresh.

'When I didn't play, I felt . . .' She wasn't about to give him the satisfaction of pulling her down. So she opted for maximum drama, which had always worked before. People love it when an artist becomes artistic; it makes it easier to pass off their behaviour as precious. Connie would rather he think her temperamental and highly strung than give him the smug satisfaction of thinking he could shake her. His interest in her past, her early years studying the violin, clearly he was trying to draw parallels between them both and didn't like the conclusions he was reaching. 'Without music in my life I felt dead.'

Daniel leaned back, sucking in his cheeks.

Connie kept her smile, expression set like stone. But her chest ached from too many years spent holding too much in. She had misspoken. That time in her life when she didn't play, she didn't feel dead. She felt free. But Connie knew that wasn't the answer Daniel sought, the one which would fit the narrative he wanted to attach to her. For him she needed to be the tortured musician.

'That's . . .' Delicately he put down his pen and notepad and rested his hands on his slender knees. 'That sounds intense.'

'It was.'

'So why did you stop? If playing was so important to you?'

'Ah, the folly of youth I suppose.'

'Young love?' His eyes narrowed.

'Something like that.'

'Was it around the time you met Mr Winchester then?'

Mr Winchester. Albert Winchester. Her Albert. With his stiff accent and ginger moustache which glowed gold in the sunlight. She'd been a young woman when she met him. He'd sent her flowers after a concert at the Royal Albert Hall. A dozen red roses. Connie had been stunned into silence when she saw them. Their petals like rich velvet. She'd seen dancers receive such gifts but never fellow musicians.

'Seems like you have an admirer,' the smooth voice of her friend, cellist Elizabeth Smith Dalton, remarked from behind her with a smirk. Connie had spun around so fast she almost made herself dizzy.

'No, no, they must be for someone else.'

Because in every book and song she'd heard until that point, you only got one true love. And that's if you were lucky.

*

153

'Was your future husband the distraction?' Daniel was reaching again for his precious notes.

Connie glanced to the window, to the rain. If it wasn't still gathering in her gutters and pooling on her driveway, this was the point where she would ask him to leave. But the manners of her upbringing were carved so deep they reached bone. It would be rude to send him out into such a storm.

'Mr Winchester was always such a fan of my music.' Even talking about him made the room brighter. Connie realised with a pang just how dull the house had become in his absence. Albert always laughed from the pit of his stomach and listened to music so loud he silenced any train of thought. His presence was all-consuming. People flocked to the light he radiated, Connie included.

'So he isn't the reason you stopped playing?'

Connie frowned. She was old. And tired. Too tired to keep playing games with the young interviewer. If he'd done his dull diligence, which it seemed he had, he'd already know the year she wed Albert. That Albert had been an investment banker based in London. It was clear to anyone tracing her past that Albert Winchester did not exist within Connie's teenage years. He came later. Into a very different world, meeting a very different Connie.

'Do you always play?' Connie could hear her voice sharpening, becoming a blade she needed to wield.

'As often as I can.'

'You're a young person, you must understand that sometimes life can get in the way of rehearsals.'

'On occasion. Yes. Certainly.' Daniel stroked his chin with the capped end of his pen. 'But I've never not played for a prolonged period.'

Connie knew what was coming next. He'd extended his line and was now hoping for a bite. Six months. That was the length she didn't play for. One hundred and eighty-two and a half days in which she didn't pick up her violin. Didn't even look at it. Because she'd sold it. Connie reached for the arms of her chair and began to get up. Manners be damned, she wanted the boy gone.

'I didn't play because I sold the damn thing when I was sixteen,' she muttered tersely. 'As I said before, I was a young girl and extremely foolish. And now I am a woman in her eighties. An old woman. And I am tired, so I must bid you farewell.' Her slippered feet started shuffling towards the hallway. It wasn't until she turned to face the front door that she realised Daniel hadn't followed. Muscles wincing, she edged back into the lounge where her interviewer remained, pen in hand, pressed to his notepad as though he were about to start writing notes. Sucking in an angry breath, Connie longed for the looming presence of her husband. Even in old age he could be intimidating. He stood 6 foot 4 with wide shoulders and a deep, baritone voice. If he were there, he'd cast her guest out into the rain without a second thought. The corners of Connie's mouth dipped low. Albert had been a good man. A good husband. And he'd left her with an empty house full of memories.

A meow. Bach pressing against her legs, his fur soft and warm. His purr rumbling through him.

'I said it's time for you to go.' She raised her voice so that it stretched over to Daniel, who peered up at her, eyes crinkled in what seemed to be amusement.

'I'll go when I'm ready,' he coolly informed her. 'I'm interested.' He leaned back into the sofa and dropped his pen to spread his arms wide across the back of it, as though it were his, as though this were his home. 'When you sold your violin, did it have anything to do with your teacher, Mr Collins?'

Connie couldn't move. Couldn't speak. The name rang like a bell in her ears.

Mr Collins.

The man who had ruined everything.

32

Then

'Who is Mr Collins?'

Robin's words were sharp, his touch firm against her shoulders as he looked at her, dark eyes wide.

'He . . .' Connie felt like she was falling. Her legs no longer of sturdy flesh and bone but something flimsy, something unable to support her. Memories that used to only flicker now burned, scorching her temple. She whimpered, staggered back from Robin. Connie blinked and she was back in her front room, fire crackling in the hearth, standing with her back to it as she faced her parents who were on the sagging sofa. Her mother still wearing the apron she'd had on while preparing dinner. It was Friday so they were having fish and chips. The whole house smelt pleasantly of grease.

'I don't understand.' When her mother spoke, she didn't look directly at Connie, she looked beyond her, to the framed picture on the mantelpiece taken just twelve months earlier, when Connie's cheeks still held the cherubic plumpness of childhood. Now you could see her bones, sharp angles appearing where before there had just been softness. 'Mr Collins is a good teacher.'

Connie looked between her parents.

A good teacher. From a distance. On paper. Yes. But being a good teacher didn't make him a good man.

'Did you hear what I just said?'

Connie had never intended for this conversation to happen. She'd thought things would have to continue as they were; closing her eyes in the dark and playing sonatas in her head until he was over. Until he was done. But now she was late. And she'd heard enough schoolyard rumours to know what that meant. What would become of her.

'I'm pregnant,' Connie said again, tears pooling along her top lip. Upon the sofa, her father, face blanched, flinched as though she'd struck him with a red-hot poker. 'Please, you have to help me.'

It was an effort to stand. Her knees knocked together, fingers picked at each other. It seemed impossible to think that amidst all the chaos, the nerves, something was growing within her. For three terrible weeks she had waited for her monthly to show. And from the way her mother's eyes wouldn't meet her own, she knew she hadn't been alone in that vigil.

'I didn't ask for this.' The fire snapped a piece of wood behind her but failed to provide any warmth. Connie trembled. 'He . . . he told me I had to. That if I was a good girl, I'd do as he said. That I'd keep it a secret.'

With a grunt her father got to his feet, swifter than she'd seen him move for years. He strode away from his daughter, the fire, out of the room, slamming the door. Connie felt the sound in her bones and her legs gave way. Crouched on the floor she pressed her hands into the thick shag of fireplace rug and peered up at her mother. 'What do I do?' She was still but a girl. What did she know about being a mother? It would ruin her. All of it. Her education. Her reputation. It would all be destroyed in an instant.

Silently her mother stood, smoothed the folds in her skirt and apron and then followed her husband out of the room, leaving her daughter to weep upon the floor alone.

★

Three days later, with her mother stiffly at her side, Connie took a bus and then a train into Manchester. They walked to an address her mother held on a slip of paper, hand shaking as she studied it. Down narrow, cobbled streets, past endless rows of houses, they eventually stopped at a blue door, marked number forty-two. The air smelt of burned rubber and beer. Connie looked down the length of the street, then at the house with the drawn curtains over its grimy windows. Her mother had not taken her to see a doctor as she had promised.

'What is this place?' she asked in a fearful whisper.

'It will be over quick.' Her mother looked ahead at the closed door, hands clasped tightly around her coin purse. 'Just do as the lady says. Ask no questions.'

'I don't . . .' Connie shook her head. She felt sick. But lately she always felt sick. 'Please, I'm scared.' She reached for her mother's hand but she withdrew from her, exhaling loudly through her nose. 'Mummy.' Connie choked out the word as her touch connected with air. It had been many long years since she'd called her mother by that name. And she thought she sensed her thaw a little but then the door opened and she was staring at a short woman with a crooked beak for a nose. She peered down it to assess who was darkening her doorstep. Then she saw the coin purse and ushered them inside with a nod of her head. Connie entered. Her mother did not follow.

It will be over quick.

That part had at least been true. Connie had laid out on a kitchen table, duly parted her legs and felt warmth slide up into her, breathing in the starched odour of strong soap that began to curdle with something else. Something she couldn't place. Then she was ordered to pull up her knickers and tights, money passed between palms and she was back on the train. Then the bus.

The next part. The part which arrived in the night while her father was thankfully working a night shift, that lasted for hours. Connie gripped the smooth side of the bathtub as she howled in pain. Her stomach burned as though the stew she'd struggled to eat at dinner had turned into hot coals. She screamed as the pain passed through her. Body covered in sweat, hair plastered to her head. And then she bled. So much more than her monthlies. It soaked the rug when she climbed out and Connie howled.

'Here.' She didn't remember her mother coming in, only the pressure of a cold flannel upon her forehead, then the softness of fresh towels beneath her. Towels she quickly soiled. The blood pouring out of her was dark, like tar. 'It will be all right.' Her mother's voice was soft, soothing, as it had once been when she sung lullabies. 'At least it's worked. That's the main thing. It worked. Be glad of that.'

The baby was gone. It felt like it had been cremated within her. Connie shuddered and leaned against her mother, body heaving.

'Shh now, child, all will be well.'

'How do you know that?' The blood. It was an ocean beneath her. Surely if she lost any more, she would die.

'Because I've been here.' Her mother's words were light, and Connie was beginning to feel disconnected from the moment, even from her pain. Blearily, she looked up into her mother's face as she lay curled within her lap, being stroked like she was just a baby. 'I had to knock on that door once, many years ago.'

'Why?' Connie whispered through chapped lips.

'Couldn't afford to feed another mouth.' A sad smile pulled on her mother's face as she looked at Connie, a single tear falling. 'You just need to rest now.'

Connie felt like a ghost as her mother tucked her up in bed, a hot-water bottle pressed to her back to ease the lingering pain. She felt like she was haunting her old life. Her old room. Because everything was changed. Most of all her. And she was so impossibly tired. She didn't feel fifteen. She felt old and used up. Eyelashes fluttering, she struggled to stay awake. Her mother stroked her cheek, smelling of Imperial Leather and tea and beneath the pain, the emptiness, a sense of contentment stirred in Connie. Perhaps everything *would* be all right.

But when her mother leaned in close to place a kiss upon her cheek, a cold look had settled on her plump features. 'You're never to speak again of what Mr Collins did, or didn't do to you, understand?'

Connie felt woozy. Detached.

'He's a good teacher. At a *good* school. Do you understand, Connie?'

She did. But she didn't want to.

'Your position there is precarious at best. Only a fool would go doing something to ruin that. Did I raise a fool?'

Connie just wanted to sleep. To slip into emptiness and forget the ugliness of the last few hours. More than that, she wanted to forget the ugliness of the last few months. How at first Mr Collins would lean in too close during lessons, then place his hands on her hips, then his lips on her neck. Her lips. Always pushing the boundaries.

Your position there is precarious at best.

He'd chosen her for a reason. Connie had no tears left to cry for this revelation. Her family were poor. They

161

could not challenge him; her word would never hold up against his. He asked for her silence even though he need not have bothered.

'And if he comes for you again, try to think of something else while it happens. Like some of your favourite music. Play it through in your hand. Chances are you won't catch again. I never did.'

Closing her eyes, Connie heard her mother move away from the bed, pause at the door. 'When I say never speak of this again, I mean it, my girl. I need you to be smart. Can you do that?'

Connie didn't speak. Didn't move. Her body ached, the most intimate parts of her still raw and smarting. Her mother twisted the silence to her own desires.

'Good girl. Now, sleep tight.'

Exhaustion met her like a brick wall.

Connie had her knees pressed to her chest, hugging them tight as Robin stroked her back, listening. They were alone now in her room. He'd ushered the others away and told her, eyes warm, that she could trust him.

At first she resisted but then the words rushed up like vomit, keen to escape. And as she finished explaining all that had happened, Connie felt light with relief. But now she had to fear his response. Since she'd told her parents, her father had been distant. Cold. A glint of contempt in his icy gaze each time he regarded her. She knew that he didn't believe her. That he thought some overeager boy from town had left her in the family way. Not decent Mr Collins. Not Mr Collins who wore a suit and drove a silver BMW.

'I can't believe he did that to you.' He ceased rubbing her back to rest a hand upon her cheek. Connie leaned into him. 'What a . . . what a fucking *monster*.' Gently he came in close to kiss her forehead. 'And your parents . . .' he whispered, heat creeping up his neck. 'I can't . . . fuck. No wonder you ran away.'

Connie curled her body towards him, no longer caring how empty the room was, how the walls were caked in mould, how when it rained the floorboards in the far corner darkened. Because she *had* run away. She saw that now. Robin had been the spark she'd needed. And now she was free. She never had to see Mr Collins again.

Only she had. There was a fire in Robin's eyes as he looked to her and then gazed at the dark space that was the window, which told her he realised that too. That Mr Collins was walking around town untroubled and free. While she was tucked away in hiding. Had been in pain. Had bled.

THANK YOU FOR THE MUSIC

Local musical star, Connie Winchester, who performed on Academy Award-winning scores including *Due Tide*, has announced that she will be retiring from music. Mrs Winchester, 68, said in a statement that she is 'looking forward to spending her twilight years with her husband, Albert, back in her home county'.

Mrs Winchester cites mounting health issues for the reason behind her withdrawal from performances. When asked if she'd possibly be mentoring future violinists over the coming years, she said it was unlikely.

33

1965

It was a moment she had spent what felt like a lifetime working towards. A moment, at times, she feared would never come. Connie was on the streets of London, in a beige mac, her violin case clutched to her side, about to attend her first rehearsal as part of a prestigious orchestra. Despite the drizzle and the grey skies, she felt buoyant. Ever since she had first held a violin, she had dreamt of doing something like this. Of playing professionally, making actual money from her talent. Being free.

Was she truly ready?

Connie lingered on the street, outside the front doors, hair growing damp. She thought back to her first encounter with a violin, how it had felt like a kind of pure magic when she placed it within her hands. Mr Collins's voice behind her: 'There, fits like a glove.' Connie felt a shadow pass over her day. Tipping her head back, she closed her eyes, whispered her mantra.

'You can do this. You can be good.'

Only today she needed to be more than good. She needed to be great. This day and every day moving forwards. There could be no hesitation, no times when she couldn't even look at her violin, let alone lift it.

It wasn't that long ago that she'd considered never playing again. Each time she reached for her instrument she saw *him*. Felt his breath on her neck. Heard him say, 'Wonderful, again.' Heard the slap of his belt as he unbuckled it. It was late, everyone else had long since gone home, the school hallways empty and still. 'You've no idea what you do to me.'

When he was gone, she feared the music was too. In her bedroom at home, she hid her violin beneath her bed, loathed it. It was her mother who brought it out, dusted off its case. Connie came downstairs one sunny morning to find it in the centre of the small dining-room table. She instantly turned on her heel, eyes blurry with tears.

'No.' It was her mother's voice that drew her back, sharp and urgent. 'You have to play, my girl. I need you to see that. If you stop playing, it was all for nothing. If you stop playing, he wins.'

Connie hadn't played that day. Nor the next. But her mother's words had burrowed deep within her, sent barbs into her soul.

He wins.

She would not allow that. Ever. The scale would forever be tipped in his favour if she didn't play again.

The first few times were the most difficult. With each pluck and draw of her bow, she sensed him behind her. Watching. Waiting. She'd find herself holding her breath through entire songs to the point of almost passing out. But somehow she pushed through. She wouldn't allow him to have *this*. To have music. Music was hers. It took weeks but Connie eventually reclaimed her form. She'd stand in her bedroom each morning and play a mournful melody, opening the window so that it drifted out to the street beyond.

After returning to school, the next logical step was to audition for orchestras. It was a daunting process, and not just because of all she had been through. Connie knew nothing of the opera, the theatre. It was an entire world she had never inhabited. All she knew of them were their songs. And how she loved them. It seemed surreal to take those songs she had played in lessons, in exams, in her bedroom, and play them before an audience. She had done recitals at school but nothing so formal as a London show. In a London theatre. Looking about her at all the stone buildings, the tidy storefronts, gilded signs, Connie felt like she was on another planet, not just in another city.

Be good. You can do this.

At her first audition she played one of her favourite pieces, Beethoven's *Sonata No. 9*, flawlessly. Though you wouldn't have known it by the straight faces of the board who had gathered to assess her. There were several more auditions, all of which she sailed through. Still, it was with a tightness in her chest that Connie opened the envelope bearing the seal of the Opera House when it arrived on her doormat back home. She had to read it over and over to ensure it was real. That she wasn't seeing things. That she had actually done it. All that remained was to pack up her few belongings and move south. It felt like both a beginning and an end.

'You starting today?' A slim redhead with intense blue eyes stopped by the doors before entering, looking at Connie. She was carrying a cello case almost as big as she was. She nodded at Connie's own instrument case by way of explanation.

'I . . . yes.' Connie nodded nervously. 'It's my first day.'

'Always a heady experience,' the redhead smiled. 'I'm Maria, cello second chair.'

'Connie.' Connie returned the smile. 'Violin, first chair.'

'First? Wow, OK.' Maria nodded in approval. 'Clearly quite special then.'

'Oh, I don't know about that.'

'Don't do that.' Maria shook her head vigorously, pushing her shoulder against the door so that they could both enter. 'Don't deny your talent. You earned your right to that chair. Own it.'

'I . . .'

Be a good girl.

'You from a small town?' Maria frowned at her.

'Yeah, I suppose.' Connie went to say more but her gaze was drawn upward, to the grand lobby they were now standing in. Everything was golden and sumptuous, from the red carpet to the drapes that bordered the door they had just walked through. Connie had never seen anything like it in her life.

'Well,' Maria hefted her case towards a distant door, 'you're in London now, Connie. Time to start developing a big-city attitude.'

Connie could only blush nervously.

'Come on,' Maria urged her in the right direction. 'I'm excited to hear you play. You must be exceptional.'

Connie followed her, turning back for the briefest moment, certain she saw him standing out on the street, beyond the glass doors, watching her. But that was impossible, he was gone.

He wins.

Connie drew in a long breath, determined not just to be good that day, but to be great.

34

Now

Connie's throat felt dry. A reed ready to snap. She suddenly felt fearful and disorientated, like she was sixteen again. But the hands she nervously wrung together felt like used leather and were threaded with blue veins. Even the callouses from her years playing had puckered with age. Bach was still weaving between her legs, pausing briefly to stare up at her, dark eyes glistening.

'So, Mr Collins—'

'Now that's a name I've not heard in quite some time,' she swiftly interrupted the young man, reluctantly tracing her steps back into her lounge. Really, she wanted to remain standing, to hold the higher ground in what she already knew was going to be an unpleasant exchange. But her legs throbbed and she couldn't help but glance longingly at her armchair.

'Sit, please.' Daniel theatrically gestured to her vacant seat. 'I feel like we have much to discuss.'

'You never came to discuss my career, did you?' Connie gripped the back of her armchair for support.

'I did.' Daniel lowered his hands into his lap. 'But I'm more interested in certain aspects of it than others.'

'Certain aspects such as my former music teacher?' She couldn't say his name. A lifetime had passed and yet it still held such power. Even hearing it reduced her to a lost teenager. A breath more like a cry escaped from her throat. She could still remember his face the last time she saw him. The stiff lines of his suit, tie loose around his neck.

'He died in most unusual circumstances.'

'So what is this?' A tremor began to snake up Connie's leg. Still she refused to sit down. 'An interview about an old teacher?'

'He was murdered.'

Connie closed her eyes, enjoyed the brief relief of the darkness she found. It was true, Mr Collins had been murdered. All those years ago. Slowly she opened them to look around her lounge, to let her gaze linger on the familiar curves of her clock, the wood of her mantelpiece, even the rough tapestry of her armchair was reassuring as she kneaded it beneath her fingers. This was *her* home. This man. This *boy* had no right to come in here and demand things of her.

'You came here under false pretences,' she told him, pushing her spine as straight as it would go. 'Your letter stated your interest in interviewing me about my career. Clearly, that is not the case. Leave my house immediately or I will call the police.'

The fight in Daniel's eyes dwindled. 'Yes, my letter was misleading,' he admitted. 'But I knew it was the only way to get you to talk to me.'

'Are you even studying music?'

He was silent. Connie exhaled loudly into the emptiness between them. 'I'm calling the police.'

'I did my due diligence.' Daniel's voice was low with menace; he rose from his chair and came to stand beside Connie. He moved quietly, easily, muscles flexing within his tight-fitting top. He peered down at her through hooded eyes. 'I told the truth when I said I researched you.'

169

Releasing the armchair, Connie shuffled back, creating space between them that he instantly filled, matching her inch for inch. While her cheeks bloomed crimson with the effort, he didn't even break a sweat. They were almost in the hallway when Connie felt something at her ankle. The firm, fluffy bulk of Bach. She wavered, felt gravity begin to pull against her. Daniel's hand grabbed at her elbows, righted her. He was so close now she could see the birth of fresh stubble along his jawline, smell the rich cologne he was wearing. His grip was tight. Connie tried to pull herself free but he was so much stronger than she was.

'I've come here for answers.'

Connie shook her head. 'I have none.'

Daniel kept hold of her elbows, pulling her back into the lounge, towards her armchair, which he unceremoniously dumped her into. Connie landed against the cushions with a gasp, old bones shuddering. She watched him neatly settle himself in the centre of the sofa, reach for his notepad and pen as though the interview had not just been completely derailed. Desperately Connie turned, glancing to the hallway and the cordless phone residing in the cradle on the small table near the front door. Daniel was so much faster than she. She'd barely make it out of her chair before he'd be able to stop her. Connie held her head in her hands. She was trapped.

'I want to know what really happened to Frank Collins.' Daniel folded his legs, watched her expectantly.

'Like you said, he was murdered. You know as much as I do.' Connie swallowed, forced her hands to rest in her lap, trying to hide how much they trembled.

You can do this.

She'd faced down monsters before. What was one more? *But you're old now. And weak.*

Connie blinked. Hardened her gaze. 'If you've come here searching for answers about a murder that occurred almost seventy years ago, you're wasting your time.'

'It was hard to locate the records.' Daniel tapped his pen to his pad. Slowly. Rhythmically. As though he were marking the passing of each strained second. 'I had to do a lot of digging around. A hell of a lot. But eventually I got hold of the documents relating to the court case surrounding the murder.'

'Good for you. Then you should have all the answers you seek.'

'I don't know if you know this, but when things are redacted from a legal document, there always tends to be a master containing all the original information.'

Connie did not know. She chose to let her silence speak for her.

'While there was an official transcript from the proceedings of the court case following Frank Collins's murder, there was another one. Kept for a long time under lock and key. The hard copy, as it were.'

Outside the rain had ceased but the sky remained murky and dense.

'The lengths I went to were insane.' Daniel smirked at the memory. Tapped his pen. 'I had to get a job in the courthouse as an intern. *Then* I had to find an excuse to work late. But that required weeks of earning the trust of those who work there. *Then* I had to steal a key and take myself down to the archives. Like the real old stuff in the bowels of the building where barely anyone went, for good reason. It was cold and spooky as shit down there. It took me a good few weeks of stealthily going down there to check, but I finally found the records for the Collins case. The original ones.'

Connie knew what was coming. The fire in the hearth had died out. The room was cold.

'Connie Lipman is all over that file.' Daniel sounded so proud of himself, like he'd solved some grand mystery. Connie almost pitied him. 'Because you were there,' he frowned at her – 'when he was murdered. You were there.'

Bach jumped into Connie's lap, making her startle. Oblivious to the tension, he turned in several circles and then dropped down, nuzzling against her and bringing much-needed warmth. Connie stroked his back, grateful for his softness, his security. He was just her cat but at least she wasn't completely alone as she faced this one-man firing squad.

'You're right,' she admitted, too tired to even feign to fight. 'I was there when he was murdered.'

'Then why did you walk away?' Anger began to stir in Daniel. His words became shorter, tighter, teeth clenched together.

'I don't understand why you . . . why you seem to care so much.'

'Humour me.' Daniel's gaze was hooded, severe.

Connie sighed and continued to stroke her faithful companion. She looked to the walls of her lounge where there should have been family portraits, images of her children captured over time. But there were none. Hers was a house which had never been filled with youthful laughter or the stampede of little feet scampering down the stairs. She had not simply walked away from Mr Collins's death.

'I want answers!' Daniel demanded hotly.

'And then will you leave?' Connie asked warily. 'If I tell you all you wish to know, will you then leave an old woman in peace?'

'Yes.' Daniel nodded. But the shadow that passed across his face made Connie doubt the truth of his words. She tightened her grip on Bach, letting his purr vibrate through her shaking hands. She was afraid.

35

Then

He curled around her as they slept. Connie drifted into a black hole where even dreams couldn't find her, as she lay listening to the whisper of his steady breaths. Come the dawn, Robin was gone. Connie awoke, cold and alone, pale light threading in through the grimy window. She showered, pulled on a plaid dress then a black turtleneck jumper she'd found in the basket of communal clothes and headed down to the kitchen, the house slowly stirring to life around her.

With porridge bubbling on the stove, it was the only room that seemed to hold any lasting heat. Arthur was leaning against a countertop, drinking coffee, while Wren perched at the table, picking at her breakfast. 'Feeling better?' she asked without looking up.

'A little,' Connie replied shyly, slipping in at the far end of the table. 'Thanks.'

Charlotte walked in, mouth wide in a yawn. 'Anyone want to tell me why Rob just so rudely woke me up?' She looked about the faces gathered in the kitchen. 'Just yanks off the blanket, tells me to get going.' Her hazel eyes settle on Arthur. 'I figured once you were up, he'd leave me alone.'

'He's on one.' Wren rubbed at her eyes. 'It was still dark out when he ordered me up.'

'Where even is he?' Charlotte demanded, striding over to Arthur and stealing a sip of his coffee.

'He's out walking.' Arthur's voice was soft; Connie had to strain to hear his answer.

'Walking?' Charlotte replied, not bothering to lower her volume. 'What the hell? It's barely half seven.'

'He needs to think.' Arthur snatched back his mug, frowning.

'Think?'

Wren rapped her knuckles against the table and then pointed along the length of it, towards Connie.

Panic unsettled the contents of Connie's stomach. 'Did I do something?' She peered at Wren, clenching her hands together. 'Something . . . wrong?'

'Nope,' Arthur swiftly replied, moving to place a fresh mug of coffee in front of her. Connie accepted it with a grateful nod, not having the heart to tell him she preferred tea. 'You've not done anything. Rob just gets like this when he . . . needs space.'

'When he's angry,' Wren added bluntly.

'Well I don't appreciate his anger depriving me of sleep.' Charlotte raked her fingers through her hair, fighting to tame it.

'Fix your attitude before we head out,' Wren noted, eyes lifted to glare sharply at her friend, nostrils flared in warning.

'Head out?'

Again Arthur spoke quietly. 'Last night was a bust. So we need to head out again. You and Wren this time.'

'Is this about money?' Connie blurted, cheeks burning with shame. Had she stayed out last night, had she somehow handled the shock of seeing Mr Collins, perhaps Robin wouldn't be out walking off his anger. 'Because you don't need to go out. I told him I'd sell my violin.'

Charlotte gave a murmur of approval but Arthur was shaking his head, drawing her out of the room by her elbow.

'You sure you want to sell it?' Wren asked from her end of the table, dark hair framing her shadowed expression.

'It's worth a lot of money,' Connie declared, remembering how many times her parents had reminded her of such a fact.

'We paid good money for that,' her mother would comment whenever the mood took her. 'Even the case was expensive. You remember that when you're lugging it around.'

'I don't doubt that we'd get good money for it.' Wren's fingers were interlocked around her bowl, fingers long and lean. 'I'm asking are you *sure* you want to sell it?'

A flutter of agitation rippled through Connie. 'I wouldn't say I wanted to sell it if I wasn't sure.'

'OK.' Wren twisted her lips thoughtfully. 'Just . . . you know. Once it's gone, it's gone.'

'I don't care.'

Wren studied her. Dark eyes shrewd. 'You do though,' she concluded. 'When you first came here, you played. You were good. To get good you must have practised a lot. A whole lot.'

'What's your point?'

'That you must be pretty attached to that violin. Don't be so quick to cast it off.'

'Maybe I don't want to be attached to it anymore.' Connie reached for her mug, sipped her coffee, recoiled at its strength and bitterness. Out of the corner of her eye she saw Wren smirk.

'Because he was your music teacher? That why?'

Connie snapped her head in the older girl's direction. The dress, the jumper, she felt none of them. Beneath Wren's gaze she felt utterly naked and exposed. Frozen with shock.

'He . . . he told you?' She wanted to scream. To cry.

'Robin tells me everything.'

'Why?' Connie snapped, face hot. 'What are you to him?'

Coolly Wren stood, taking her bowl with her. She gingerly placed it within the sink and then turned to face Connie. 'Not what you think I am.' She tucked a strand of black hair behind her ear. 'Not anymore.'

'Then why would he—'

Wren dropped into the space at the table directly across from Connie, eyes burning. 'He told me because I knocked on a door once.'

Connie was silent, the coffee she'd swallowed lingering on each strained breath.

'I went in one way. Came out another. He's worried about you.' Wren's fingers began to drum against the table. 'Christ, I need a cigarette,' she muttered, her glare slipping away from Connie. Palm slapping the wood, she pulled herself back into the conversation. 'He didn't tell me because he's secretly in love with me or any shit like that. He told me because he cares about you. And honestly,' Wren flicked her gaze between the door and Connie as though fearing someone might walk in, 'I'm angry too. Men like him, like your teacher, they get away with too fucking much. Some men . . . the war softened them. Others,' she rubbed the bridge of her nose, sorrow tugging the corners of her mouth low, 'it turned them to stone. Just . . .' Wren looked to the cupboards behind Connie, to the closed door and the hallway beyond, as though searching for what to say. 'Know that you're not alone, OK? This house, this place, it's like a family. Remember that.'

Connie sniffed as overhead floorboards creaked and then music began to play. 'Thanks,' she offered weakly. 'I'm sorry about losing it last night. I'm sorry I—'

Wren stretched out a hand to silence her. 'Don't waste another second worrying about it, OK? We'll figure it out. And Charlotte is due some more time out, she's been getting lazy.'

'Seriously, I can sell my violin. I can—'

'Robin won't say it because he cares too much,' Wren smirked, 'but I'm not so burdened with feelings here. So trust me when I say that if you sell it, you'll regret it. He's already taken so much from you, are you going to let him take your music too?'

Connie swallowed as she considered this. Elvis was singing somewhere in the house, voice rich and deep. 'There will be other violins . . .' Her voice lacked the conviction she tried to instil in it.

'Well, it's your call.' Wren got to her feet. 'Sell it. Don't sell it. Do what makes you happy.' She moved towards the kitchen door and then turned back, fingers closed around the handle. 'I'm sorry you went through what you did. With him.' Wren looked to the floor, to the heavy boots she was wearing.

'Yeah.' Connie tried to look in her eyes but they remained downcast. 'Same.'

Two days later Connie sold her violin. It fetched half of what was originally paid for it. If her parents had known they'd have been livid.

36

Then

Questions drifted like leaves from Robin over the coming days. Some mornings merely one or two, others a flurry.

How are you?

Are you all right?

How long had it been going on?

Did he know about the baby?

When did he last touch you?

Were there others?

When he asked, a hole would open up beneath Connie that she struggled not to fall into. She did her best to piece together the answers he sought.

I'm fine.

I'm OK.

Months.

I think he suspected.

Months ago.

I don't know. Maybe.

In the quiet of night, they'd lie side by side, fingers interlocked, digging up ghosts. And Connie would feel Robin tense beside her, drawing in breaths he'd hold for a beat too long.

During the day Robin was absent from the house. He told her he was out getting money, keeping things afloat. But the cupboards grew barer by the day. Connie didn't leave. The small back garden became all she saw of the outside world. She'd sit on the slabs, legs drawn up against her chest, chin balancing on her knees as she peered between the house and the heavens, studying the thick grey of the sky, wondering if soon it would snow, how far off Christmas must be.

'You're going to catch your death if you keep sitting out here.' Charlotte joined her one particularly cold morning when their breath caught in the air, the weeds on the ground stiff.

'I'm fine,' but Connie shivered within the coat and gloves she wore. Both several sizes too big.

'You're freezing.'

Connie nodded in reluctant acceptance. 'Yes, but this is the only way I get to be out of the house. It's the only way to get any fresh air.'

'He still doesn't want you going out on walks?'

She pushed her chin harder into her knees. 'No.'

'He's out a lot lately,' Charlotte observed, lowering herself to sit beside Connie, both of them peering up at the house where shadows drifted within.

'We need money.'

'Hmm.'

Connie turned to face the other girl. 'You don't think he's out getting money?'

Charlotte's round face tipped to one side, eyes narrowed in thought. Where Wren looked sharp, she was soft. Her curves gave her a maternal presence. 'Not always,' she finally replied. Connie frowned at the cryptic nature of it.

'What does that mean?'

'Take today,' Charlotte sighed wearily and looked up. 'He's out. Alone. God knows where, doing God knows what.'

'Just ask him,' Connie urged.

'Why?' Charlotte countered sharply. 'He'll only lie.'

'What, no, he—'

Charlotte groaned so loudly Connie fell silent. 'Don't tell me you're under his spell too?'

Connie flinched. 'What?'

'You sound like Wren, she's always defending him.' Charlotte rolled her eyes as she shook herself, reached for a nearby frigid weed with a gloved hand and plucked it clean from the ground. 'She thinks Robin hung the bloody moon. I mean . . .' Chewing her lip, she looked at Connie. 'How far would you go for him?'

'Sorry?'

'Because Wren would follow him into a burning building.'

Something in her tone made Connie uneasy. 'I'm not sure what you're—'

'Look.' Charlotte's hand landed on Connie's shoulder. 'I'm not trying to be a bitch, believe me. This is the opposite and it's just coming out wrong. Robin, he . . . he has a way of securing people's loyalty.'

'OK . . .'

'He has a habit of doing these things. These . . . these grand things to make sure someone is forever indebted to him. Clever really,' she shot an angry look towards the house, 'because honestly, who would choose to stay here? The place is a fucking dump. Yet here we are, loyal and stuck. Because Robin is smart. Really smart.'

'Is that why you're here? Because you owe him some debt?'

Charlotte cracked a half-smile, warmth returning to her face. 'No. I'm here because I'm a fool. Because I followed Arthur when he chose to come here. And half the time he barely acknowledges what I gave up. Yet here I am, here I stay.' The smile faltered. 'Love seems to make fools of us all.'

'Does Wren love Robin?' It was the question Connie nurtured in the dead hours, when Robin's breathing came deep and easy beside her. She clutched it to her chest, felt it grow with the passing days and weeks. Felt it get heavy.

Charlotte's eyebrows lifted, a fresh smile of approval pulling on her thick lips. 'So you're not just another dumb blonde?'

Connie felt bile making its way up her throat as she waited on the answer.

'She certainly did once. Now . . .' She lifted her hands as though they were a pair of scales, tipping this way and then that. 'Who knows with Wren. Not sure if you've noticed but she can be kind of closed off.'

Connie laughed dryly. 'I've noticed.'

'She's definitely indebted to him,' Charlotte continued. 'Which is why she stays. And why she will do anything he asks.'

Wind clawed through the small garden, scratching at their cheeks.

'That's the other thing about Robin.' Charlotte's face bloomed red from the cold, eyes tearing up. 'He's as dangerous as he is smart.'

'No.' The word was instantly out of Connie's mouth. Robin was kind. Gentle. Safe. In his arms she found peace.

'Perhaps I waited too long and you're too far gone.' Charlotte got up, dusted herself down. She extended a hand towards Connie. 'Come on, it's too bloody cold out here.'

'Where do you think he is?' Connie wondered as they reached the back door. 'If he's not out getting money, where is he?'

Charlotte pressed her back to the door, keeping them in the garden a few moments longer. 'That's what worries me,' she admitted, voice low. 'I think he's out finding a way to keep you here indefinitely.'

'I'm not going to leave.'

Charlotte smiled at the younger girl, eyes crinkling with sadness. 'Aren't you?'

Connie felt herself growing angry. And hot. The bitter wind no longer holding any bite. She had chosen to come here. To the house. To run away. She was safe. Why would she return to her old life? To school? To *him*?

He'd known. Mr Collins had read the paleness of her pallor, noted her absence from school for several days. Yet he said nothing. They resumed their lessons. School broke for the summer and Connie considered that perhaps it was all done. She was free. But come September, her tutoring commenced anew and at first he was just friendly. Chatty. Then he started to ask if she needed a lift home. A hand would linger on her shoulder for a second too long. Then on her waist. Connie felt it coming, like a storm slowly drifting in from the horizon. And without even her parents to save her, their constant inability to hear her truth, this time she would just drown.

'I can't go back,' Connie was sobbing as Charlotte embraced her, 'I can't go back. I can't go back.' They stood like that as the wind whipped at their backs, the house standing over them like an old guard.

37

Then

'So here we are again.'

Connie jumped at the sound of Wren's voice, wrenched from sleep. Slowly, blinking languidly, the room came into focus. First the long table, littered with browning banana skins, half-empty jars of jam and breadcrumbs. Then the window, the slice of darkness outside.

'What the . . .' Connie could barely speak, still held in the dream world.

'I keep debating telling him,' Wren said coolly as she perched on the table and reached for a jar, sticking a finger inside and scooping out a dollop of crimson jam which she placed directly on her tongue. She sucked on her finger long and hard, watching Connie as she regained consciousness.

'Telling . . . telling who what?'

'Telling Robin how you sleepwalk.'

Connie blinked. Felt the tell-tale quickening of her pulse that told her something was wrong. 'Look . . .'

'I mean, I think he knows,' Wren fed herself some more jam, 'but I don't think he *knows* knows. Like, he's mentioned you being weird in the room.'

Connie suddenly flushed. 'He has?'

'Mmm.' Wren sucked on her finger, on the sweetness of the jam. 'I told him it will surely pass soon. That it's just, you know,' she tilted her head in an overtly sympathetic gesture that was clearly fake, 'trauma.' Wren pouted play-fully as she said the word.

'I don't sleepwalk.' Connie wasn't even sure why she was bothering with the lie. She probably just didn't want to give Wren the satisfaction of being right.

'You do,' Wren confirmed in a sing-song voice that didn't suit her. 'Most nights in fact. I come down here and find you either staring at the garden or, well,' her dark eyebrows lifted, 'holding a knife or some shit.'

'A knife?' Connie felt cold. She thought back to that first time, her kitchen, her mother.

'Uh huh,' Wren confirmed. 'Should I be worried?' she asked mockingly. 'Do you intend to stab us all in our sleep and then blame your nocturnal antics?'

'What? No.'

'Then why the knife?' Wren pressed.

Are you going to peel potatoes?

Connie closed her eyes, hugged her arms to her chest. 'I don't . . . I don't know.'

'I get it.' Wren placed down the jam jar, sans lid, and reached in her pocket for a match and stretched for a nearby candle, striking the match and adding a glimmer of much-needed light to the gloom. Connie studied the shadows and tried to assess what time it was. The darkness outside seemed impenetrable. 'I know what it's like to be afraid,' Wren offered in a rare moment of openness. 'To want to hurt someone.'

'I don't want to hurt anyone.' Connie's teeth were beginning to chatter, something that often happened when she suddenly awoke while sleepwalking.

'Yes, you do.' Wren rolled her eyes as though Connie were being droll. 'Hence the knife.'

'No. I'm—'

'You're doing weird shit in your sleep, Connie. Lots of people sleepwalk, sure. But few actually *arm* themselves.'

'The knife is just—'

'Don't sweat it,' Wren interrupted. 'I had an uncle, war vet, he came back and started walking in his sleep almost straight away. He'd go out to the shed, load his old rifle. Every night. My aunt would find him there in the morning, asleep with it at his side, pointing at the house.'

'The house?' Connie echoed with alarm, wondering where the story was going. None of Wren's stories had a happy ending.

'Anyway, weeks pass and then one morning she goes out to the shed, she sees him, she screams.'

'What had happened?'

'He'd blown his brains out.' Wren reached for the flame of the newly lit candles. began to dart her fingers through its tip, seeming to savour the brief burn.

'Jesus.'

'Yep.'

'OK, but I'm not . . . I'm not going to hurt myself.'

'I know.' Wren smiled wolfishly at her, her face eerily illuminated by the flickering candle beneath it. 'If I thought that was going to happen, I wouldn't say anything.'

'Gee, thanks,' Connie deadpanned, feeling alarmed at the admission but refusing to give Wren the satisfaction of showing it.

'What concerns me is that you might hurt someone else. Say—'

'I'd never hurt Robin,' Connie blurted instantly.

'You say that . . .' Wren stared at her, dubious.

'It's the *truth*. I care about Robin.'

'As do I, hence . . .' Wren extended her arms, explaining her presence within the whole conversation.

'Why do you think I'd hurt Robin?' Connie demanded.

'Because I think you're going to hurt *someone*,' Wren stated, 'and I need it not to be him.'

'I'm not going to hurt Robin.'

'He's been through enough.'

'I know. I'm not going to hurt him.'

'I'll destroy you if you do.' Wren stood, extending herself to her full height, which against Connie wasn't exactly formidable, but the gesture made her uneasy all the same.

'I'm not going to hurt Robin,' Connie repeated, temple beginning to throb. She needed water. Rest. How long had she even been in the cold dampness of the kitchen before Wren found her?

'I get that you're troubled.' Wren's shoulders lowered slightly and she reached again for the jar of jam. 'Find someone here who isn't and you've found a liar.'

'I promise I won't hurt him.'

Wren waggled a jam-coated finger at her. 'Don't make promises you can't keep.'

'He knows I sleepwalk,' Connie stated icily.

'But not about the knife.' Wren lifted her eyebrows slyly.

'You don't—'

'If he knew about the knife, he'd remove them all from the house. He's no fool.'

'So why don't you then? Remove them?'

Wren shrugged nonchalantly. 'Because maybe, just maybe, you'll be like my uncle.'

'You're a real sweetheart, you know that?'

A serious look suddenly settled upon Wren's face. 'Look, if you want to sleep at night, stop stalking our halls like some phantom. Own your shit, Connie. Stop ignoring what's wrong.'

'I'm not ignoring anything.'

'You can't kid a kidder, my sweet,' Wren purred at her. 'Until you sort your shit out, I guess I'll need to keep following you, keep taking the knife from your hand.'

'Thanks . . .' Connie muttered awkwardly. 'I guess.'

'Anytime,' Wren replied dryly. 'Anytime.'

38

Then

'Where do you go?'

The air in the room was still. Connie was on her side, tracing a finger along the ridges of Robin's spine. His presence warmed the bed but the bite of early winter lingered on the fringes of their shared space, hungry and eager.

'Mmm?' He gave a sleep-clogged murmur and Connie rolled onto her back, exhaling with annoyance. She'd let him drift away too far. Lately it was dark when he left the house and dark when he returned. Connie filled her daylight hours wandering room to room, cleaning where she could, tidying piles of abandoned clothes and crockery. Escaping to the garden when the temperature outside didn't sink too low. But still there was too much space for things to slide into it. She was thinking of home more. And music.

In the emptiness that followed her question, she thought of one of her favourite arias, 'Habanera' from *Carmen*. She imagined the opening chords, the accompaniment to the strings. An entire orchestra swelled in her mind as she lay beside Robin, who was lost to sleep. Connie replayed the aria over and over, until her limbs grew heavy. It was Mr Collins who had introduced her to it.

'I think you'll like this one,' he'd said with a gentle smile as he placed the needle upon the record. It was early spring. The sky was eggshell blue and golden daffodils were beginning to unfurl. But it remained dark in the music room. Full of oil-slicked wood and the coppery odour of worn strings.

'What is it?' Connie asked as she listened, already picking out the various notes, the parts played by her beloved violin.

'It's an aria, from an opera called *Carmen*.'

An opera.

Connie had heard of them, sure. But had never been exposed to their music, their theatre, their power. In her home all music came from the wireless, out of the mouths of popular musicians. Opera felt other-worldly in its exoticness. She listened to the record, enticed, failing to notice how close Mr Collins came to stand beside her, his back pressed up against hers, large hands on her narrow shoulders.

'*Carmen* is a tale of desire . . .' His breath was hot against her ear but still Connie turned cold. 'Of lust. And ultimately betrayal.' She swallowed, throat feeling paper-thin. 'It is a tale,' one hand lifted to stroke her cheek, Connie felt the rough callouses of the fingers he used to play guitar, 'of how wanting a woman can drive a man insane.'

Robin stirred and then woke, gasping like a fish freshly caught on a line. Connie could feel the nightmare lingering in the spasms that moved through his chest.

'Hey, hey,' she tried to soothe him, drawing up close and gently smoothing his hair out of his eyes, which were wide and wild. 'It's OK, I'm here.' The music had stopped. There was only the loud rasp of Robin's agitated breathing.

'Fuck,' he exhaled, shuddering.

'Another nightmare?'

He looked at her, face ghostly in the darkness, and nodded. Connie didn't press him. Most nights were like this; he'd tremble and burst to the surface of consciousness, fearful and shaking as though the demons of his dreams were still chasing him. Connie wondered if he saw his mother falling. Or something else. Something worse.

Robin was fully awake now, back pressed to the wall as he dropped his head in his hands.

'You can talk about it, if you like.' Connie gingerly placed herself at his side, pressed her head to his shoulder. Everything about him was so familiar now. She knew every curve of his slender body, the patchwork of each mole pebbledashed across his back and upper arms. Even the slight dent in his upper lip from an old scar. He was a map that she had studied, committed to memory.

'I don't want to talk about it,' he yawned, lowering one hand to rest it upon her knee, his skin burning as though he were in the grips of a fever. But Connie knew he wasn't. They all just ran shot when they hadn't had access to their drugs for a while. And it had been a while now. Money was low. Which meant their stash was low. Along with the contents of the cupboards. And the days were just getting colder.

'Where do you go?' Connie asked again, louder, bolder, than before.

'Huh?'

'Every day you slip out before dawn and when you're back, it's dark. Where do you go?'

Beside her his body remained loose from sleep, the power of his nightmare receding. 'I go out.'

Connie snorted through her nose. 'I know that, genius. What I want to know is *where*.'

'Around.' He nuzzled into her neck, distracting her.

'OK.' She pushed him back, tingling at his touch. 'But around *where*?'

A shrug. 'Town. Places.' Another shrug. 'It might have slipped your attention but money is getting pretty low around here.'

'I've noticed.' Connie dusted a strand of hair away from his face, tucking it behind his ear. He was so boyishly handsome, even in the dim light, but the sad glaze to his eyes, the dip of his rich lips, aged him in a way that made Connie's heart ache. 'Let me help,' she urged, pressing a kiss against his mouth. 'I want to help.'

'No.' He was shaking his head as he pushed her away. 'I want you here. I want you safe.'

'I want to help.'

'You are helping.' He pressed his lips to her neck and Connie felt herself begin to melt. Pleasant thoughts tumbled like unfurling ribbon in her mind as he pulled her into him. She had always thought it was meant to be like this. Without pain. Without friction. Without fear. 'You help by making me so happy.' She was on her back now and Robin was peering down at her.

'I love you.' She barely had chance to whisper the words before he was kissing her.

PAROLE DENIED FOR
HOUSE OF HORRORS TRIO

Today a high court denied a second appeal from Robin Strand and his accomplices, for their double life sentences to be shortened to twenty years.

Currently all three convicted for the murder of Frank Collins and his wife ten years ago are each serving a sentence that exceeds eighty years. Meaning they will most likely never be released in their natural life. The presiding judge over the appeal stated that: 'Given the scale of the crime, I cannot in good conscience look to even consider reducing the sentencing.' The judge also passed a ruling forbidding future hearings since 'it would be futile and a waste of time and resources'.

39

Then

The window in the kitchen was laced with frost. Connie studied it as she peered through clear gaps out into the garden, which glistened. Even though the sun was high in the sky, it had failed to thaw the ice of the morning.

'We need to smash it off.' Wren's face came from behind her.

'Huh?' Connie spun around.

'The ice.' Wren pointed to the window, dark hair covering her eyes as she slid onto the bench before the table. She had a thick scarf snaked around her swan neck, finger gloves drawn up her arms. They were all dressed this way as the cold of outside continued to penetrate the house. Fires were lit but they dwindled long before they could push back the freeze of December. Not enough wood. Or kindling.

'We need to smash the ice off all the windows,' Wren continued. 'Although it will only come back again tomorrow.'

'It's definitely getting colder.' Connie shivered as she said it. The cold. It was like a new person within the house who refused to leave, invading every room. There was no warm water. No respite. Except for the occasional cups of tea. Connie would hover around the kettle on the hob as she waited for it to boil, enjoying its limited halo of warmth. Several people had left in the past week. Those that stayed buried themselves in as many layers of clothing as they could find.

'We should be all set by Christmas.' Wren smiled tightly.

'Oh?'

Christmas.

Connie reached for the sink behind her, gripped it tight. She didn't like to think about Christmas. About whether or not her parents would be putting up their small, single tree in the front room and covering it in tinsel. Whether they had bothered to buy their runaway daughter any gifts.

'You all right?'

Blinking, Connie felt the sting in her eyes from gathering tears. She quickly forced them away. 'I'm fine.'

Wren frowned at her, unconvinced. 'Well, like I said, we should be all set for Christmas. Rob's working on a big score.'

'Oh?'

He never told me. The pang of jealously Connie felt was enough to subdue the homesickness. She watched Robin leave her bed every morning, return to it every night, having no idea where he had been, having only cryptic answers to cling to.

'Yeah,' Wren continued, 'he's got us casing a big house.'

'He has?' Connie felt foolish in her confusion. She knew none of this, was left in her empty room while Robin was out in town making plans. With Wren. Fire pricked at her cheeks, causing Connie to bow her head. She didn't want Wren to see the flush that was surely colouring her.

'Uh huh.' Wren shoved a piece of toast into her mouth. It had no butter, they were out. And Connie was certain the bread was mouldy but they were all too hungry to care. 'This place over on Old Mill Lane. Real nice, with iron gates and big windows. You can see they've already got their tree up.'

'Old Mill Lane?' Connie repeated.

'Yep.' Wren smacked her lips against her dry breakfast. 'He reckons the place will be full of stuff we can sell. You know, like the family silver. Maybe a TV. There's a woodland opposite so we're taking it in turns to watch the place, get the rhythm of the family.'

'A family live there?'

'Uh huh.' Wren greedily drank water to wash down her toast. 'Mum, Dad and three boys by the looks of it.'

'I see.'

'But they're all out most of the day.'

'So that's when you'll go in? During the day?' It made sense since Robin was always back by nightfall. They all were.

'I think so.' Wren was getting up, dusting crumbs off her gloves and jumper, both with holes in.

'Has he said what he intends to do?' Connie hugged her arms to her chest, hating the nerves that slithered within her like fetid worms. Every day he went out. Every day she stayed put. He went back to the same place. An intended place.

'He'll say when the time is right.' Wren was preparing to leave, approaching the kitchen door.

'What if he gets caught?'

Connie's question drew her back. She studied Wren, cheeks sunken, her face thick with shadows. 'Robin is always careful.'

'A big house, in a nice neighbourhood, it sounds . . . dangerous.' It wasn't just some pub in a rough part of town. This was a home. With a gate. And a family within it.

'Who said it was a nice neighbourhood?' Wren straightened with challenge. Connie was shaking her head, instantly backing down.

'I just . . . I assumed it was. Given the gate, the tree being up.'

'Well.' Wren cocked her head thoughtfully. 'I think that's why he picked it. You know, affluent family inside. The woods opposite make it a bit remote; the next house over is set back quite a bit because they have these long driveways.'

'And cars,' Connie noted, remembering how it felt to ride the bus, to see her peers pull up, not soaked from the rain, dropped off right at the entrance to the school.

Wren nodded. 'Nice beamer out front at night.'

Connie opened her mouth to ask if it was silver but something silenced her. A swirl of nausea twisted in her stomach. So what if it was silver, it meant nothing. Many nice cars were silver. It was a popular colour choice.

'So are you going there today?' Connie wondered as Wren slipped into the hallway.

'Sure am,' Wren confirmed with a roll of her tired eyes. 'Off to freeze my arse off hiding under an oak tree. I hope Robin makes a move on this place soon, for all our sakes.'

'Mmm, me too.'

'See you then.' Wren didn't wave as she let the door slam closed behind her. Alone, Connie turned to face the ice-covered window. How easy it would be to shatter it all, to let the delicate shards crumble to dust. But come the dawn it would be there again, renewed. The cold wasn't going anywhere.

40

Then

The night was stone around her, cold and hard. Connie felt it press in on all sides, the pressure drawing her from sleep. Rubbing her eyes, she rolled onto her side and realised she wasn't alone. A figure. She exhaled in surprise as she made herself small, peering at the silhouette standing in the square of moonlight near the window.

'Robin?' His name was cracked when she said it, sleep had made her hoarse, words thick in her throat. 'What are you doing?'

He was standing, peering out at the night, dressed in a long woollen coat and a hat pulled low over his eyes.

'Are you going out?'

'Don't worry about it, go back to sleep.'

Something twisted within Connie. Fear. Anticipation. She got to her feet, hurried to his side. 'Are you going to that house?'

'Go back to sleep.' His words were smooth, coaxing, as he gripped her shoulders and placed a warm kiss on her forehead. 'I'm sorry I woke you.'

He made for the door but Connie kept him tethered by his wrist, holding on, keeping him in the icy darkness of their room. 'It's the middle of the night. Where are you going?'

'Seriously,' he shook her free with ease, 'don't worry about it.' Connie withdrew to the slab of moonlight, pressing her arms to her chest. Sometimes she forgot that with the tenderness Robin showed, there was another side. A stronger side. In bed he could flip her over with ease. In those moments it was exhilarating. But Connie had felt pinned by the power of a man before. She felt her chest constricting just thinking about it, breaths growing short and pained.

'Please don't be upset.' His face was crumpled with concern as he returned to her.

'It's not . . .' Connie fought to level out her breathing. 'Why are you going to the house tonight?'

Robin cupped her chin, smiled. 'If you must know, we're going to hit it tonight.'

'While the family are home?' She felt cold, even with the warmth of his hand pressed against her skin.

'We are low on money. Seriously low.'

'What about the money from my violin?'

'Gone.' He dropped his hand, pulled it through his hair and began to pace near the doorway. His steps were quick, shoulders rigid. Connie could feel the tension radiating off him. 'We need food, clothes. Coal for the fire.' He rapidly listed items on his fingers. 'Winter is coming and we aren't prepared. We need to get money now. Tonight.'

'And what of the family inside?'

He reached for the door handle, not looking at her.

'Robin?' She grabbed his shoulder and he shrugged her off, sending her skittering across the room. He strode out, onto the landing, floorboards wincing. Connie took a moment to orientate herself, then she was fumbling for clothes from the pile in the far corner. A jumper. Gloves. A hat. She tugged them all on, shoving her feet into boots that didn't quite fit. She stumbled after him, down the narrow stairs, into the hallway. Robin heard her approach and turned, frowning. 'Look, please, just go back to bed.'

'Why can't it wait until morning?' Connie asked desperately, still pulling on her coat. 'Why enter the house tonight, when people are home?'

'Is she coming?' Arthur fired a confused glance in her direction from where he stood waiting by the front door.

'No.'

Someone was behind her on the stairs, shouldering their way past. Wren joined Robin and Arthur in the hallway, bundled up in her warmest clothes. 'Right, are we ready?' She turned to look at Connie. 'What's she doing up?'

'I'm coming,' Connie declared, lowering herself off the final step.

'The hell you are,' Robin growled.

'We don't need you fucking anything up,' Wren stated tightly.

Robin cleared his throat, looked at the faces in the hallway. 'Where's Charlotte?' He angled the question at Arthur, who raised his hands, gave a quick shake of the head.

'She won't come.'

'Typical,' Wren muttered sourly.

'She's just . . . uncomfortable with it all,' Arthur explained awkwardly.

'But she'll eat the food. Wear the clothes. Stay here,' Wren's voice began to rise with rage.

'Yeah, but this isn't to do with that.' Arthur stepped close to her, words hissed, a sideways glance thrown towards Connie, who lingered at the base of the stairs. 'This is different.'

'What's happening?' She edged forwards. 'Why are you going tonight?'

Robin clicked his fingers at her. 'Just . . . just go back to bed. The less you know, the better.'

'Wait.' Wren slowly closed her long fingers around his wrist and lowered his arm, lips pursed. 'With Charlotte flaking, we need a lookout.' She stared purposefully at Connie.

'No.' The word fired like flint from Robin's mouth.

'We'll all be inside and—'

'I said no.'

'Let's . . . consider it.' Arthur nervously scratched at his elbow. 'Wren might have a point. Do we really want to go in there blind?'

Robin sighed tersely. 'We won't be blind.'

'I know but—'

'I don't want her involved. At all. OK?'

Wren and Arthur were silent, faces blank. Connie tentatively approached him. 'I want to help,' she assured them all. 'I've been . . . here. Doing nothing. Let me help.'

Robin turned his back, shoulders hunched. When he finally turned to face her, his eyes were filled with sorrow. 'I can't ask this of you,' he almost choked the words.

'Let her come,' Wren sharply filled the space which followed. 'It's all for her anyway, right?'

Connie shuddered and peered back up the stairs. It felt tempting to slink back up them, back to her bed, to the darkness, to close her eyes and pretend she had never seen him standing in the moonlight. She sensed that she had intruded upon something she was never meant to see. When Robin spoke, she saw how he still wrestled with his feelings.

'Really . . . just . . . go back to sleep. It will all be done come the morning.'

'What will be done?' Connie asked desperately, searching each of their faces for an answer.

No one moved. No one spoke. But then Wren obliterated the silence by reaching for the front door and swinging it open to let the velvet night welcome them. 'Revenge.' She tossed the word over her shoulder as she trotted out into the street, Arthur quickly turning to follow. Robin lingered, staring at her. 'I have to do this,' he finally whispered.

'Then I'm coming too.' Connie reached for his hands and he knitted his fingers through hers, taking her with him as he followed the others out into the street.

41

1971

Her feet were wet. That was the first thing Connie noticed. The dampness. The cold. With a sharp intake of breath, she looked around. Heard something roar. Tasted salt.

The beach. She was at the beach.

Panicked, Connie looked around. It was dark, the ocean a smooth black slate ahead of her. Moving back, she left the waves that had licked against her toes and let herself sink against wet sand. Her nightdress fluttered in the evening breeze.

'Shit.' Connie hugged her chest, turning, looking for someone who might notice how crazy she surely looked. How had she even reached the beach? Had she driven there? Taken a bus? Wincing, she did her best to dredge up her memories of that evening, of going to bed. Everything had been so routine. She'd returned home to Albert after a day of recording, together they ate dinner out on the patio and before bed she had taken her usual sleeping pills, read two chapters of her current book and gone to sleep. So why was she now standing on a beach beneath a pale moon?

'Shit!'

The beach was quiet, deserted save for a few figures Connie could just about make out in the distance. Fear began to snake around her.

What is going on?
Where am I?

Anxious thoughts fought for dominance in her mind. 'Connie!'

Upon hearing her name, she froze. Looked up the beach. She had heard it, hadn't she? Or was this her mind playing tricks on her?

'Connie!'

No, there was definitely a figure running towards her, calling her. Connie squinted, hands still clasped to her chest. It was man, tall and lean. There was panic in his voice. *Robin.*

Connie stared hopelessly, reminding herself that it couldn't be. Unless she was still dreaming, unless none of this was real. She turned back to the sea, foaming as it caressed the shoreline.

'Connie!' The man had now almost reached her. Connie blinked and gone was any image of Robin she might have conjured; instead she was looking at her husband, Albert. Handsome in jeans and a white t-shirt, hair tousled by the breeze. 'What are you doing?' As he reached her side, she saw the worry in his widened stare. He grabbed her, pressed her to his chest, breathed her in. 'Sweetheart, what's going on?'

'I don't . . .' Connie shuddered within his grip, trying to make sense of it all. 'One minute I was in bed and then . . .'

'Christ.' Albert hugged her tighter. 'I knew you were sleepwalking again. The second I heard the car pull out of the drive and realised you weren't in bed, I panicked.'

'The car?'

She had *driven* to the beach? How was that even possible?

'It's getting worse,' Albert said, stroking her hair as he protectively held her close to his chest.

'No,' Connie tried to counter, but she knew he was right. Initially, when she placed an entire ocean between herself and her past, Connie felt better. She began sleeping more normally, having fewer nightmares. But after only two months of living in Los Angeles, it all started up again. First Albert would find her downstairs, loitering in their hallway as though she couldn't quite decide if she was staying or leaving. Then he would find her in the kitchen, emptying cupboards, in the lounge rearranging furniture. The next day Connie could never remember anything; the only sign that anything had even happened was the pounding headache that she was left with.

'This is getting serious.' Albert was taking her back up the beach, towards the lights of the parking lot. 'We can't have you *sleep* driving. Or whatever the hell it is. You're in these, like . . . these *states*. Connie, you need help.'

'I just need more sleeping tablets, that's all.' She was cold in her nightgown; LA always carried a chill come sundown. And her bare feet felt sore.

'You need to see someone,' Albert insisted. They reached his Mustang and he opened the passenger door, helped Connie slip inside. 'You need help, sweetheart,' he told her as he climbed into the driver's seat. Connie could see her own car parked close by; they were the only two vehicles there. 'Shit, keys.' Albert climbed back out and she watched him approach her white Cadillac. He tried the door and it opened easily. After barely a few seconds rummaging, he straightened, closed the door again and locked the car. 'Someone could have just taken that,' he said with disdain as he got back in his own car.

'I know.' Connie bowed her head and looked at her hands. It scared her. All of it. How she could do something like take her car keys, leave her home and drive to the beach, all while in some sort of slumber.

'Has this happened before?' Albert had asked after those first few times.

'When I was a girl,' Connie remembered, 'sometimes, I'd sleepwalk downstairs.'

She forgot to mention going in the garden.

Down the street.

Picking up a knife.

'It just doesn't seem normal, to be able to do so much while just . . . sleepwalking.'

'I know,' Connie had agreed. None of it was normal. She kept telling herself she just needed time. Time to heal, to grow. To forget.

'Maybe you need to take a break from playing.'

'No,' Connie had snapped, suddenly panicked. 'Not that, Albert. If anything, playing keeps me sane.'

'I'm just worried about something happening to you. I'm scared you might get hurt.'

'I'll be fine,' Connie assured him.

'Sweetheart—'

'I just need better sleeping tablets. That's all.'

Albert wore his worry the entire drive home. The streets of LA were quiet but not still. As they wound their way up towards the house they were renting, Connie wriggled her toes, feeling sand between them.

'I'm going to have to start hiding all the keys.' Albert was half talking to her, half to himself, formulating a plan. That was what Albert did: he planned and he cared for her. He made her feel safe.

42

Then

He was high. Connie could tell from the way he listed to the right as he walked, the way he craned his neck too far back to peer up at the stars as though they burned even brighter for him. Together they navigated the streets barely uttering a word. There were no cars. No streetlights burning. It was like moving deeper into a black hole. Connie tried to study the faces of Wren and Arthur but they walked with their eyes cast down, expressions hidden from her. It all felt so dangerous just for silverware. They needed money, yes. But weren't there easier ways?

Revenge.

That's what Wren had said just before they left, the crimson slick that was her mouth rising in a slight smirk. So was Robin lying when he said it was about money?

'Can we slow down?' She tugged on his hand, tried to be an anchor to his manic pace, but it didn't work; he merely dragged her along, further into the tunnel of the night. The moon was a slice of marble above them. Connie shivered.

As they walked, the houses around them thinned. Terraces became detached. Driveways appeared. And front gardens. They were edging into the nicer part of town. Connie peered at blackened doors and faceless brickwork, trying to recognise something. But beneath the veil of night, it was all foreign to her. Yet there was a tension in her muscles that told her she had been here before.

'Where are we?' she asked loudly, inviting anyone to answer.

'Close.' That was all Robin said.

'OK, but *where*, what street are we near?'

He didn't respond. Within his grip Connie's hand grew numb.

They passed by a low red brick wall that gave way to large metal gates. Connie peered through the bars, at a driveway housing a pair of cars. At a house three storeys high with long sash windows. She must have slowed because beside her Robin stumbled.

'Come on.' He pulled sharply on her wrist. 'We can't be seen lingering here.'

Seen by who? Connie thought. It was so dark and the streets were deserted. Everything was still. Quiet. The eye of the storm. Then she heard a gentle rustling, like whispers at the back of the classroom. For a moment she was transported back to her school, breathing in chalk, fearing that it was her name being traded between girls.

'The woods.' Wren stormed ahead, hurrying across the road towards a flank of trees. Many of their branches were spindles held up to the sky, only a few leaves clinging on, fluttering, sharing their secrets.

'Let's go.' Robin followed her, bringing Connie along. Together they gathered at the base of a grand oak, its rippled trunk providing brief shelter from the wind that scratched at them. 'Are you all right?' Now he looked at her. His eyes were wide, his stance unsteady.

'Are you high?' Connie's voice rose in accusation.

'So what if he is?' Wren scolded, pacing beside the tree. 'You try doing what we're about to do with a level head.'

'Stealing?' Connie wondered dubiously. 'Surely you need a clear head for that?' No one spoke. Twigs cracked as Robin crouched, making himself small like an animal preparing to pounce.

'The lights are off.' He was speaking to the others but Connie followed the line of his gaze across the street. Over the red brick wall, past the iron gates to the grand house beyond. All of its windows as black as the night beyond. All bar one. Downstairs, to the left of the black front door, a tree glistened. An array of perfect baubles caught the light, mirrored it amongst the emerald branches. It was beautiful. Connie imagined the family who lived there carefully decorating the tree, laughing together, lifting a little one up to secure a star at the top. In the background Bing Crosby crooning from the record player. They'd hug one another, stand back to admire their handiwork, smiles wide.

'Who lives here?' she asked, trying to ignore the stab she felt in her stomach when she thought of her own home. Of the slip of a tree that had no lights. But sometimes the firelight would catch the tinsel and it would sparkle just as beautifully as the one in the grand home across the street. A sob tried to slip from her but Connie caught it in her throat, twisted it into a cough.

Home.

Perhaps it was the call of the season or the primal desire for warmth, but she missed it.

'So they're all in?' Robin was speaking to Arthur, still pressed low to the ground.

'As far as I know, yeah.'

Connie glanced from the tree-filled window to the single car in the driveway, partly obscured by the walls. From her vantage point she could just see the curve of its boot. It was too dark to tell colour or make.

'So are we doing this?' Wren was still pacing, unable to keep still. Was she also high?

'Stay here.' Robin turned to face Connie, held her in a steely stare. 'If you see anyone, anyone at all, shout fire as loud as you can.'

'Fire?'

'Don't worry.' Wren's quick breaths gathered like stiff clouds around her. 'If you shout it, we'll make one.'

'A fire? I thought you were just going to rob the place. Now you want to burn it down?'

'Only if we have to,' Robin barked. He rocked back and forth on his heels, keen to move.

'We need to go now,' Wren snapped. 'We're wasting time.'

'She's right,' Arthur agreed, stamping his feet against the ground. All three of them were constantly moving, full of a restless energy that made Connie nervous.

'Cut them,' Robin ordered and Arthur reached for something beneath his coat and then scurried away.

'Cut them?' Connie repeated, voice dry and sharp. 'Cut *what*?'

'The phone lines,' Robin explained stoically, staring straight ahead, at his prey made of brick and mortar. 'I don't want them being able to call for help.'

'Robin—'

'It's done.' Wren darted forward, responding to a signal Connie didn't see. 'Help me get over the wall.' She tossed the request over her shoulder as she moved. Robin sprang up and followed her, keeping close. The words he slipped to Wren weren't as soft as he'd hoped and when Connie heard them, she turned to stone.

'Remember,' he said as they passed across the street, 'make them suffer.'

43

Then

It was the time of night reserved for prowling cats and watching owls. The air was so cold it felt like it might snap. Connie watched the others boost one another over the wall and disappear from sight. A few seconds later and there was the tinkle of breaking glass, so easily mistaken for the gentle ringing of a bell. But Connie knew better. In the shadows she strained to see movement in the grand house until her temples throbbed with the effort of it all.

She was meant to be keeping a look out. Casting her gaze about for anyone. Ready to raise the alarm. But instead of studying the street, she watched the house. Considered its neat walls and long windows. The car in the driveway.

The drugs made her mind slow. She would later dwell on this, when everything in her world had shifted. How, when on them, she made connections fast and furious, lightning constantly sparking between each thought. But without them it was like trying to see through a fog. Answers took a while to materialise. This effect lingered for about a month after her last trip and then things just . . . reset. Were normal. Though by that point, normality was a completely unobtainable goal.

As Connie crouched beside the oak tree, her sluggish thoughts scrambled to piece themselves together.

The house.

The street.

The car.

She was certain she'd never been in the house. Yet the street . . . it was familiar. With a grunt she pressed her hands to her temples.

Think.

Think.

Wren had said when they left their house, that this was about revenge. So it wasn't about breaking in to steal some silver. It was about something else.

Make them suffer.

Those last words caught against Connie like a fish hook, tugging at her, hurting her, drawing her up to a surface she didn't want to see. In the darkness, in the depths, she was safe. She longed for blissful ignorance.

The house.

The street.

The car.

Connie whimpered as the memory finally came.

She had been lost. A young student, barely into her second week at her new school, trying to navigate her way to the bus stop. At some point she'd turned left when she should have gone right and now she was on a street she didn't know, surrounded by large houses with vast gates. And there was a woodland up ahead. No sign of a bus stop. Connie berated herself, struggled with her satchel, which grew heavier with each step.

The whirr of a car engine approached. Connie kept her head down, kept walking, waiting for someone to wind their window down and demand to know why she was there, sullying their neighbourhood. She froze in shock when she heard her name.

'Connie? Connie Lipman?'

Turning, she saw a silver BMW hugging the kerb, a familiar figure at the wheel.

'Mr Collins?' she squeaked, almost stumbling over her own feet, feeling clumsy and awkward.

'What are you doing around here?' He stopped the car, climbed out, bringing with him the smell of cigars and leather. 'Are you all right?'

'I was just looking for the bus stop and . . .' A hot tear fell down her cheek. 'I got lost,' she admitted shamefully. By now she'd have missed her bus. Which meant she'd be home late. Which meant she'd miss dinner. Already she heard the thunder in her mother's voice when she finally walked through the front door.

And where have you been, young lady?

'Hey, hey . . .' He hugged her, pressed her against the starched surface of his shirt and waistcoat, buttons pressing sharply into Connie's cheek. 'It's all right.' As he moved away, his hands remained on her shoulders and he stooped down a little. 'Why don't you let me give you a lift home?'

Connie's eyes darted about. 'No, no, really it's—'

'Really it's no trouble.' He was possessing her elbow within his large hand, guiding her back to his idling car. 'I only live just there.' He pointed to the house at the end of the road, with black gates and a curved driveway. 'I insist on helping you get home.'

The leather in his car stuck to the back of Connie's knees. She awkwardly positioned herself in the passenger seat, feeling impossibly small. The engine grumbled and he turned around, flashing her a warm smile. 'Try to relax,' he encouraged. 'I don't bite.'

As he drove, he turned on the radio, letting music fill the space between them. Connie listened, relaxing against the stiff leather, thankful to have been saved.

★

She focused on the lights of the Christmas tree. Bright, like jewels. Connie watched them until they swam in her vision. This was his house. Mr Collins's. Of course it was. It all made sense. Robin had been planning to come here since she'd been so spooked that day. Because he cared about her. Because he loved her. He was doing what her own father should have done when he found out what the music teacher had done to his daughter.

Standing straight, Connie kept one hand against the roughness of the oak tree as she leaned forward, eyes never leaving the house.

Later, over a year after that first drive in his car, Mr Collins would suggest that she'd deliberately got lost, ended up on his street in an effort to lure him. Connie had been quick to correct him, to tell him that she'd genuinely taken a wrong turn. That nothing about her being there was planning. That she had always only ever been the prey.

Connie began to shake from both the cold and the cocktail of nerves flooding her body.

This house.

This street.

His car.

She knew this place. The family within. Mr Collins would be sleeping beside his wife, their two sons tucked up in their beds. All of them so safe. So warm. So oblivious.

Connie listened for more tinkling of breaking glass but all was still. Silent. She didn't know what Robin's intentions were once he made it inside. She just knew that she was not the one who had brought the wolves to Mr Collins's door; he'd done that himself.

NEW MUSIC HALL

Blackhill Girls Grammar today saw the unveiling of a new wing for musical study at the school, funded and dedicated to former student, Connie Winchester. Unfortunately, due to ill health, Mrs Winchester was unable to be present for the ceremony but said she was 'thrilled it was finally happening'.

The new wing will house four classrooms and a 200-seat theatre. Headmistress Annabelle Clements said, 'Here at Blackhill Grammar we cannot wait to nurture the next generation of musicians who we hope will follow in Connie's footsteps and go on to great things.'

The wing will incorporate the previous music room, which was dedicated to the late teacher, Frank Collins.

44

Now

The rain was a whisper against the window. Connie shuddered as her old bones remembered the cold from that night, when she'd stood beneath gnarled branches and played lookout.

'So you watched them go inside?' Daniel's nostrils were wide, veins pushed against the taut skin of his neck. His anger. Connie felt it from across the room, wilted beneath it. His youth was in his muscles, the volume of his voice. She was powerless against the storm he was unleashing.

'Yes.' She nodded in recollection. She kept rubbing her hand against Bach, trying to distract her trembling limbs. 'But you know that.' Her tone sharpened, hand freezing atop the softness of Bach's fur. Her body failed her daily. Her mind sometimes too. But being dragged down memory lane reminded her that some days, she could still be shrewd. 'You've read the complete transcript. You know what happened.'

'Here's what I know.' Daniel scowled at her. 'I know that you were there that night. That you watched the others go into the house.' The fire in the hearth had all but died. A chill began to fill the air. 'That you didn't try and stop them.' The accusation was there in the burning of his eyes, the way his mouth dipped down with disdain. Or disgust.

'I . . .' Connie pursed her lips. 'I wasn't to know,' she admitted with a sigh. 'What they would do once they were inside. I thought . . . I thought they were there to steal silver.'

'Liar.' The word unfurled between them like the crack of a whip. Connie pressed herself against her chair, Bach silent upon her lap since she'd ceased to stroke him. 'You *knew*. How could you not?'

Tap. Tap. Tap.

The rain on the window. Fingers beckoning to be let inside. Little fingers. Childlike fingers. Connie winced. Too often when it rained her joints seized, her lungs ached. But whatever pains her body inflicted were nothing to the torment her mind gave her. She'd only need to feel the spatter from a grey sky or notice the sheen of a puddle on the pavement to be reminded of that day, to see his face within the bus stop.

'You've read the transcripts.' She fought to keep her voice level, to be calm. 'You know all that I can tell. I watched them go inside, thinking they were merely going to steal some valuables.'

'No!' Daniel jabbed a finger in the air, rose to his feet, face twisted with dissatisfaction. 'You were a smart girl. A bright girl. You *knew*. And you did nothing to stop them.'

'If that was the case then I wouldn't have been allowed to walk free.' Connie felt the pulse of discomfort blooming from the base of her spine. She needed to move from her armchair. To rest. But Daniel was looming above her, exhaling sharply.

'Why? Why spare you? You were *there*. You were a part of it.'

'I didn't go inside.'

'Yes, but . . .' With a groan Daniel edged away from her, hands in the air. Connie watched him, her fear slipping over into bemusement.

'Why do you even care?' she wondered plainly, too old and too tired for games. 'You're asking me questions about a crime committed *decades* ago. Long before you were born. Long before even your parents were born.'

Calming, he sank back onto the sofa, eyes glimmering. 'You make a fair point.' He pressed his hands to his knees. 'It must seem strange to you to have me here, pretending to talk about one thing but asking about another. Asking about something you've clearly spent a lifetime trying to run from.'

The pain in Connie's back pressed harder, higher. She resumed stroking Bach, needing the rumble of his purr, the strength of his presence.

'Because you're right,' the smile he gave her was manic, 'it is absurd, what I'm asking.'

Connie glanced to the window, to the rain, wishing there was someone due to call by, someone who could arrive any minute and intervene. But there was no one. She felt the isolation of her existence pressing in on all sides, smothering her.

'I wasn't born when it happened,' he agreed, eyes never leaving her. 'Nor were my parents.'

Connie inhaled, took a moment to close her eyes, to try and rest, if even for a few fleeting seconds.

'But my grandfather, he was alive when it happened.'

Her eyes flew open as she studied the young man anew, a pit opening up in her stomach.

'You see . . . Mr Collins, your late music teacher, he had two sons. And they were the first ones to find their parents murdered in their bed that night, slathered in blood.'

She dropped her gaze to her knees. This she knew. But it was a truth she kept locked away, in a box within her memories that she never opened. It was padlocked. Wrapped in chain. Because to open it was too painful. All of it was too painful. Connie used to wish that when they'd redacted her name from the official court files, they could crack open her skull and take it all away from her mind too.

'My grandfather, Marshall, he was the eldest. He said he never forgot how it felt, the warmth of his parents' blood on his hands, how he and his brother kept shaking them, trying to wake them,' Daniel informed her icily.

'Look . . .' Her heart fluttered in her chest and Bach jumped down, not appreciating her restless energy. Connie reached a blue-veined hand out towards the young man, clutching her armchair with the other. 'I've told you.' Her words felt flimsy and weak, like paper about to rip. 'I never went into the house. I stayed outside. That's all. I didn't—'

'If they didn't go in to steal silver then what?' Daniel's voice was thunder and Connie crumpled back against her chair, hand reaching for her throat. Out of the corner of her eye she saw Bach's tail held up like a question mark as he disappeared from the room. She gasped for air, feeling utterly abandoned.

'I deserve answers!' Daniel's face burned red. He stood once more, pointing at her. 'That night . . . what happened in that house . . . it ruined my grandfather. He . . . he . . .' For a moment he turned and Connie watched his shoulders lifting and falling. When he turned back around, his cheeks were damp. 'He was a cruel man because of that night. He treated his own son badly because he could never work through his grief. And in turn . . .' Daniel hung his head, breathed deeply.

'In turn your father was a cruel man, who treated his son badly,' Connie quietly concluded for him.

'You did that to them,' Daniel rasped, 'you and your friends. You ruined more than one life. You ruined many. So, so many. How was my grandfather ever supposed to get over something like that?'

She had no answer to give.

'You failed him. You failed all of them when you stayed outside and stayed silent. So tell me the truth that the court failed to get from you. Why did they go into the house that night?'

'You know, it's strange,' Connie threaded her hands together, tried to ignore the ache in her spine, 'back then, nobody wanted the truth. Yet here you are, demanding it.'

'Well?'

She felt that his patience was about to snap.

'They didn't go into the house to steal silver,' Connie admitted, seeing Daniel swell with pride at being right. She wondered how many hours he'd pored over those old documents, trying to piece together the story that in the past others had fought so fiercely to hide. And Connie had played her part. Protected those she shouldn't have. But she supposed that didn't matter. Not now. 'They went into the house because of me.'

Daniel pressed his hands to his temples, folded into the sofa. 'I knew it,' he spat, spittle filling the air. 'That makes you just like them. That makes you a monster, too.'

45

Then

Robin had only ever been truly mad at her once. It was a moment Connie tried to push to the back of her mind, but it kept coming up, like a record stuck on repeat. She had been downstairs talking with Arthur, swaddled in a cardigan and chewing on stale crackers when Robin called her name so loud and so long that she knew something was wrong.

'Oh fuck.' Arthur had looked at her, stricken. 'You all right?'

'She's fine,' Wren offered from the far side of the kitchen where she was curled on a countertop, looking out the window. 'He'd never kick his favourite puppy.'

'I'm fine.' Connie tried to give Arthur a confident smile as she stood up, though inside she was reeling. She hurried upstairs to where she found Robin in their room, the mattress they shared propped against a wall. And upon the floorboards where it usually rested, a scattering of tablets, round and perfect like discarded confetti.

'What the hell is this?' Robin gestured to the floor, face red.

'Let me explain.' Connie dropped to her knees and began picking them up, one by one, gathering them in her palm.

'Connie,' he knelt at her side, reached for her chin and turned her head to face his, 'have you been lying to me?'

'No.'

'Then what is this?' He cupped his hands around the hand she was collecting tablets with. 'I thought you always took the pills.'

'I do.'

'Then what is *this*?' He squeezed her hand.

'I can explain.'

'Then explain.' He eased back from her, face flushed and hurt. His chestnut eyes glistened as he waited for Connie to speak.

'I . . . I take the tablets,' she told him. This was true. She did take the tablets. And she liked how they made her feel. Except . . . 'I just don't take *all* of them.'

'Why not?'

'Because . . . because I don't like how they make me feel. Too much is . . . is too much. I don't want to be switched off, Robin. I want to be . . . to be present.'

'No.' He shook his head savagely. 'You *need* them, Connie. You need to take them.'

'No, I don't.'

'You do,' he insisted, scrambling towards her, reaching for her shoulders. 'The tablets . . . they make you better. Things like . . . like the sleepwalking.'

'Have you been talking to Wren?' Connie felt the sting of betrayal burn within her. 'Because whatever she said isn't—'

'I don't need to talk to Wren about it. I've seen you. Many people here have. It's a busy house.'

'So what? You're all just talking about me behind my back?'

'No, we're all just concerned about you.'

'I'm fine.'

'The tablets will help, Connie, trust me.' He stroked her shoulders, his touch tender, but Connie shrugged him off.

'What are you? A doctor?' she yelled. 'You don't know what's best for me. These . . . these *pills* do nothing except trap us all in dreams.' In anger she slung the tablets she had so carefully scooped off the ground, sent them skittering across the bedroom floorboards like hailstones.

'That's not true.' Robin's voice hardened. 'The tablets *help*. I know that they do. Because they helped my mum.'

'I thought your mum died,' Connie retorted, instantly wishing she hadn't, as she saw pain flash bright and awful across Robin's face. His mouth was a hard line as he looked at her. 'I'm sorry.' She reached for him but he moved away. 'I didn't mean to—'

'My mum did die,' Robin glowered at her, 'but before that she was ill. Really ill. She was sleepwalking and—'

'I'm not like your mother,' Connie snapped.

'Yes, you are!' Robin suddenly grabbed her wrist, drew her close to him. 'You're broken, Connie. Just like my mum was. I'm trying to help. Let me help.'

Connie snatched her hand back and scrambled to her feet. 'I am absolutely fine,' she declared indignantly. 'You're just upset that I'm not playing your silly little game like everyone else is. That I'm not as obedient as Wren.'

'No, that's not it, Connie.' Robin approached her, moving with purpose. 'I care about you.' He was close enough to stroke her cheek and she let him. She only had to look into the softness of his eyes, glance at the velvet of his lips and she felt the anger leeching out of her, replaced by longing. 'Please, don't be mad, just listen to me.' He pressed his forehead against hers and closed his eyes. 'I care about you *so* much.'

Connie didn't want to admit the truth to him; that the pills seemed to be making everything worse. When she took them too much, everything became blurred, she lost track of what was a dream and what was real life. She lost track of herself. She had thought that if she hid them away, pretending to take them, she could keep him happy while keeping herself sane. As she felt his breath hot on her face, she knew she should have just flushed them. Had been more careful.

'I just want to help,' Robin mumbled before kissing her. Connie kissed him back. There was nothing gentle about their connection. It was full of hunger. Behind them the door creaked open and Arthur peered inside.

'Hey, I'm just . . . Oh shit, OK.' Then the door promptly closed again.

Soon Connie and Robin had forgotten all about the tablets. There was just one another, their flesh pressed together. This was what Connie longed for – the place he could take her to, where there was just their heartbeats, nothing else mattered. As they tumbled together to the floor, they crunched the tablets beneath them to dust.

46

Then

There was no rustle of leaves. No chime of broken glass. There was only the rushing of Connie's blood in her ears. A river running through her, restless and overflowing. How long had she waited in the shadows? Five minutes? Ten? The house beyond was stoic, impassively surveying the woodland she stood within.

But everything changed. It happened like a finger snap. Fast and sudden. Connie was beside the oak, stretched on tiptoes, watching the distant twinkling of the Christmas tree adorning the downstairs window, trying to find some meaning in its glow, some reflection of passing movement. The screams reached her first. Taut with fear. They ripped apart the velvet richness of the night. But on her next shaky inhale they were gone. Wiped out with a breath.

'What the . . .' Connie stepped away from the tree, edged closer to the street, to the house. Who had screamed? It sounded high. Female. She desperately scanned the wall. The windows. All was as it had been. Had she imagined the screams? Was the cold curdling with fatigue in her mind and conjuring illusions? Once Connie had stayed up all night to study for a Latin exam. In the small hours she kept rolling the ancient language around on her tongue until it felt fluid, natural. The next day her head ached and she saw spiders in the corner of every room, skittering just out of view. Was that what was happening now? Were the screams some internal echo?

No. Now there was movement. Footsteps whispering over gravel. Then the grunting of bodies lifting over the wall. First Arthur dropped down. Then Wren. And finally Robin. The trio hurried to Connie and for a moment the change was hidden from her, concealed by the night. But as they edged closer, she saw. Blood. It was spattered across their coats, their cheeks, sinking into their gloves. It shone like silk and as they approached the woodlands, they brought with them the smell of copper. The taste of iron. Connie recoiled, pressing a hand to her mouth.

'We need to get out of here.' Robin was like a ghost, his skin pale as the moon. He reached for Connie's arm but she staggered back. 'I said we need to go,' he hissed at her. Connie looked up at the splashes across his cheeks, the parts of his hair that were already hardening.

'What happened in there?' She scanned his body, wanting to believe the blood might perhaps be his. But there was no way. She'd watched him ascend from the wall, land with catlike grace upon his feet. 'What did you *do*?'

'Less talking, more moving.' Wren grabbed Connie's elbow, nails digging deep, and forced her forwards.

'It's not safe to stay here,' Robin uttered by way of further explanation as they scurried like rats from a sinking ship. In a daze Connie followed them, Wren remaining cuffed to her wrist.

A scream. There had been a scream. But whose? Connie looked between her companions, all moving with ease. They rounded a corner, the house with the twinkling lights now gone from view, and Connie snatched back her hand. 'The . . . blood.' Three faces looked back at her, all tarnished. The smell . . .

Connie shook her head, hands instinctively dipping to clutch her stomach. She was back in a pool of her own blood, shaking with despair. Squeezing her eyes shut, she pushed her back to the wall of the closed corner shop they'd just sprinted past.

'We need to get back.' Robin moved to grab her and she flinched like a scared animal.

'Fuck this.' Wren was backing away from them. 'I'm not going to wait around for the police to find us.' She ran, feet kicking up high and fast. Arthur gave Robin a pained look.

'She's right.' He rubbed at the blood smeared on his cheek, lowering his stained fingers and staring at them. 'We can't be out here. We need to lie low.'

'Go,' Robin told his friend. 'Just . . . just go.'

'What did you do?' Connie was shaking as shock moved through her. Because she *knew*. The sordid certainty of it gathered like a rock in the pit of her stomach.

'Not now, we need to get back.' That same crazed energy was within him. He hopped from foot to foot as Connie looked up at him.

'What did you do?'

'For you.' He clasped her chin in his hands and Connie grimaced, feeling the wet slide of blood on his fingers. 'I did it for you.' He kissed her and tears slid from Connie's eyes. Somewhere in the dark the peel of a siren. Robin instantly withdrew, but kept holding her face. Connie's lips trembled as she looked up at him.

The scream. Someone else had heard it. Time was running out.

'You need to come with me.'

She shook her head frantically. 'I can't.'

Grief reduced him to a boy. He stared at her, face falling in shock. 'I did this for you. Because I love you.'

Another kiss that felt more like a bite. Connie's lips burned from the sting of it.

'Connie,' he urged, pressing his forehead to hers, their breath mingling in the icy air. 'Please, you have to come with me.'

'It was his house, wasn't it?' She trembled.

'You know it was.' His voice was soft.

'What did you do?'

A kiss. Hard and searing. 'What had to be done.' He placed the words gently against her ear. 'Come with me.' He was edging away, a hand extended, a final invitation. Around them the streets were beginning to stir, windows lighting up, the screech of the sirens nearing.

Connie gave a brisk shake of her head. A door slapped shut and Robin withdrew into the swelling shadows of the street, head darting about in fear.

'I have to go,' he told her, his tears streaking the blood.

'I know.'

'Please.' His hand remained held out, palm turned to the moon. Connie looked at it, considered what would happen if she took it. How they'd run together back to the house. How they'd hide. She looked into Robin's eyes. Still so wide, so wild. Then she turned her back on him and moved as fast as she could. She kept running until her legs burned while behind her Robin dropped to his knees and howled.

47

Then

The streets blurred around her as Connie ran. Darkened windows watched like lidless eyes as she fumbled through the night, knees high, heart pounding. The squeal of sirens shrieked in the distance and she moved ever faster. Cold air rushed into her lungs, stalling her, icing her from within. Connie fought against it, against the quaking in her legs that told her she had nothing left to give. Existing on fumes she kept moving. To stop. To stop would be suicide, out here in the frigid night with the police surely searching for a handful of trespassers.

What did they do?

The question pressed like a hammer against her skull.

There was so much blood.

And none of them hurt.

Connie was skittering down a hill, rounding a corner, powering past shadow-filled parks, shops with their shutters down. The houses became more clustered, long rows of slim terraces with small stretches of front garden. She moved along them, struggling to draw breath. Snaking past hedges, a neat brick wall. So few lights were on, only the stars and the streetlights glowed. The rest of the world was lost to slumber. Reaching out a hand, Connie finally slowed, grabbing at a small black gate to steady herself. Her chest rattled as she doubled over, wheezing. She felt her knees sag, so keen to release her and let her drop to the hard ground.

The gate groaned as she pushed it open, then turned to fiddle with the latch to close it. Turning she looked down the path, glazed with ice, towards the front door of the house whose garden she had entered. Connie gulped, feeling ever so brittle. She was home.

Instinct or longing had guided her. Perhaps both. Nervously she edged closer to the door, reaching for the brass knocker in the heart of it. She noted the darkness within. Her parents were probably tucked up in bed, lost to exhaustion. Would they even hear her?

Her desire for warmth, for respite, it was feral. An animal desperately seeking shelter. And safety. Connie glanced behind her, at the empty street and the pools of streetlight that were speckled along it. No one was chasing her. But how long until they were?

You know what happened in that house.

A flutter breath escaped from her, chest aching. Reaching for the knocker she clasped it tightly and rapped hard against the door three times. The sound was hollow. Connie hugged her arms against her chest and edged back, peering up to search for life within the walls.

Nothing.

Perhaps it had been a mistake to come home. Even if her parents did answer the door, it did not mean they would welcome her back.

A flicker.

Connie saw it above, as quick as the snuffing out of candlelight. A curtain had been peeled back. A slice of light had disturbed the darkness. Someone had seen her.

She thought to knock again but then she heard the thump of footsteps. Then the light in the hallway came on, burning like the sun. Behind the door a lock twisted.

Thunk.

Then a chain was rattled loose. Finally the door creaked open, the pinched face of her mother peering out. Her hair was up in curlers and beneath a blue net, and she wore her warmest dressing gown, the one that reached all the way to the floor and was covered in faded roses. It had once been soft but now it was so threadbare it was barely holding together.

'Connie!' Her eyes widened and her arms opened. There was a slight pitch of surprise to her voice but as Connie fell against her mother, breathed in her talc, her warmth, she realised the shock on the woman's face was mild. She did not look like someone who thought they were seeing a ghost. She had not thought her daughter perished.

Connie began to weep, convulsing with the power of it. Her mother moved to close the door, to seal them inside.

'Hush, come on now, it's all right . . .' Soothing words were whispered as her mother stroked her hair with a tenderness Connie hadn't been expecting. Through her tears, her shaking, Connie realised that her mother had been waiting on this moment, on her return. Which meant that her parents had probably always known where she'd gone. That her running away had only ever been an illusion. Her sobs turned to hiccups as her sorrow washed out of her. 'Shhh, now. Come on. I'll go fix you some tea and start the fire.'

But Connie couldn't move. Could only clutch at her mother and tremble.

'Hush, hush, you're home.' Her mother looked down at her daughter's ruby cheeks, dusted away the blonde hair slick to her forehead. 'You're safe now,' she told her gently. 'So let's get you warmed up, all right?'

Connie shook her head. She didn't deserve this. This welcome. These open arms. She deserved to be left out in the cold until her bones rattled within her. She looked up from her mother's arms, almost overpowered by the feelings of relief that were passing through her. She was home. But . . . Her face twisted as she hiccuped over fresh sobs and wrestled to find her voice. And then two words uttered on a harried breath: 'Something's happened.'

48

Then

It made the papers. Both local and national. Of course it did. How could it not? Even poker-faced reporters on the BBC were talking about it.

The House of Horrors.

That's what they dubbed it. The story leaked through the town, in lines at the post office, across garden fences. Come dusk the following day everyone knew that Mr Collins and his wife were dead, discovered by their young sons like some grotesque Shakespearean tragedy.

Connie was cocooned at home. She wept as she told her mother all that happened and come the salmon-pink dawn, she was holding the heavy phone receiver in a trembling hand and making a call to the local police station. She was taken for interview and there were so many questions.

How did you reach the house?

How many of there were you?

Did you know what they were going to do?

How did they get inside?

Question after question. All delivered by a stern-faced officer with a heavy orange moustache that twitched as he spoke.

Connie answered them all, hands clasped before her on the cool surface of the metal table, her parents waiting for her in the next room. Their lips were drawn tight, eyes shadowed as they escorted her to the station.

'Tell them what you told me,' her mother urged her. Her father said nothing. But Connie was grateful for him being there, in showing solidarity simply by showing up. Normally after a night shift, he'd creep back into bed and snore beneath the covers for six hours. But the fatigue had left him when he saw his daughter. With renewed energy he listened, grim-faced.

'She's already called the police,' her mother explained. 'We're to head there first thing.'

'Good.'

Rumours would quickly swirl like leaves in a storm. Her parents knew it was best to get ahead of them, to offer the truth up as swiftly as possible.

'We need the names and address of those individuals who went inside the house,' the moustached officer told her, leaning back in his chair. Connie looked at her hands. She felt so impossibly tired, as though she hadn't slept for a month, not just a single night. 'The names, miss,' the officer pressed.

Where were the others now? Were they sleeping back at the house? Or had they run off for fear of repercussions?

Connie swallowed. Robin's name was already known to the police. Maybe the others too.

'I'm sure you understand the gravity of the situation,' the officer continued. 'We don't have time to hang about.'

'I told them not to.' Connie peered up at him, eyes aching.

'Not to enter the house?'

'I told them to turn away, I tried. But they . . .' A strangled sob left her throat. 'They wouldn't listen. They *threatened* me.'

You're a good girl, she reminded herself. *Good.*

'They told me what they'd done when they came out and I was so *afraid*.' Her chin wavered along with her voice.

'Just tell me what you know,' the officer urged. 'If you weren't in that house, you're a witness. Nothing more.'

Connie cleared her throat, squared her shoulders. 'I didn't go inside. But I'll tell you who did.'

Her mother tutted over the evening paper as though she were reading the terrible news for the first time.

'Awful, just awful,' she clucked before placing it down on the kitchen table and returning to stirring the soup on the hob.

'What will happen to me?' Connie watched her mother's easy sway between cooker and sink as she prepared dinner.

'Hm?'

'Am I going to go to prison?' It was all she could think about. Imagining existing within four small walls, bars across a window.

'No,' her father answered as he came to sit across from her at the table, picking up the paper and skipping straight past the front page. 'You'll surely need to go to court. But no prison. You've done nothing wrong.'

She heard the intake of breath from beside the stove.

'I should have stopped them,' Connie admitted.

'You weren't to know what they'd do,' her father stated bluntly in the tone of voice he used when he wanted a conversation concluded. 'You weren't to know what monsters you were living with.'

First came her day in court the following February. Then her return to school after the subsequent Easter holidays. Normality resumed. At first it felt stiff and awkward, but like easing in a pair of new shoes it eventually became comfortable and familiar. By June it was almost as if events of the previous winter had been a terrible dream. The school even gave her a new violin. Connie accepted it graciously, knowing what it was. When she played it, she thought of the silence it had bought.

All anyone wanted from her were the names of the others. No reasoning. No excuses. Mr Collins died a saint, mourned by his community. The media considered the attack random, making it all the more terrifying. People started to lock their doors and eye their neighbours with unease.

In quiet moments, when it was just Connie and her thoughts, like when she lingered on the cusp of sleep, she thought of the others.

Wren.

Arthur.

Robin. Dear Robin. Her heart clenched each time she imagined him locked up somewhere. It was his name that had been strewn across headlines most of all. The Manic Mother Killer. A little digging and the press had drawn their terrible conclusions about what happened to his mum. It tied in so nicely with their narrative about the murders.

Crazed Cult Goes Rampant.

Connie wondered if Robin ever told them the truth about Mr Collins. And if anyone listened. Or believed him.

Everyone accepted her truth so eagerly. She was the pretty grammar school girl who'd been lured by the devil in disguise in the dilapidated house. She'd followed her heart instead of her head before finally waking up. Her truth was convenient. Palpable.

Sleep never came easily for Connie after she returned home. She'd often end up playing her violin by moonlight, needing the pulse of the strings against her fingers to remind

her that she was alive, that she was OK. That these grey
clouds would pass. She played so much she passed over
from being great to exceptional. In the fires of her misery,
she forged herself into a legend.

DEATH IN

HOUSE OF HORRORS CASE

Wren Adams, one of the three teenagers found guilty of
killing beloved schoolteacher Frank Collins and his wife,
in 1954, has died.

Two years ago she developed breast cancer. Despite
receiving treatment, the cancer spread and she passed
away last night. She was still serving two life sentences
for the crime that shook the community of Blackhill to
its core.

49

Now

'I'm no monster,' Connie told him deftly, her voice thickening like the tide drawing in. 'I never went into the house.'

'In the court transcript,' Daniel frowned as he tapped his temple and then pointed at her, no longer needing his notes, relying purely on memory, 'the others, all three of them, they all went to prison. But you,' he released a slow, steady breath, 'you walked free. Explain that to me.'

'I told you.' Connie sensed that her feet had become numb through lack of movement. It would take an age to get the blood flowing again, to get the sensation to return. 'I didn't do anything wrong.'

Just talking about it made it so easy to slip back into the courtroom with its cheap, functional tables and strip lights forever veiled by a cloud of rising smoke. Connie, upon her solicitor's advice, had worn her school uniform to every court appearance. The school had paid for the solicitor and his advice had been simple and effective: say nothing of what Mr Collins did. There had been whispers about him, other students whom he had been close with. No one wanted the scandal of it all. The soiling of his legacy. All Connie was to do was name names. If she did that, her freedom was all but guaranteed. So Connie did as she was told. She was reprimanded for poor judgement in the company she kept. Given some community service and then set free, like a caged bird suddenly expected to soar. A violin was thrust into her hands her first day back at school, gifted by the head teacher. 'You have a gift Mr Collins would not want squandered.'

'Why not punish you for being there? For being part of it?' Daniel demanded.

Connie was shaking her head. She could almost smell the cheap tobacco, feel her legs sticking to the plastic of the chairs, hear the hum of the heating system trembling in the thin walls.

'I understand how it must look.' Where her body wasn't numb, it was heavy. Connie was tired. The secrets she'd guarded for so long, she no longer had the energy to keep them locked up. 'My sentence appears most lenient. But I paid for it.'

'How?'

'With my silence.'

'Being redacted from the records?' Daniel asked, confusion pulling on his features, knotting them.

'No.' Connie's response was clipped. Perfunctory. 'That was the idea of my school and solicitor. To help ensure my future.'

She saw the young man's gaze harden at this.

'My sentence was as such because I wasn't permitted to talk about why they entered the house.'

'Not to steal silver?'

'Not to steal silver.'

'So it was all your fault?'

Connie tipped her head, felt blood rushing in her inner ear. 'I . . . yes. I was partly the reason they were there. But really, Mr Collins had only himself to blame for their presence.'

Mr Collins.

Saying his name singed her tongue, made her stomach lurch in revulsion. And shame. Some nights she still woke sensing the pressure of him above her. Hands gripping her hips, pinning her down, demanding entry. Coffee-scented words whispered against her neck.

'It's fine, it's meant to be like this. Just relax.'

'Whatever my great-grandfather did, he didn't—' Daniel's chest puffed out as he began his self-righteous speech.

Connie wasn't about to hear it. She'd suffered these remarks for too long. After his death, Mr Collins became a martyr. An entire wing of the school was named after him. There was a plaque erected in the music room and every year silence was held to mark his death. Everyone batted about what a *good man* he was. How it was a *waste*. A *tragedy*. And Connie had to soliloquise about him along the rest of them. Which was perhaps the worst part of it all. The part that truly made her feel like she'd sold her soul for her freedom. Only the pitch of her violin could drown out the self-hating thoughts that played on a loop in her mind.

'The house is empty,' she interrupted the young man, firing words like needles. 'It always has been. My late husband and I were denied a family. Because of your great-grandfather.'

Daniel fell silent. Coughed.

'In the simplest terms, he raped me. I understand that now. He groomed me. Used his power to coerce me into silence. And then when his indiscretions produced evidence, I had to have it stripped out of me. I had to suffer.'

Daniel watched her, face still. In the ensuing silence, Connie pressed on.

'I ran away because of it all. Ran away to hide with Robin and his friends. And when I confided in him, he was . . . consumed with rage. Maybe I should have stopped him. Maybe I didn't want to.'

Still Daniel said nothing.

'Even after his death, the school were determined to preserve his, and their, reputation. Even they knew what he did. I had clearly not been the first. But I was at least the last. So the truth of him got buried.' Connie looked to the rain-splashed window, the leaden sky beyond. 'The world is a different place now.' Her voice was small. 'If a girl spoke up now about such things, she'd be heard.' She glanced at the sofa suddenly when she heard Daniel rising to his feet.

'And his two young sons?' he said through gritted teeth. 'Colin and Marshall. What had they done to you?'

Connie looked into her lap, face burning with shame.

'They were three and five. What do you think it does to someone to witness something so horrific so young? Did they deserve to lose their parents? They went into care because of you! They lost everything!'

'Look—'

'Where is it?' he roared over her.

'W-what?'

'The violin!' Daniel raged. 'The one the school gave you in payment for your silence. Where is it?'

She wanted to say she no longer had it. That something so ill-gotten did not stay with her. But it had. And he didn't have to look far to find it. Connie's gaze strayed to where it rested in a gap between her fireplace and a nearby bookcase, crammed full of autobiographies and thrillers. The case was battered and worn, just like her.

'Get it.' Daniel clicked his fingers as though he were ordering a dog. Connie looked at him, trying to decipher his intentions. Was he going to burn it? Take some joy

241

from watching flames lick across its curved edges, hearing strings snap in the heat? 'Get it!' He was shouting now. Connie forced herself up, joints creaking. Her feet shuffled against the floor as she scurried to the fireplace, struggled to stoop low enough to grab the case. It was coated in a fine film of dust that she didn't bother to blow away. Case in hands, she turned to the young man, chest tight. 'Open it.'

She placed the case on the arm of her chair and unfastened the latches. It had been years since she had done this. Since she had peered into the velvet bed in which her beloved instrument lay. She smelt varnish and dust. And ink and copper. Sweat and tears. Joy and sorrow. It was all there, within the case. Within her violin.

'Now pick it up,' Daniel ordered darkly. 'I want to hear you play one last time.'

50

Then

The thing Mr Collins was always best at was listening. And not in terms of music. Though of course, Connie loved how his mouth would lift at the corners in delight each time she played, how he would visibly swell with pride as she drew her bow back and forth. It was how he listened to her as a person. Not like the other teachers did, who forever seemed to be looking over her. Mr Collins *listened*.

When Connie broke down during one of their sessions, sobbing until she shook, Mr Collins held her. He said nothing, just waited for her body to calm. Then, slowly and controlled, he used his thumbs to wipe away her tears and looked into her eyes. 'You can always tell me anything.'

So she did.

Connie told him about her father. How he drank. How violent he could be. How afraid she felt. And Mr Collins listened. When she cried, his arms enveloped her. She would lean against his strong, firm chest and feel heard. Feel safe. The darkness from home that followed like a shadow began to ease.

'Thank you,' Connie would whisper tearfully to her teacher, 'thank you for being there.'

She had been crying the first time he crossed a line. Though he'd been toeing the line for many, many months. Circling it, assessing it. A hand on a shoulder, a kiss upon a cheek. Then the hand moved to her thigh. And he kept on listening and Connie kept on crying and talking.

'You have no idea, do you?'

'Sorry?' Connie wiped her eyes, confused.

'Oh, Connie, Connie, Connie,' he said her name as though he were singing. 'No idea at all.'

'No idea about what?' She was becoming mildly irritated by his vagaries.

'About how achingly beautiful you are.'

That was when he first kissed her lips. Hard and sudden. Connie was too shocked to push him away; she could only remain in place as his breathing grew deeper, louder. Words whispered into her ear as her back was pushed against the rough fibres of the carpet of the music room.

'I know you want this as much as I do.'

'You know what you're doing, when you cry in here, when you look at me.'

Fresh tears bloomed in Connie's eyes as she turned her head to the side and endured it.

'You ruin me, Connie Lipman, you ruin me.'

When he was done, she hurriedly pulled up her pants, her skirt, hands shaking. A girl no more.

Connie did not like to reflect on what occurred in that music room. It stirred up ugly, awful feelings within her. Feelings that made her retreat into herself, and when she was strong enough, into her music. But as she grew older, as time awarded her the gift of hindsight, she understood that one of the worst things Mr Collins had done to her was to take away her confidant. Her safe place. No longer could she go to the music room and cry, talk about what was happening at home. She had to stuff it all inside. And not just what was happening at home. The music room became another storm to weather. Her violin ceased bringing her joy. With nowhere to turn, Connie had no choice but the internalise everything. Push it all down. She made attempts to save herself. She told her mother she wanted to quit the violin.

'Over my dead body,' her mother instantly told her, puffing out her cheeks in anger. 'Your father and I paid good money for that violin. Good money, you hear? I'll not have you quitting on some whim. I didn't raise a quitter, Connie.'

Connie stayed. Connie played. Mr Collins stopped listening. He'd stand behind her during a sonata, lacing her neck with kisses, which made Connie's skin creep. She thought of telling another teacher but could just imagine the look of disgust that would spread across their face.

'Mr Collins? Our beloved music teacher?' Who was she, a scholarship student from the shit part of town, to challenge someone so supported within the school community? All Connie could do was run away. So she did.

She ran to Robin. Because he listened. He cared. She ran to Robin and tried to find safety there, in his arms. But when she saw Mr Collins again, she knew in her heart that she didn't want to spend a lifetime running. He had taken so much from her, it was time she took something from him.

51

Now

It used to fit so easily in her hand, her violin. Her arm would bend from memory, chin tilted upon the rest. It all felt so seamless. So natural. Now the instrument was foreign in her grasp. Heavy and awkward. Connie fumbled with knobbly fingers to try and raise it up.

'I don't . . .' She grunted with the effort. 'I don't think I can hold it.'

'Try.'

As she attempted to heft the curved pieces of maple, she tried to recall the last time she had played. The last time she'd drawn her bow across strings and been able to lose herself in the music. It had been years. She knew that much. Since before Albert died.

'I'm sorry,' Connie panted, cheeks salmon pink. 'But I can't lift it.'

'Can't or won't?'

'I'm an old woman.' She hated the mirror he was holding up to her frailty. 'My muscles don't work like they used to.'

'You're going to play.' Daniel moved with an ease Connie envied as he stooped down to open his satchel, the flap slapping against the outer leather. He fumbled within it and she felt each second like a knife in her side. She *should* be moving. Running away. But escape was impossible. Her legs ached just from the act of standing in the centre of her living room. When Daniel straightened up again, he had something in his hand. Something small. Something deadly.

'You're going to play or I'm going to kill you.' The gun wavered slightly in his grip as though in a breeze, but the barrel was firmly aimed in Connie's direction. She looked down it. Into its dark depths.

'You think that scares me?' she wondered, continuing to look at the weapon. 'The prospect of death?' The violin was cradled in her hands like a baby, but she couldn't raise its weight higher, to rest upon her shoulder. A dry laugh rustled out from her. 'I am surrounded by the prospect of death. Every day. It's called being old.'

'I'll shoot you, I swear it.' His jaw clenched and Connie nodded.

'I've no doubt. But look around . . . I'm all alone. I do not fear death.'

'Then I'll shoot the fucking cat.'

Connie heard the breath that left her as her mouth fell open. Not Bach. Dear, loyal Bach, who curled up on the edge of her bed every night, woke her with the press of a soft paw to her cheek and a rumble of purring in her ears.

'I'll bring him in here and paint the walls with his guts.'

Connie whimpered at the image.

'Just like you did to my great-grandparents.'

She shook her head so furiously she made the room spin. 'No. No, I told you. I didn't go in. I didn't know what was going to happen in that house. I didn't—'

'I did so much research.' Daniel's voice broke over hers, snuffing her out. 'So much. I spent hours poring over the various court transcripts. Did you know that the statement from the others present that night didn't match with your own?'

Connie continued to cradle her violin.

'But no one believed them. Why would they? Robin was already a suspected murderer, for his own mother no less. And Wren and Arthur . . . they were runaways. Drop-outs. Nobodies. You were the golden girl from the good school who could play the violin. Who was gifted.'

Behind her Connie heard the meow of a hungry, impatient Bach. Her lower lip began to tremble. 'Please don't hurt him,' she whispered hoarsely. 'He's an animal. He's innocent.'

'Everyone believed *you*,' Daniel continued, 'your story. The school were so eager to cover it all up. Which makes sense given my great-grandfather's transgressions.'

'Please . . .' Connie felt a tear follow the crevasses of her cheek. 'Just leave.'

'But do you know what doesn't make sense?' Daniel cocked his head as Connie heard Bach pad into the room and begin rubbing against her legs. She felt her organs liquefy within her. Her own end, that she could handle. But not Bach's. She tried to nudge him away but her old legs were too slow. It felt like wading through tar.

'Michelle Rivers. Does the name ring any bells?'

It did not. Connie flicked her gaze from Bach to Daniel. 'Should it?'

'She lived next door to the Collinses'. She had a one-month-old baby. The night of the break-in, she was up doing a night feed. She'd kept the lights off so as to minimise the disturbance to her newborn.'

Connie swallowed. Bach continued to press himself against her legs, eager for attention.

'She said she heard voices outside. She came to the window and saw bodies climbing over her neighbour's wall. Assuming the worst, she tried to call the police but her phone line had been cut. Fearing for the safety of herself and her baby, she stayed inside and attempted to wake her husband. Eventually he got up and went three doors down to find the nearest working phone. By that time the deed was done. It was too late.'

The violin felt heavy in her grip. Connie imagined it slipping from her grasp and crashing against the floor, wood snapping and splintering.

'Her testimony was easily dismissed as the police felt that due to sleep deprivation, it wasn't reliable. But it got noted down all the same. Kept within the case files.'

Daniel shifted the direction of the gun towards Connie's feet. Towards Bach.

'Please!' she implored, voice high.

'Do you know how many figures Michelle saw climbing the wall?'

'Three!' Connie's heard hurt. She felt nauseous, faint. 'She saw three.'

'No!' Daniel yelled. 'Four. She saw four figures break in.'

'Impossible!'

'Four figures because you went in. I'm not here because you waited impassively outside.' Daniel took a second to swipe the back of his hand across his nose, sniffing loudly. 'I'm here because you did it. Because you killed them. You killed my family.'

52

Now

No. He had to be wrong. What he was saying was impossible. Three people went into Mr Collins's home that night. Three. Connie had watched them clamber over the wall, had heard the distant shattering of breaking glass. The new mother next door was mistaken, had to be.

The violin in her grasp was beginning to feel like it was filled with stones. Connie kept her gaze ahead, locked on Daniel and the gun, willing her geriatric limbs to not fail her. His words had opened a plug in her mind; she felt so many thoughts seeping out of her.

In court. In her uniform, back poker-straight, hair held in an austere bun, she had spoken clearly, let her words carry across all the heads assembled in the room beneath the cigarette smoke.

'I watched them climb the wall.'

It was all held in her memory. Verbatim.

'Are the people you saw in this room?' the man in the navy suit asked her. Connie nodded.

'Can you point to those who you saw elevate themselves over the wall of the property?' She angled her finger towards Arthur, Wren and Robin in turn. Arthur was holding back tears, Wren's face burned ruby with rage as she glowered at her, while Robin kept his head down, unable to look at her.

'Were you aware of the concealed weapons?' the suited man asked.

'No, I was not. I thought they were entering the home to steal silver.'

'Did you know it was the residence of your music teacher, Mr Collins?'

'No, I did not.'

Then how had Robin found the house? The question pricked at Connie, causing her eyes to smart, the violin to tremble within her weak arms.

He'd found the house himself. Had asked around. Gathered knowledge like a squirrel gathers nuts. Then he'd spent weeks watching the gate, the windows. Had he been crouched in the woodlands when the family gathered to put up their Christmas tree?

He knew the address because you gave it to him.

'No!' Connie barked the word and saw Daniel startle, barrel of the gun briefly lowering. 'I . . .' She blinked, looked to the violin.

'We want you to continue making music,' the head teacher had told her as it was passed into her waiting arms. 'We don't want this awful, awful tragedy to be a reason for you to squander your gift.'

'I didn't kill anybody.' The words fell from quivering lips as she looked helplessly at Daniel. 'Please, I'm an old woman.'

'And they were young boys.' The iron in his voice wrapped chains around her. 'Children. Yet you stole their parents from them. Ruined their lives.'

'I didn't go in,' she rasped.

A memory flickered, bright and insistent in her mind. In the lounge, her mother at her side, clasping her hands, her touch unusually cold, her father standing with his back to the fire, staring down at them both.

'You need to say you stayed outside,' he ordered, looking to his wife, not his daughter. 'They need to know that she stayed outside.'

Connie was nodding and shaking as snot and tears formed a river down her face, her mother's large hands still clutching her so tightly.

'That's what you'll say, right, sweetheart?'

Connie nodded more aggressively. 'Yes, I'll tell them. Dad, I'll tell them, I swear it.'

When they decided Robin's guilt and led him away, he looked to his feet, hair falling to cover his face. Connie watched him leave, heart pounding in her ears, willing him to look at her. Just a glance. She wanted that thread of connection between them. That chance to say sorry.

'I . . . I'm sorry.' Connie had to move. She tottered towards the armchair, wilted as she placed her violin against the cushions, grabbing the plush back and leaning into it.

'For killing them?' His voice was rain on a glass roof. Sharp and urgent.

'For . . . for . . .' Connie closed her eyes. Smelt the smoke from the courtroom reaching through time to engulf her once again.

'You did so well.' Her mother had embraced her tightly when it was all over. 'You did it, sweetheart. Now we can move on from this.'

Blood. Connie remembered there being so much blood. Underneath her. But not on tiles. Dark and slick like oil, concealing grains in wood. She shook her head, swatted at her ears as though there were a nuisance fly. Her thoughts. Her memories. Why weren't they making sense?

'Well?' Daniel demanded shrilly.

Blood. On her hands. In the air. On the knife.

Connie's hand fluttered between her mouth and her throat. She gaped at the young man, trying to find the words. Old age was a cruel mistress but this one kindness he was now taking from her. Her denial. Her ignorance. They protected her and Daniel was hacking them away. She blinked, breathed deep to steady herself. 'I'm sorry,' she tried again, seeing the hate which shone in his eyes as he watched her, 'I'm sorry for forgetting.'

53

Now

'My mind, it . . .' She pressed a prune-like fingertip to her temple. 'It hides things from me. Changes things.'

The arm aiming the gun at her straightened with certainty.

'But not the music.' Connie gave a wry smile. 'I never forget the music. Every note. Every arrangement. All remembered.'

'So what happened the night my great-grandfather died?'

A papery sigh left her. It was all still so muddled. There were the words she had uttered in court.

But blood.

It had been on her hands. Her cheeks. Her clothes. Slick and warm.

A look of horror had fallen across her mother's face when Connie darkened her doorstep. Face ashen, she'd ushered her daughter inside. 'Come on, we need to get you cleaned up.'

Connie shuddered. Looked at the gun, at the man holding it. Had she rewritten history? In her old age, had she allowed fiction to replace fact? 'I . . .' It all felt as futile as trying to catch snowflakes. The moment you had them in your palm, they melted away. Gone.

Someone had seen them. She'd said as much. Four figures climbing the wall. Not three.

The sputtering of a final breath. The warm tide splashing against her. These were moments buried deep, in the graves of the past.

'I went into the house,' she told him, words uneven as she dragged them across the coals of her consciousness. Connie sagged beside the chair, had to clutch its firm back to stay on her feet. So what was she now? A liar? A murderer? 'I went in and . . .'

Stinging in her ears. Screaming. Connie slammed her eyes shut, pressed her free hand against the side of her head. Needing silence. Clarity. It was all rising up. Boiling water in her mind, bubbles pounding her skull, desperate for release. The blood. The screams. All of it. Connie remembered.

'Hearing what happened.' She gulped in air, lungs ablaze. 'It won't change anything.'

'Not for you.' Daniel's lips curled with contempt. 'But maybe for me. Your truth might bring me closure.'

Pulling her mouth into a tight line, Connie shook her head. He was asking her to steer them both into the heart of a storm. A storm that could crush her.

'I was angry . . .' The excuse tumbled out of her. 'I was lost. No one would listen to me about what he . . . what he did to me. I ran away and still I didn't put enough distance between us.'

'He didn't deserve to die.'

Connie had no rebuttal.

'Nor did his wife,' Daniel continued, sniffing loudly. 'But you . . . you got to have your life back. While the others rotted away in prison.'

'Some rot there still,' Connie commented, regret darkening the edge of her vision. She knew that Robin lived. That he remained locked up. That he'd see out the end of his days in a cell. On the rare occasions she went to the library, she forced herself to use the internet there, to search his name. There were posts about the crime, mostly from sites interested in past, iconic murders. Nothing recent. Nothing about his death. It was during one of these searches that Connie learned that Arthur died in the 1970s, Wren in the '80s. Natural causes for both. It felt strange to think of them gone, when in her mind they were forever teenagers.

'I'm going to give you the chance to play one last time.' Daniel quickly pointed the gun at the violin, then it was back on Connie. 'Since that seems to be what mattered most to you. And it was apparently what bought you your freedom. So let's hear how good you actually are.'

'I've not played in years. I was good once. Great. Not now.'

'Play.'

Connie blinked away tears. At her feet Bach meowed, yellow eyes peering up at her earnestly. Daniel lowered the barrel of his gun. Aimed it at the cat.

'Play.' He icily repeated his order.

Connie reached for the violin, thin muscles burning. She awkwardly reclaimed it, pushed through pain and arthritis to hold it against her shoulder. Her chin used to fall upon it so easily, so effortlessly. Now the gesture felt alien and painful, her neck throbbing from the angle Connie forced it into. But at last it was in her grip. Desperately she grabbed the accompanying bow, fingers throbbing as they eventually closed around it. Sweat pooling down her back, across her brow.

She could do this.

She *had* to do this.

She had played through pain. And grief. In the music she always found safety. Release. If these were to be her final moments, let her spend them doing what she loved. Connie positioned her fingers, grimacing as sparks of pain fired in her hands, then tipped the bow to the strings. Then suddenly she glanced over at Daniel.

'Please don't hurt my Bach,' she beseeched him. 'He's a loyal, loving cat. Take him to a shelter. Let him find happiness in another home.'

Daniel raised the gun to aim at Connie's chest. 'I can do that,' he told her with a curt nod.

'Thank you. I . . .' She drew in an even breath. 'I appreciate it. Truly.'

She needed to play. The melody which came to mind was 'Meditation' from *Thaïs*, a melancholy piece where a beautiful courtesan reflects on her affluent life when asked to give it all up to follow God. It was a piece Connie often played those first few months when she returned to school, when what she'd done haunted her at every turn. She saw Mr Collins in every crowd and at night when she closed her eyes. She kept hearing the gargled gasp of his dying breath like a record being played on repeat. And the blood. No matter how many times Connie scrubbed her hands raw, she swore it was still there, embedded beneath her fingernails. A permanent stain.

Gingerly Connie pressed down her fingers, drew back her bow. She didn't think of Daniel and his gun. Or Mr Collins. Or Robin. She thought only of the music.

SECOND HOUSE OF
HORRORS DEATH

Arthur Hedges, part of the notorious gang who brutally murdered music teacher Frank Collins and his wife in their bed in 1954, has died.

Mr Hedges was still serving two life sentences in Wakefield Prison. Last year, as his health began to fail, he applied to be moved over to Shrewsbury Prison so he could be closer to his home county. The appeal was denied.

This leaves only the ring leader of the group, Robin Strand, still alive. Robin was believed to have led a cult-like group of teenagers in the 1950s, who all lived in a communal terrace and regularly stole from ale houses and stores to fund their existence. Strand also encouraged the group to take hallucinogenic drugs. They attacked the home of Mr Collins while high, which many believe explains the heavy-handed approach and graphic nature of the crime.

Mr Strand is also still serving two life sentences over at Wakefield.

54

Then

The night was still. The stars burned white-hot in their distant dwellings. Connie was beside the oak tree, on a patch of grass flattened by the increasing vigils held there. Where she had crouched beside Robin and pointed, whispering, 'This is the house.'

Now without the sheen of sunlight it stood ominous and dark. Already a tomb. The phone line had been snapped, the cord to life beyond the four tall walls severed. It was time.

Connie followed the others across the street, keeping her movements low and swift. Like a cat stalking the shadows. In the pit of her stomach, the coal of her pain had been turned over so many times it now gleamed like a diamond and poked at her, reminding her of all she had suffered. All she had lost.

They were almost at the wall. Just two feet from the iron gates. Gates his car had so seamlessly glided past, one hand on the wheel, casually returning home with that same hand which had earlier reached across for Connie. Her knee. Her inner thigh. Always advancing. Always conquering her defences.

'Make them suffer,' Connie hissed. She heard the hot exhale of breath, of agreement.

★

Robin cradled his hands and crouched low to boost her over. The wall was rough beneath her hands, the thick wool of her gloves catching on it. Drinking in icy breaths, she hauled herself up. First one leg, then the other. Finally she dropped onto the other side, the impact pulsing up to her hips. But it was done. She was in. Looking back up, she waited for Robin to appear against the night sky. It didn't take him long. And then he was beside her.

'Let's go,' he remarked stoically. Together they crept to the window on the left side of the house, the one out of view from other homes, watched only by the woodlands. Robin stroked a hand across the glass, assessing it.

Wren searched a nearby flower bed and then passed a stone to him. 'Here.'

Gripping it tight, Robin thrust it against the glass which instantly shattered. Carefully he punched out the remaining shards, ensuring all that remained was the wooden frame. Then he hoisted himself up and disappeared inside.

Connie kept searching the driveway. The windows. Braced for a face to appear, for her internal alarm bells to start ringing. But all remained still. 'Do you think anyone heard?' she whispered to Wren, who shook her raven hair.

'It's late. Everyone here will sleep soundly.'

Connie nodded. Of course they would. Fear couldn't reach their gates, their tidy front lawns. People like Mr Collins believed the world belonged to them.

Locks turning. The trio outside scurried to the back door, which swung open to reveal Robin, sweat dappled across his forehead. He jerked his head, ordering them inside.

Connie joined him in the kitchen. She could make out the shadows of a long table, a grand stove. The room still smelt of roast dinner. She pictured the family gathered around the table, laughing widely, pushing forkfuls of potatoes and chicken into their mouths. Would Mr Collins smile adoringly at his wife and thank her for cooking such a wonderful meal while reaching for her hand? Did she even sense what he was? What he did? Or was she willingly blind to it?

Robin advanced into the house, passing through the kitchen into the hallway. Connie followed, noticing how a nearby door was cracked ajar, revealing the lounge and the glimmering Christmas lights, which winked out at her. She was watching them as he tugged on her wrist, nodding upward.

At the foot of the staircase he paused, pressed himself flush to the wall and listened. Around them the house moaned. Pipes expanded. Floorboards settled. But no people moved. The family were still. Oblivious. He took the stairs two at a time. Connie followed, not daring to breathe. When she reached the landing, her lungs burned.

The darkness felt thicker up here. Connie had to wait several seconds for the shape of a side table to come into view, the lines of the doorways to show against the flower pattern of wallpaper. Robin reached for her arm and guided her along, towards the final door on the right. He stealthily pressed an ear to it and listened. Then he raised his hand and clicked his fingers. Breathing within. A bedroom.

Wren and Arthur positioned themselves at another door, where they too listened and waited for the tell-tale rise and fall of someone sleeping. They both raised their hands in confirmation.

This was what they knew – it was a four-bedroom house but only two were occupied. The boys shared a room and had a bunk bed. All of this information had been pulled together from snatching scraps of conversations that carried over to the woodland in which they alternately hid. They'd been able to paint a picture of the family. Husband. Wife. Two boys. Cricket for the boys on Tuesdays. Rugby on Thursdays. Church for all on Sunday.

Robin raised four fingers. From beneath their coats, they each withdrew what they'd been concealing. Connie's knife felt heavy in her grip. She wanted to whisper that they should stop, that she couldn't do this. But to speak now was to risk being discovered. To damn them all.

'What is it you wish for him?' Robin had asked previously while drugs swirled in their systems, loosening tongues. Connie had stared around the room, the colours within suddenly so vivid. So real.

'I wish for him to suffer.' She'd thought this since the moment he first touched her. Since he took all choice from her. But until she told her parents, she'd considered this a girlish notion. Some impotent anger. But when she told them of the baby he'd put inside her, when she saw their fear, their panic, their utter desperation, she understood. No one would ever believe her. Mr Collins could do as he wished. To whom he wished. And each girl like her would have to suffer what came next. Either bring up a bastard alone or face the grim door. While he kept teaching. Kept smiling at his wife over roast dinners.

The tears that rolled down her cheeks burned. 'He needs to suffer,' she said, shaking with her own fury.

'I know.' Robin pressed her against him, let her anger pulse through him. 'And he will. I promise you, he will.'

The drugs made everything looser. Dreamlike. When Wren asked about the boys, the answer had seemed obvious: 'Because they could wake, alert neighbours, shout for help.'

'If they wake, we silence them too,' Robin announced. And no one challenged him. Because it felt right. It seemed right. All so simple. So clean. Like doing something in your sleep. The detachment from reality, it was delicious, intoxicating. The removal of not just Mr Collins but his entire family if it came to it. *That* was justice. Wasn't it?

'But they're just kids,' Wren whispered. Robin gave her a hard look, one which made her pale. 'Robin—'

'They'll be asleep,' he stared at her, unblinking.

'Don't go too far.' There was a tremor in Wren's face. 'Not again.'

'I'll go as far as I have to,' he told her coldly.

'Robin—'

He made a rough sound in his throat, silencing her.

'Let's just hope they keep sleeping,' Wren said, voice low.

Robin grunted at her, whether in confirmation or agreement, no one could tell. For a moment, no one spoke, just breathed, feeling the world pulse around them. Ethereal. Beautiful. Nothing felt real.

Finally Robin held up three fingers.

Connie swallowed. Looked to her blade, which gleamed like a slip of moonlight within the darkness of the landing. She could smell Imperial Leather. The bathroom must be close by.

Two fingers.

She turned the handle within her palm. Many times she had held it, thrust with it. Considered pushing through flesh. Hitting against bone. Her pulse was rising, skin clammy beneath all her layers. She should have taken more drugs. She needed to feel more distant.

One finger.

A fist.

The door was opened quickly. One wincing on an old hinge.

Robin entered the bedroom first, Connie followed. The air within was thick, tinged with sweat and slumber. Together they approached the bed and then divided. Connie moved to the pillows and the head that sagged within them.

Mr Collins. Eyes closed peacefully. He groaned in a dream and shuffled beneath the covers.

His wife was not such a deep sleeper. As Robin approached, her eyes flew open. A scream burst from her. Connie felt the sound splinter against her. Then she heard the thrusting of blade through skin and the woman was swiftly silenced.

There was no waiting. Connie drew back the covers and forced the knife into Mr Collins's bare chest. He gasped as it pierced him. Connie withdrew it and dived again. It was harder than she expected, forcing it into his taut flesh. Again and again she stabbed, pushing as hard as she could, his breath catching and gargling in his throat. It began a repetitive motion. Thrust down, withdraw, repeat. Over and over. It smelt worse than it did that day in the bathroom, when Connie felt her own blood seep out from within her. The air in the bedroom was copper-laced and sharp.

Thrust down, withdraw, repeat. Thrust down, withdraw—

'Enough.' Robin's arms closed around her. Pinning her. 'We have to go,' he whispered against her cheek. Shaking, Connie stepped back from the bed, arms aching.

They found the others on the landing, blood-spattered and pale. It was done.

'Let's go,' Robin urged them all as they hurried back through the house, back through the kitchen. It was only when the night air slapped against her that Connie gasped and looked around as though waking from a dream. Her gloves were sticky against her hands. Her coat peppered with crimson.

'What have we done?' she whispered, teeth beginning to knock together.

'She's in shock,' Wren stated sharply, pulling on Connie's wrist. 'We need to get her out of here.'

They left as they came in. Back over the wall, back across the street. Back into the night.

With each step, the fog in Connie's mind cleared a fraction more. Until several streets from the house, she found clarity.

The knife. The blood. It couldn't be real, could it?

While the others kept running, she stopped on a corner, turning to Robin. Needing to see something in his eyes that absolved her. But he was crazed, face smeared with blood that wasn't his own. He grabbed her, kissed her, urged her to keep running. But she couldn't. This wasn't her. She hadn't done this.

'It was his house, wasn't it?' She trembled.

'You know it was.' His voice was soft.

'What did you do?'

A kiss. Hard and searing. 'What had to be done.' He placed the words gently against her ear. 'Come with me.' He was edging away, a hand extended, a final invitation. Around them the streets were beginning to stir, windows lighting up, the screech of the sirens nearing.

Connie gave a brisk shake of her head. A door slapped shut and Robin withdrew into the swelling shadows of the street, head darting about in fear.

'I have to go,' he told her, his tears streaking the blood.

'I know.'

'Please.' His hand remained held out, palm turned to the moon. Connie looked at it, considered what would happen if she took it. How they'd run together back to the house. How they'd hide. She looked into Robin's eyes. Still so wide, so wild. Then she turned her back on him and moved as fast as she could. She kept running until her legs burned while behind her Robin dropped to his knees and howled.

55

1982

'I think it is time for us to go home.'

It was Albert who made the decision for them, as Connie swung in a hammock on her patio, back and forth, watching the stars blur together in the sky above her. At first she ignored her husband, considered leaving her hammock to get yet another glass of wine. Lately, it was the only thing that helped her sleep. Originally just by the glass, but more recently by the bottle. And Albert had noticed.

'You're drinking too much,' he'd comment each morning when he spied the green bottles propped up behind the bin.

'I'm fine,' Connie declared, though her mouth felt like sandpaper and her head throbbed so terribly she almost couldn't see.

'Darling, you have a problem.'

She kept playing her violin. Kept going to auditions, and then jobs. Working on a high-profile film was a great way to get more work in Los Angeles. Whatever room Connie walked into, people were keen to see her, talk to her. She should have been living her best life. And yet six months ago she began not just walking in her sleep, but climbing into her car and driving it. Albert spent hours hiding away the knives, the glasses, the keys to absolutely everything. Still Connie would float through their home, troubled and restless.

'It's worse than being a ghost,' Albert had told her once. 'It's like you're there, but not. Your eyes are open, but no one is there. Honestly, it scares the shit out of me.'

The sleeping pills, the wine . . . Connie kept throwing them all down her throat at bedtime in an attempt to drown her demons.

'Did you hear what I said?'

Albert came and stood over her. His hair, jet black when they met, was now flecked with silver. He was still so handsome, still able to make Connie feel an ache in the pit of her stomach.

'I heard you,' she mumbled, still swinging.

'Connie.' He placed a hand upon the fabric, stilling the motion. 'I need you to focus here, sweetheart.'

'I'm still booking jobs.'

'It's not about that and you know it.'

'I'm still playing.'

'We have money enough, Connie. This is about you. Your health.'

Connie turned on her side and then slid out from the hammock, padding her way to the end of their garden. Their house was wedged into the side of the hills that bordered Los Angeles and at night the hillside sparkled with the glow of countless homes. It was a beautiful sight to see, one which soothed Connie. Many evenings she would sit out on her patio and look out, listening to the cicadas.

Behind her, she sensed her husband's presence. 'Darling, you're unwell.' He rubbed her shoulders as together they looked down at the city. 'It's time to go home.' He leaned close and kissed her cheek.

Home.

The thought reverberated within Connie.

Home was something she'd fought so hard to escape. Even when her parents died, she didn't return. Couldn't face it. Though of course she missed the greenness of Shropshire, the familiarity of it all. But she didn't miss her past. Not one bit.

'Being here isn't helping,' Albert continued. 'You're getting worse.'

She knew he was right. She wasn't a fool. Things were escalating. What would come next? First driving a car, then what? Deep down, Connie knew what she was capable of and it left her cold. Left her numb.

'I know you have painful memories of what happened,' Albert said carefully, one hand rubbing her back, 'but we can face them together. I think you'll be happier once you confront things. Don't you?'

Always someone telling her what to do. How to be. How to feel. How to heal. Connie sighed and walked away from her husband. The truth was that she would be tormented and miserable wherever she was. Why not go home? At least there the world made sense. She missed the sound of the rain, the fog of her breath on a winter morning. 'OK.' She kept looking at the glittering hillside. 'Let's do it. Let's go home.' She felt it closing the moment she said the words: her chapter in film. Her time playing musical scores. She had come so very far. Achieved so very much.

'It's time to rest.' She could feel Albert's eyes on her. 'You need this, sweetheart. Time to focus just on yourself.'

Connie had some stipulations. She wanted a house in her home county, but not close to where she grew up. And it had to be alone, with a private driveway and no neighbours to bother her. She wanted to go days, weeks, without seeing another living soul if she wanted to. Albert agreed to everything.

When Connie returned to England, she expected to feel a great weight settle upon her, but in fact it was the opposite. As the plane touched down, she instantly felt lighter, liberated. She wasn't the Connie who had left. She was older, wiser. More tired. It was with relief that she retired from music. It was only when she gave herself permission to fall apart did Connie realise how exhausting it had been to hold herself together for all those years. It was time for Connie to grow old gracefully, quietly. With Albert by her side.

The sleepwalking persisted, though with less ferocity. She would awaken in the bathroom, or the spare bedroom. She never even made it down the stairs. Connie read books, watched television, took walks in the woodland. She still thought about *him* but it happened less. She even visited the graves of her parents, leaving a bouquet of lilies. It was when she lost Albert that loneliness truly set in. Connie began to feel less like a person and more like a shell. Until one day a letter arrived, kindly written and gushing over her musical accomplishments. Perhaps, she thought, it might be nice to chat about something positive, to hear another voice in the home that didn't just come from the television.

56

Now

It was agony and ecstasy to play. Her old bones burned with pain but her heart pulsed in time with the music. This was the place she had always felt weightless, free. Within the melody. But the spell had lost its potency over the years. Her fingers struggled on the swifter notes, unable to apply enough pressure, to move fast enough. Her musician's ear heard where she faltered. And she was back in the room, bow in hand, staring at the boy with the gun. Beside her the fireplace was still, only tendrils of smoke curling up from the ash. The chill of the room began to sink into her. Against her legs she felt the soft pressure of Bach, returned to remind her that his bowl had yet to be refilled.

Blood.

She blinked and she was there. In the bedroom, hands damp, Robin's grip on her shoulders, drawing her back. Connie struggled to play on. Her fingers were cramping, her arms trembling.

'Music . . . music saved you,' Daniel seethed from across the room. 'Everyone believed your lies, even when faced with the statements of others who were there that night. You were spared because of your talent. Because of the glory it would bring the school.'

Connie winced as she kept playing. She wanted to think he was right. In so many ways music *had* saved her. It gave her somewhere to hide. Built a ladder to a better life. Let her swim amongst the stars in Hollywood.

That first time she held a violin she'd felt her stomach dip with excited anticipation. Like she'd known something special was about to happen. And Mr Collins had looked on with hungry eyes, a wolf surveying his lamb. Music might have been the thing to save her, but it had also been the very thing to condemn her.

Panting, she had to stop.

'I said *play*.' Daniel stepped forward, gun presented at her temple. 'I want to hear what is so fucking special about your music that makes you worth saving.'

Connie gave a rueful shake of her head. 'They weren't saving me,' she rasped. 'They were saving *him*.'

No one had wanted it. The truth. They wanted Connie outside, oblivious. Innocent. Because if she was inside, it was all too much of a coincidence. People would have started asking questions, wondering why this teacher had solicited such an attack from a student. Others like Connie might have spoken up. The reputation of the school was on the line.

'Did you even care about what you did?' Daniel demanded, lips curling with disgust as spittle flew from him.

'I buried it,' Connie admitted. 'I had to. It was the only way I could cope. I let the . . . the lie become my truth.'

'They were *boys*. Children. And you could have stopped it. All of it. You didn't need to kill their father. Their *mother*.'

Connie hung her head. She knew all this. Yet she'd crept into the house, blade within the lining of her coat, pressed to her chest, aware of what was about to happen. Willing it. Her desire for vengeance needing to be satisfied.

There were pictures of the boys in all the papers afterwards. Their names constantly uttered on the wireless. Connie tuned it all out with her violin.

'Shoot me,' she whispered, looking down the barrel of the gun, seeing only darkness. 'Shoot me but spare my cat.'

'You deserve to be fucking shot!' Daniel raged. 'To die here, alone, in a pool of your own blood. To be left here to rot.'

'You're right,' she agreed coolly. 'My fate is now sealed. Either here now or a few years down the line, I die alone. This house is a crypt.'

'I should just shoot you!' His arm trembled as tears sliced his cheeks. 'You brought my family so much *pain*.'

Connie dropped her gaze to the ground. She understood pain. How motivating it could be. She welcomed the bullet that was about to come. Let her join her beloved Albert in death. Living was so lonely. So long. And now the truth of what had happened that night had been disturbed, she knew any further days would be agony.

'Please,' she uttered, letting her favourite sonata commence playing in her mind, 'just end it.'

Connie Winchester sucked in a breath and waited for absolution. For the crack of bullet through air.

Instead, something clattered to the ground. Then footsteps, manic and quick, someone brushing past her. The front door wheezing open, the wind rushing inside, rattling the framed pictures on the wall. Connie opened her eyes, feeling dizzy, surprised to find she was alone. The gun was on the floor where Daniel had been standing, his satchel gone, papers scattered across her sofa. Connie shuffled into her hallway, Bach following, turning to see the driveway beyond her open door and the figure retreating along it.

He'd spared her.

Connie numbly went to the door, closed it, turned the locks. Tugged the chain into place. Then she pressed a hand to her chest, struggling to catch her breath. Hot tears were rolling down her cheeks.

Daniel had spared her. Which was the cruellest thing he could have done.

The thing with a fractured mind is that it can conceal things from you. Your brain becomes a labyrinth in which you often lose the way. Connie Winchester wanted to believe that this was attributed to her age when truly, she knew it was not. It was an internal war that had been raging since she was a teenager. Things happened that were stolen from her. She sleepwalked. She picked things up. Sharp things. She drove cars.

Sometimes old memories would surface like debris along a shoreline. It was always sudden and unexpected. It was as she stood alone in her home, the silence surrounding Daniel's departure deafening, that one such event occurred. It must have been all the talk of the past, of Mr Collins, which caused it. With a whimper Connie pressed a feeble hand to her chest and recalled the time, some years ago, that her house phone had rung and she'd made the terrible mistake of answering it.

It had been a rainy Wednesday morning mid-June. Albert had taken the car into the village to stock up on milk, bread and eggs. As he did most Wednesday mornings. Though had the day been clear, he would have walked. Connie knew not to expect him home until after eleven, that he liked to idle in the grocery store, chat with Malcolm, the owner, before enjoying a stroll along the riverside. When her phone began ringing in the hallway, she was instantly rigid with anticipation. Her phone rarely rang. There was no one to call her.

Albert.

Panic guided her swiftly to the hall where she picked up the handset and forced herself to answer calmly.

'Hello?'

'Will you accept a call from Reckton Prison?'

Connie turned to stone.

The caller repeated the question in the same flat voice.

Auto-pilot kicked in, Connie responded in the affirmative. The following seconds felt unbearably long. There was a crackle on the line as she was connected elsewhere. All the while her mind raced, was it *him*? Was he calling? But why after all this time? Was he going to shout at her? Rage into whatever handset he was holding while released from his cell?

'Connie?'

Instead, it was a raspy woman's voice that filled Connie's head. One that she didn't recognise.

'Connie, you there?'

Connie closed her eyes, found the part of the voice that was still tangible, still held that fire.

Wren.

'I . . .' she paused, cleared her throat. 'I'm here.'

'Good,' Wren replied with purpose. 'I don't have long. Five fucking minutes they give me. The bastards.'

Connie glanced nervously down the hallway, at her front door, hoping against hope that Albert didn't cut his morning trip into the village short.

'I'm dying,' Wren announced with steely pragmatism.

'Oh.'

'Not that you care,' Wren continued, unphased. 'Cancer. Bad. We all know how it goes. But anyway.' She inhaled

276

as though she was smoking a cigarette, though Connie doubted she was, unless the rules within the prison changed when someone was terminal. Maybe it was just something Wren did out of habit, or comfort. 'I got my diagnosis last week. We are talking months at best. And I couldn't, I can't go, without speaking to you.'

Connie didn't dare breathe. The phone felt like a portal through time and she imagined Wren as she had known her on the other end; dark-haired and dangerous. She didn't want to think of her frail, old. Dying.

'Do you have any idea how much I hate you?'

Connie pursed her lips, said nothing.

'How many hours I have dedicated to wishing you the worst? And look where it's got me? I've tried to put it out of my head, what you did, but how can I when I'm trapped in a box. I told them, you know.'

Connie's gaze flitted towards the front door, heart beginning to race.

'The cops, I told them everything when we were caught. How it was all you. Though of course no one believed me. Why would they? Me, Arthur and Robin, we all had priors. You were the clean one, the *good* one.'

Connie felt her palms growing slick against the phone.

'I told them how you set it all up; that we were going to go in and steal from Collins. That's it. Pinch some silver, maybe grab some of the wife's jewellery. In, out, done. Only when we got inside, you changed.'

The wind whistled around the house and Connie felt her body grow icy cold.

'It was like a veil had come down. And I'd seen it before, that glassy, distant look. I told Robin we needed to turn around, to stop you. But he was too far gone. He followed you inside. I suppose more's the fool that I went in too. But he had me, just as you had him. Arthur and I rummaged around downstairs while you went up, alone. Robin remained on the landing, keeping watch. He told you to be quick. When you came back out of the bedroom covered in blood, he screamed. That's when the little boys woke up.'

Connie pressed a hand over her mouth to stop herself from crying out.

Just hang up.

But she couldn't; it was like being paralysed within a nightmare, incapable of doing anything other than watching it all play out.

'He told me how he had to grab you, drag you down the stairs. How you both heard the little boys fearfully calling out for their mother.'

'You're lying,' Connie managed to rasp.

'You came downstairs covered in so much fucking blood. Robin panicked, he ran back up into the bedroom, tried to see if he could help anyone. Covered himself in the shit. Then he called for me and Arthur, we ran up, tried to help. We were too late. All the while you stood in the kitchen, eyes wide, like you were on another fucking planet. Robin had to leave the bodies, come down and shake you. Suddenly you snapped alert, looked right at him and said "Make them suffer." It was terrifying. And then you bolted out of the house so we all gave chase. You left him, left us, and ran home to Mummy and Daddy.

'And what's worse is one of those little boys saw us as we hurried along the landing, wearing their parents' blood; they had cracked their door open and glimpsed us. We must have looked like something out of a fucking nightmare. Those poor, poor boys. Orphaned because of you.'

Connie's fingers were pushing so hard into her cheeks she was drawing blood. She felt her knees buckling as she slumped down to the floor, back against the wall.

'In court you lied so beautifully.' Wren sounded almost impressed. 'How easy it was for everyone to believe *your* version of events. Hell, I think even you believed it. Pretty blonde Connie Lipman. Such a talent. Such a *good* girl. It was only me, Robin and Arthur who knew the truth. Who paid for what you did. The eldest boy recognised Robin in a line-up, you know, helped to finger him for it all.'

Connie was shaking from the effort of suppressing her sobs.

'The only mistake Robin ever made was loving you. He thought he was helping you but I knew, I saw it. The darkness. The madness. And I can't go to my grave without you knowing what you did: that you killed Mr Collins and his wife, you alone. That you're a fucking monster and because of you, your so-called friends have rotted in jail. Hate is too gentle a word for how I feel about you. I just hope that—'

She hung up. Connie could take no more. She slammed the phone down and stared at it as though it were a deadly rattlesnake preparing to strike. Her breathing grew fast. She grew hot. And then she passed out.

When Albert found her, she was lying in the hallway. He panicked and called an ambulance. Connie came to as the paramedics were loading her onto a gurney. She spent a day in hospital being assessed, but no one could find a medical reason for what had happened. Connie told them about her spells in her youth, learned they were termed 'psychogenic blackouts'. When the doctors asked if anything could have caused this latest blackout, Connie looked at them earnestly and told them no. There was nothing. Because already her mind had buried the call, to protect herself.

★

In the aftermath of Daniel's visit, Wren's call was suddenly fresh in her mind and Connie could think of only one person. The person who so often haunted her dreams. And so she forced herself to sit down and write one final note.

Epilogue

Dearest Robin,

It seems more than redundant to announce that I hope this letter finds you well. Although that is my hope. That despite the years which have stretched between us that you are indeed well.

I should have written to you sooner. I accept this along with many other things. I'm at fault. Forgive me. But please don't think this letter is me seeking forgiveness, for it is not.

You and I, we are both old now. Our lives wound out behind us like fraying rope. I wonder if you know where my life, my music took me. Or if you even care. I'm not ashamed to say that it has been a full life. Rich with music, travel and success. Even love. I don't say that to wound but merely to defend my actions. I know what I did. I followed the advice of others and I let you, Wren and Arthur hang for my mistakes. And then I disappeared. Into myself. Into music. I tried to blot it out. All of it. And somewhere along the line I was so utterly successful at this that the lies blurred with truth and I believed my own innocence. I was wilfully blind to all I had done. So what does that make me? A fraud? A liar?

I imagine you must hate me. I certainly would if our roles were reversed. I can only hope that time has softened your anger.

For so long I hid behind the life I had created for myself. The decades slipped away and my history with them. Only recently a young man darkened my doorway. He pretended to be one thing but turned out to be another. He so keenly wanted to excavate the past. He pierced the bubble of my ignorance, which had been sharpened by senility, the God-awful affliction that seems to want to come for us all, to mock us at our weakest. And I'm now left with the truth of what I did. Who I am. And a world without music or any place to hide. My hands can't play like they used to. I've found myself thinking of you. Wondering what you must think of me.

I know that what you did, you did out of love. To protect me. Defend me. And I let you. I was young and falling in love was like tumbling down a well. For so long my stomach flipped in that oh so pleasant way, as if we were at the fair, but eventually you hit the ground. And find darkness. Or at least I did.

I see you in my dreams. As you were. As you will always be to me. Chestnut eyes, that crinkle in their corners and that wry smile, too old and too cynical on such a boyish face. Have the years hardened your features? Thinned the silky mass of your hair?

I'm not asking to come and visit. I want to keep you as you are. Forever frozen. Forever mine.

Perhaps this is where I say that if I were given the choice to do things over, I'd change things. That I'd come forward and demand to own my guilt. But that would be a lie. I like the life I've had. What I now dread is this final act. I get to watch my house and myself gather dust. Alone. It is deserving.

I loved you. Wholly and completely. Ever since that night on the Ferris wheel. Despite what you surely think,

I've never stopped. Not truly. It's as if there are two parts to me. There is Connie Lipman, young and lost. She is forever yours. Then there is who I became, Connie Winchester. I found all the things I'd been searching for. All but one.

I'm sorry your life has been lived in a cage. You deserved more. You deserved to see the world, to watch dawn break against a flat ocean, to scale mountains that touch the stars. Yours was a spirit of adventure that would never be tamed. I imagine you losing yourself in books to escape your cell. Hiding out in Middle Earth or Middlemarch to help pass the time.

Time is now running out for us both. Maybe there is something that comes next. Some beyond. I suppose I should hope not, since I am surely marked for the darkest of places.

Thank you for trying to save me. For seeing me, all of me. Continue to visit my dreams. To keep those lingering embers of what we once were burning.

Until we meet again,
Yours,
Connie
x

Acknowledgements

This book has been on quite the journey but I've loved shaping Connie's story into what it has become. Firstly, I'd like the thank my lovely editor, Rhea. Your kindness has always shone through and you helped talk me back from a much more severe ending!

I set out with big ambitions for this book about tackling the nature of cults and the power of personality and I hope I've come some close to achieving that. Also, having many parts of the book set in the 1950s has given me so much respect for writers of historic fiction. I've never had to do so much research for a book before!

Thank you to my family for continually putting up with my madness. And for always encouraging me to follow my dreams.

And the biggest thanks of all to you, the reader. Thank you for taking the time to read Connie's story.

Credits

Carys Jones and Orion Fiction would like to thank everyone at Orion who worked on the publication of *The Final Score* in the UK.

Editorial
Rhea Kurien
Sahil Javed

Copyeditor
Clare Wallis

Proofreader
Jane Howard

Audio
Paul Stark
Jake Alderson

Contracts
Dan Herron
Ellie Bowker
Alyx Hurst

Design
Tomás Almeida
Joanna Ridley

Editorial Management
Charlie Panayiotou
Jane Hughes
Bartley Shaw

Finance
Jasdip Nandra
Nick Gibson
Sue Baker

Comms
Corinne Jean-Jacques

Production
Ruth Sharvell

Sales
Catherine Worsley
Esther Waters
Victoria Laws
Toluwalope Ayo-Ajala
Rachael Hum
Ellie Kyrke-Smith
Sinead White
Georgina Cutler

Operations
Jo Jacobs
Dan Stevens

Don't miss the other addictive and emotional psychological thrillers from Carys Jones . . .

'*Someone needs to bring her down a peg or two . . .*'

When Pippa's best friend goes missing on a school run, no one thinks twice. Heather is pretty, popular and more than a little wild.

Most people think she ran away for the attention . . . Others say girls like her always get what's coming to them.

Pippa's mother, Abbie, has never liked Heather. Or her mother Michelle, a successful doctor who thinks she's too good for the school mums' group.

But when Heather turns up dead, everything changes. Because Pippa was the last person to see her alive . . . and now Abbie's own house of cards is about to come tumbling down.

Five names on a list. The first two are dead. The third is *yours*.

Beth Belmont runs every day, hard and fast on the trail near home. She knows every turn, every bump in the road. So when she spots something out of place – a slip of white paper at the base of a tree – she's drawn to it.

On the paper are five names. The third is her own.

Beth can't shake off the unease the list brings. Why is she on it? And what ties her to the other four strangers?

Then she discovers that the first two are dead.

Is she next?

Delving into the past of the two dead strangers, the truth Beth finds will lead her headlong into her darkest, deadliest and most dangerous nightmares . . .

We're best friends.
We trust each other.
But . . .

Allie, Stacie, Diana, Emily and Gail have been by each other's sides for as long as they can remember. The Fierce Five. Best friends forever. But growing up has meant growing apart. And little white lies have grown into devastating secrets.

When Gail invites the increasingly estranged friends to reunite at her Scottish cabin, it could be the opportunity to mend old wounds and heal the cracks in their friendship. But when a freak snowstorm rocks the cabin and one of the girls is found dead on the ice, their weekend away becomes a race against time – and each other – to get off the mountain alive.

And in the end, whose story can you trust, when everything was founded on lies to begin with?